THE
WINE MENAGERIE

A DASH RAMBLAR MYSTERY

RANDOLPH E. ROGERS

Dedications:

To Hope Haywood Boland:
An unrelenting supporter, friend, and muse.

To Joan Singleton:
A beguiling editor who defines the art of the tale.

The Wine Menagerie

Invariably when wine redeems the sight,
Narrowing the mustard scansions of the eyes,
A leopard ranging always in the brow
Asserts a vision in the slumbering gaze.

Then glozening decanters that reflect the street
Wear me in crescents on their bellies. Slow
Applause flows into liquid cynosures:
I am conscripted to their shadows' glow

Hart Crane

1926

Part One: Saignee

Translation (Fr): *Bleeding. The non-machine process of bleeding the grapes by their own weight to make rosé wine from red grapes.*

Part Two: Veraison

Translation (Fr): *Ripening. The natural process of green grapes ripening to deep purple.*

Part Three: Vendange

Translation (Fr): *Harvest. The wine grape harvest is called Vendange.*

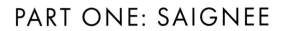

PART ONE: SAIGNEE

Chapter One:

WINE SISTERS

Claudia missed her flight to London on Thursday. Claudia had enjoyed the buzz she got from an evening of superb wine, yummy food, and the congenial company of The Wine Sisters. She had walked alone to her parked car located in the familiar blocks that surrounded the park plaza. A few of The Wine Sisters had carpooled, but no one felt it necessary to accompany anyone to their car on a quiet Wednesday night. The small town of Great Oaks grew eerily still steps away from the park plaza in the late hours. Leaving the restaurant, Claudia checked her cell phone for messages from her fiancé Greg, who texted that he couldn't wait to have her in his arms, punctuated with a heart emoji.

Claudia had parked three blocks away to the north of the downtown blocks. This area had zero restaurants and bars, consisting of bank branches and real estate offices, all devoid of nighttime commerce.

Claudia walked the three blocks in a happy trance, pulling out her car key, hitting the button that opened her doors, lighting the door handles, welcoming her with a friendly beep. Her black sedan was wedged between two trucks on Fifteenth Street. She settled into her car, turned on the radio, and started the engine.

A tall sturdily-built man in a hooded sweatshirt got out of the driver's side of his truck in front of her car, motioning that he was going to move his car forward, giving her more room to exit. Claudia smiled broadly at the man, thanking him with a gestured short wave from behind her windshield. She left her car in park, waiting for the truck to creep forward when the truck behind her nudged forward, bumping her bumper. She was momentarily startled, then the driver got out of his truck and approached her. He was shorter and stockier than the man who had moved his truck, similarly dressed in a hooded sweatshirt, jeans, and work boots. She moved her window down, assuming the man was going to apologize for bumping her car. Before Claudia could greet him, he grasped her neck violently with a gloved hand, causing her to collapse into unconsciousness. The perpetrator opened her door, moving her limp body to the passenger seat, putting the running car in drive, turning off the radio, and slowly pulled away from the curb. The driver in the truck in front of her car followed the perpetrator in slow procession.

The shorter, stockier man drove Claudia's sedan across the Thirteenth Street Bridge, down River Road, parking along a dark stretch of the Salinas River arroyo. The dry Salinas river bed was a mile wide marked by thickets of undergrowth, mulberry and scrub oak trees, and scattered homeless encampments. He parked Claudia's car near a city utility station at Twenty-Sixth Street and near an overpass of Highway 101. The other man stayed in his truck with the engine and lights off, acting as a lookout. The perpetrator then pulled Claudia out of the car, dragged her across the road, to a path that ran underneath the giant cement piers of the overpass, into the underbrush, laying her on the ground. He struck her with his fist when she started to regain consciousness. Resting and taking a deep breath, he then dragged her to a scouted location. Catching another breath, he fumbled with his sweatshirt, which hung loosely over his pants, then pulled out a long slender folded knife from the sheath attached to his belt. He slit her throat with one sweeping motion from ear to ear, a motion that he had learned from harvesting lambs on his family's farm. He then tied her ankles together with a rope maneuvering her warm corpse over a tree branch, pulling her two feet up off the ground. The blood poured from her neck wound, drowning her face in a scarlet mask. Claudia's cascading brunette hair was washed in a henna dye of blood. Her body was hidden from view by the massive underpass cement piers that marched across the half-mile expanse. Her body would not be visible from the road or from the makeshift trail that ran adjacent to the bridge piers. The killer had surveyed the area earlier, choosing the ideal spot, placing the rope in a secure spot. Sweating and breathing heavily, he got into Claudia's car, giving a thumbs up to the accomplice sitting in the truck, then drove back to the same parking space on Fiftieth Street, turning off the car, leaving the car keys in the passenger seat, walking to his parked truck around the block to Pine Street, where a lonely dive bar pretended that the night was still young.

A homeless male in his late forties, who looked sixty-five, found her two days later on Friday, but being fearful, he didn't report it until the following Tuesday, when he was picked up for loitering. By the time the coroner arrived, Claudia's body was disemboweled and tattered from animal encroachment.

Earlier that evening, The Wine Sisters sat at the large banquet table laden with wine glasses, fresh flowers, and plates for sharing. The warm evening lent itself to dining al fresco in the brick-walled courtyard with trellised ivy vines.

An abundance of sparkling rose animated their monthly dinner gathering. The eleven sisters devoured the lamb lollipops and crab cake appetizers, moving on to the lobster bisque, a bit heavy for late August, a butter leaf salad with watermelon dressing, then the main course: beef medallions with a cherry and Syrah reduction sauce and fingerling potatoes with haricot vert. Dessert was a lighter lemon soufflé drizzled with raspberry puree. Smiles broke out as the chef introduced each course, cheers as she presented each wine pairing, progressing from a fun Picpoul Blanc to a lively Grenache, then to a denser Petite Verdot.

They chatted about the wines, the winemakers on the rise, and wineries on the decline. Inevitably the conversation turned to relationships. The Wine Sisters ranged in age and status representative of the new era, mostly divorced, single, and a few clinging to their marriages.

When the Petit Verdot was opened and served, Mona lifted her glass in a toast, "To my dear friend Claudia: Cheers to your engagement, your eventual nuptials, and finally, safe travels to London."

The group clapped and cheered, lifting their glasses, tasting the dark plum-colored wine.

Claudia beamed at the toast. She was the youngest sister present, in her late thirties. She wore a white blouse covered by a short-waisted denim jacket. Her taupe-colored slacks, simple flats, and little jewelry reflected her Mormon upbringing. She had shoulder-length brown hair pulled back, a small mouth, narrow sparrow eyes. She was lovely, not pretty, shapely, not voluptuous, clever with learned confidence that belied her insecurity. Claudia possessed a comedic wit adding to her winning personality.

Claudia stood up and spoke to the sisters, "Thank you, Mona, for the kind words. My fiancé, Gregg, is my latest and final victim. He's no Brad Pitt, but I love it when his mother calls, droning on, as he fidgets. After the call ends, he retaliates by giving me a proper rogering." The sisters laughed and cheered, raising their glasses in another toast.

Claudia had met Gregg Perigold when they both were taking sommelier classes in St. Helena. She became a wine barrel salesperson; Gregg's family owns Jasper Wine Estates.

Mona was a wine writer for a local magazine and a contributor to national publications. Mona drank a vodka martini, wore big oversized dark-rimmed glasses, querying Claudia about her agenda.

"You're going to have to try the fabulous Indian food while you're in London, there's nothing like it here in California," Mona said.

"I'll add that to my list after watching the changing of the guards," Claudia laughed heartily, "If we ever leave Gregg's apartment."

Claudia sat at the large banquet table between Taylor and Mona. Taylor was the quirkiest of the wine sisters; she dressed for herself and her mood. A handsome brunette who wore retro capri pants, a bare shoulder blouse, and flip flops. Her hazel eyes glistened with laughter, and her heart was lifted with friendship. She was the best friend a woman could have— she kept secrets and wasn't flirtatious or catty. She was supportive, loving, and kind. Taylor was never without male attention, preferring her single life and its pursuits to committed relationships. Taylor was a marketing and media consultant to the wine industry—a whiz at online social media. Taylor agreed to watch Claudia's cat in her absence.

"When do you return from London?" Taylor asked Claudia through the background din.

Claudia raised her voice, "Tomorrow afternoon—I fly out of LAX on the red-eye, and I'll be back after Labor Day weekend, on the eighth."

When Taylor said, "Too short for Gregg, too long for me," everyone cheered her pronouncement, raising their glasses for a final toast.

The conviviality of the evening was heartfelt, renewing friendships and contacts. The Wine Sisters felt enlivened by these monthly meetings.

Dash Ramblar was at home on his ranch, just eight miles away from the restaurant. He knew a few of The Wine Sisters and was especially close to Claudia. When he first moved to Great Oaks, Claudia was among the first people he met. Claudia was the one that got away, but he was happy for her and her fiancé. The pain of her death only was magnified by the sense-lessness of it. She was a shining light in the dim shadows of the one-horse industry town of Great Oaks.

Chapter Two:

DASH RAMBLAR

Dash was a nascent grape grower and winemaker. Dash was a fit fifty-year-old, of medium height and weight. His sturdy shoulders and chest and firm handshake confirmed his farming hobby, belying his years in the insurance business. He found the local wine industry on the Central Coast to be cordial and welcoming. The industry was comprised of men and women from all over the world, all ages and varied educations—who have a passion for wine. There was a familiar pecking order. The billionaire class owned the most prestigious properties. They hired their winemakers and vineyard managers. The millionaire class from other careers started more modestly, hoping to catch lightning in a bottle. There were the millennials who worked non-stop, bartered, begged, and talked wine from sun up to sundown, learning the ancient craft. Lastly, the workers who pruned the vineyards, picked the grapes, ran the crushing and bottling lines, and spent Sundays with their families. Dash did not fit into any of these groups. He was too old to be a millennial. He was a billionaire only in taste—his passion was as a grower and producer, not solely as a winemaker. Dash hired seasonal help but did much of the vineyard work himself. He came from another career, insurance brokerage, investing his meager savings into the enterprise. Wealth is a relative measurement in coastal California. He was not a dilettante, nor was he an expert, simply a man who loved the smell of the earth.

He met Claudia at a fundraising roast at a posh winery and wedding venue near his ranch. The vineyards were part of the backdrop and their donated wines a tax write off. Dash was taken by Claudia's youthful vitality, wine knowledge, and her sense of humor. She told him early on that she was in a relationship halting any romantic notions. She was open to drinking and dancing the night away with him on her arm. Claudia seemed to know everyone at the annual roast, honoring a giant in the local wine industry. She introduced Dash to winemakers and winery owners, whom he had previously only known t by name. She needed a companion. He needed an entrée to the industry.

A year later, he ran into her again at another fundraiser at Red Fox Winery. She was best friends with the Red Fox Winery owners, Bryson and Jackie Jackson. Dash got the opportunity to meet them and taste their fabulous reserve wines. Red Fox was known for its Rhone varietal wines.

The Jacksons were a handsome couple, invited to every soiree in Great Oaks. Bryson was a large man with a receding hairline, powerful handshake, and an engaging sincerity. His wife Jackie was a petite brunette with sparkling blue eyes. Photos of their children were proudly displayed throughout the tasting room.

Dash asked Bryson Jackson how he got into the wine business.

Bryson smiled, "I was a hedge fund manager living in Westchester County, and my wife Jackie wanted to go home to California. We started the winery and immediately starting bleeding money. We were into the business five years before we made a nickel. Now we're making nickels by the barrel full," he laughed. "Enjoying the Central Coast lifestyle—learning how to make a drinkable wine." Bryson lifted his glass. "How about you, Dash?"

"You've succeeded. This Rhone blend is superb," Dash lifted his glass, "Like you, it was about quality of life. Ultimately, you have to make a go of it. I have a small vineyard, have a private investigator's license, and do mostly insurance fraud," Dash said. Bryson Jackson excused himself to greet other guests. Dash connected again with Claudia, who indicated that she wanted Dash to drive her home. She was a bit too buzzed to drive her own vehicle.

Dash drove her home—she invited him in for another glass of wine. She lived in a modest two-bedroom house. One bedroom was a home office with floor to ceiling wine racks full and cases of unopened wine on the floor.

Claudia grinned as she showed Dash her wine supply, "One of the benefits of being a barrel salesperson." She lifted a Zinfandel from the rack, "This is a classic Great Oaks Zin—fruit-forward, big, juicy, almost edible."

Dash laughed. They walked out to the small patio, drank wine, under the canopy of the star-strewn sky, "You can see most of the constellations from here, how lucky for us."

Claudia was a bit tipsy but managed to call out the major constellations, "Orion, Big Dipper/Ursa Major, Ursa Minor. There's Orion's belt and the North Star," Claudia said, pointing to the heavens. "I could sit out here all night."

Dash admired her childlike enthusiasm for the stars. Claudia was eventually chilled by the evening air, and Dash accompanied her back to her house. Dash steadied her as she maneuvered herself down the patio steps. She had a little foot slip, and Dash held her fast in his arms. He looked at her bright face and kissed her lightly on the lips. She responded with a fuller kiss, holding him tight for balance and warmth. They continued into the bedroom, where Claudia invited Dash to share her bed. They fell into a frenzied embrace, letting the fatigue and wine consumption of the day slip off as quickly as their clothes. They embarked on a night of passion and exploration. Dash never forgot how sumptuous she looked that night, an enchanted memory that lingered on, well after she was gone.

Two weeks had elapsed since that meeting at the winery when Claudia's murder became front-page news. Her murder occupied a full week's news cycle in local daily and weekly publications, on radio, on local television—even garnering some regional and national news. There was the notion that a single woman attending late-night functions alone was an easy target. Her funeral was in Arizona, where her only living relative lived—her brother, Frank Bowers.

A few days after the funeral, Dash got an unexpected call from Bryson Jackson, owner and winemaker at Red Fox Winery, asking him to find Claudia's murderer.

Dash was taken aback, "The Tribune didn't give many details. It appears that it was a random act. The police even suspect someone from out of the area—an opportunist. I didn't know anything about her private life. I can't say we were more than just casual friends," He lied.

"You knew Claudia. You had mentioned that you're a licensed private investigator," Bryson said.

Dash didn't elaborate on their relationship, "I will meet with you and Jackie, but I can't assure you that I will take on the investigation, or that I will take your hard-earned money."

"Can you come over after we close the tasting room tonight at five?" Bryson was adamant.

"Sure, it'll cost you a bottle of wine," Dash felt his levity was ill-timed.

"Of course—see you at five," Bryson confirmed.

The Red Fox Winery tasting room sat behind an old farmhouse. It was located in a restored barn next to a lovely picnic area and in front of a large crushing and storage area that mimicked the architecture of the barn. The tasting room was wainscoted with weathered redwood and was warm and inviting. The Jacksons' were intensely proud of their wines and the revitalization of an old homestead. Bryson took his passion for winemaking to a discipline and craft. Unlike his last visit to Red Fox Winery, there was now a somberness and rigidity in the air. It made Dash uncomfortable.

"Can I get you a glass of wine?" Jackie asked Dash.

Dash didn't feel like drinking, "Just some water, please."

They sat at a large oaken table that was raised. They all drank water.

Dash listened to their appeal to investigate Claudia's murder.

"We've known Claudia since she moved here three years ago after an ugly divorce in Los Angeles. She made a clean break and wanted to start a new life. She was a determined go-getter. I think we were her first clients," Bryson said.

"I knew she was divorced. She told me that when she got divorced—she studied to be a sommelier, and that was her entrée into the wine business. She didn't discuss her private life with me other than she had a long-distance relationship with an American living in London," Dash said.

Bryson nodded, "We know all that, but you probably are not aware of her romantic liaisons and her political activities. We started a Save the Oaks action committee after Jasper Winery cut down fifteen hundred ancient oaks to make a reservoir. She became a vocal member of the action committee. It served her well in Great Oaks, hurting her business with some of the big boys. They believe no one can tell them what to do with their property."

Dash responded, "I know that to be true, but what has that have to do with her murder?"

"Bryson pondered the question, "She got in their crosshairs. I know it sounds provincial. More to the point—it was complicated by her liaison with a married winery owner."

"When did that so-called liaison end?" Dash asked.

"Over two years ago," Bryson answered.

Dash was intrigued, "Who was the winery owner?"

"Bill Lyons, Lyons Wine Estates, direct competitors to Jasper Winery," Bryson added.

"It was my understanding that the competition comes from Napa and other appellations. The competition is not local. You mentioned her activism, her affair, what else could be pertinent to her murder?" Dash asked.

"The gold rush here on the Central Coast!" Bryson blurted out.

Dash flinched, "What gold rush?"

"The aquifer, the water we're sitting on—the biggest west of the Sierra. Imagine a big reserve of water with four hundred wineries, a dozen breweries, small manufacturing, and fifty thousand residents, all with straws sucking water from that aquifer. There will be winners and losers. The owners of Jasper could give a damn about wine. They're after the water rights."

"What's that have to do with Claudia?" Dash asked.

Bryson hesitated, "Her former lover, Bill Lyons, was sounding the alarm about the water grab, and he was using Claudia to stir up the pot."

Bryson looked at Jackie, and she moved her lips. "His million case production dwarfs every other winery in the region. He's not a billionaire like the Jasper owners, but he's close, and he has immense political clout."

"You're saying that Claudia was a pawn in a high stakes *Game of Thrones*?" Dash asked.

Bryson got up from the table and went over to the bar snatching a bottle of Reserve Syrah and three stemmed glasses setting them on the table and pouring three fingers into each glass. Bryson took a swallow and smiled, "This is my best work, not over-extracted, balanced, and elegant."

Dash drank and concurred, "My regards to the winemaker." Dash got back on topic. "Okay, I see where you're going with this scenario. I don't think these folks, the winery owners, would murder a barrel salesperson to make a point."

"It's more complicated than that. Gregg Perigold, the man in London who she's engaged to and his father Jason Perigold own Jasper Winery, among other holdings. Gregg is the heir to the throne. His relationship with Claudia, a vendor, was frowned upon by his parents. They were from a different class and tribe. "

Dash took another swallow of the Syrah and pause, "Claudia was very active. I guess I didn't know her as well as I thought. I live here—I'm reluctant to get involved in other people's personal business and schemes. These folks can crush me and put your winery out of business. I'm not frightened—just practical. They probably can pay off the police, the county supervisors, the district attorney, and anyone else they chose. What can be gained?" Dash asked.

"Justice for Claudia, peace of mind, revenge, and a giant fuck you," Bryson squeezed his wine glass.

"We're willing to pay you twenty thousand dollars and one case of wine for two months work," Bryson looked squarely at Dash.

Dash lowered his head, "I'm not in the fuck-you business. Let me think about it."

"Get back to us tomorrow. We've already cut a check. We don't expect a miracle, Bryson said."

Dash got up from his chair, leaving a finger of Syrah in the glass, "Okay, that's fair. Thanks for the wine. If I say no, I hope you'll understand."

Jackie walked Dash out to his car. It was still hot out in the eighties. Dash went to shake hands with Jackie. She gave him a hug.

"She was like our daughter. She didn't deserve to die like that. We don't expect that it will change anything—consider Claudia—consider how she was killed—consider that she's not at rest."

Dash hugged Jackie. She seemed frail, "Yes. I'll consider Claudia. You know, the truth probably won't change the outcome if I get anywhere near it. I don't want to set you up for further disappointment."

"We know."

Dash drove off. His place was just ten minutes from Red Fox Winery. It wasn't the money—it was the grave. We all end up in the same place, and sometimes we're better off.

He wished he hadn't had the glass of Syrah. Wine always complicated things.

Chapter Three:

CLAUDIA BOWERS

Claudia stayed on Dash's mind through the night. He realized he barely knew her—they had spent only four or five social outings together, not really dates. He'd spent one memorable night with her when they were both above the legal limit. They were never truly intimate; they were simply acquaintances trying to maneuver through life.

Dash knew a little about her background gleaned from casual conservations with her. She lived by herself in a little rental cottage on a horse ranch. She worked from home for a Spanish barrel-making company headquartered in Barcelona. Claudia traveled extensively between Europe and the west coast, enough to maintain a relationship with a Londoner. Her brother lived in Flagstaff, Arizona. Her ex-husband, whom she never spoke of, lived in Southern California. Her passion was wine. Following college, she had been determined to work in the wine industry. She went to college on a cheerleading scholarship and had a gymnast's body—she was petite and athletic until she started drinking wine. She complained that she was carrying ten extra pounds on a five-foot three-inch frame. Dash was never comfortable when a woman mentioned her weight; they all did—no man with any sense would dare complain. After she was divorced, then passing her sommelier's course exam, where she'd met Greg Perrigold, in Napa, she settled in Great Oaks, the home to four hundred bonded wineries.

She was very discreet about her lovers and liaisons—never mentioning them to Dash. He never asked. This was the tricky part for Dash. He was okay with the investigation into her murder—the pay and his clients. He was not okay snooping around into married men's affairs, online hook-ups, and indiscretions. That was the very reason he never took on domestic surveillance cases involving cheating wives and husbands. Carl Jung said we all have three lives: public, private, and secret. Dash knew that Claudia lead an active public life, a guarded private life, and a complicated secret life.

On the positive side, Dash could use the money for vineyard improvements, had another six to eight weeks to harvest, and was getting bored with his social life. He called Bryson in the morning, telling him that he'd take on the case. He would limit it to two months with no renewal. He would not divulge their names, nor would he use their names for entrée. They would be silent partners, and, if needed, he would hire a social networking expert at additional expense. Travel, lodging, or lab reports would also be additional; all meals, tips, hush monies, and bribes would be incurred by Dash, out of his pocket.

Dash knew one detective with the Great Oaks Police Department; FJ Evans, sixty years old, grizzled, thirty pounds overweight, reminding anyone that would listen how many days and hours he had until he retired. He put everyone on notice that he'd be in a foul mood until that day arrived.

Dash knew FJ from twenty years ago when he had a better attitude and a waist. They would run into each other at some civic events or at the gym where they both swam laps. FJ grew up in Southern California, and swimming was second nature to him. Dash was taller, leaner, and in better shape, but FJ was a much more efficient swimmer. They had cigars, donuts, and whiskey in common. Dash called FJ at the new public safety building.

"Hello Floyd, this is Dash. Could I meet you for coffee and donuts?" Dash knew that calling FJ Floyd Joseph would push all his buttons.

"Damn you, Dash. Don't ever call me Floyd. There's not a decent donut in this broke down one-horse town. They figure if they put enough frosting, sprinkles, and candy on them—no one will know how lousy the cakes are. I can still taste the donuts from Doug's Donuts in Huntington Beach. Enough about donuts. What are you up to, besides being a pretend private investigator and grape grower?"

"I've been hired to look into Claudia Bowers' death. She was a friend."

"Here we go again—amateur hour. I suppose you want me to divulge some insider information that will placate your clients and send you on your merry way. First off, I don't have any information. Secondly, if I did, I won't tell you, and thirdly—what makes you think you can solve this murder from your pathetic vineyard when we have the labs, the crime scene photos, and the autopsy. We also have her vehicle and the testimony of all her friends she had dinner with the night she disappeared. Here's your takeaway. She was either in the wrong place at the wrong time, or a jilted lover cut her throat O. J. Simpson style."

Dash was nonplussed. "I guess that means the donut date is off."

"You could say that, but I will still say hello to you on the pool deck at the club," FJ Evans hung up the phone unceremoniously.

Dash gathered two things from the call. He now assumed they were focusing on jilted lovers and that her throat was cut. The paper did not indicate how she was killed; the Tribune simply said she was slain. Dash knew that FJ was sitting on a largess of resources, whereas Dash was sitting on squat.

Dash went over to Red Fox Winery to meet once again with Bryson and Jackie Jackson. They handed him the check and shook hands. They took him into a private room just off the tasting room. Jackie asked if he'd like his case of wine now. He deferred until the end of the sixty-day period.

They both looked fatigued and out of sorts. Dash gave them the tidbits of information that Evans had given him.

Bryson Jackson laid down some guidelines, "I don't know if Bill Lyons dumped her or vice versa, but I would immediately take him off the shortlist. He's a stand-up guy who fell for Claudia's charms. If you do talk to him—don't tell him that we are the source of the info on his infidelities. We can't think of anyone she jilted other than you," Bryson said.

Dash laughed uncomfortably, "When I get jilted, I contemplate redemption, not revenge. Claudia and I were never more than friends. I know most men believe friendship with a woman to be improbable at best and unnatural at worst. Yes, we had mutual attraction—flirted, but that was the extent of the relationship. I can't provide another tale of woe."

Jackie ruminated, "I've had male friends, but usually they wanted more, and it ended. I consider many of Bryson's friends to be our friends, but that's different. I don't think Bryson would appreciate me having coffee with a male friend."

Dash redirected the conversation, "Did you know of any other friends, lovers, or liaisons that Claudia could have had with other men?"

Bryson paused, his face reddened, "I suppose I know a couple of her clients who bragged about her, but I can't say that they were being honest."

Jackie looked at her husband hard, "What do you mean by that? You're talking about Claudia like she was merchandise?"

Bryson retreated. "No, never—I won't mention names, but several winery owners imagined her as more than a vendor. "

Dash interjected, "I'll need to know their names. I won't mention yours, and I won't betray your confidence. Write them on a pad. What do you think the police know about her affairs?"

"Damn little, but I can assure you that The Wine Sisters are blabbing. Claudia bragged about her conquests to her friends. She embellished the facts for entertainment value."

Dash was tired of sitting in the meeting room just off the tasting room. He had his check, a little information to go on, and he didn't want to witness an argument between the Jacksons.

"I suppose I'll start with The Wine Sisters. I want to know what the police know. I appreciate the payment upfront," Dash got up to leave.

Bryson went behind the wine bar, where there were two tasting room employees pouring tastes to the tourists. He nabbed a bottle of his Bordeaux Blend of Cabernet and Merlot and handed it to Dash. "Taste this—it scored a ninety-two in Wine Spectator. It pairs well with bone-in steaks, chocolate desserts, and divorcees."

Dash laughed, "That pretty well covers my every desire."

Dash thanked him for the wine and went out into the hot part of the day. He drove to the bank and deposited the check. He was driving his vintage grey Range Rover. He didn't take along Barney, the blue merle Aussie, because it was too hot even with the air conditioner on. He went home and relaxed on the couch with Bixby and Barney at his side. Bixby, the big white Anatolian shepherd, never left the ranch, whereas Barney was always ready to go anywhere.

He got up and starting writing down names on a notepad. He began every investigation the same way. He would write names, dates, and places with a short description. His process was by elimination, not discovery. Dash thought discovery was overrated. Discovery came later when the pieces were all in place after he'd eliminated every scenario and suspect.

He began with the obvious—Claudia Bowers was a knifing victim murdered in mid-August. Bryson and Jackie Jackson were clients and mutual friends of Claudia. Bill Lyons was a former paramour. Gregg Perigold was Claudia's fiancé living in London. Of the infamous Wine Sisters, Dash knew: Taylor Thorngate, Mona Morgan, and Brenda Brown. The other seven or so were not known to him

His tack was simple—go through the names, add and subtract to the list of suspects. Unlike the police, Dash had no political axes to grind or any loyalties to honor. He could follow his nose until it got bloodied. He was under the radar for now, but since he spoke to FJ, even those bets were off.

Soon enough, Dash got a call from Detective Evans, "This is FJ, I wanted to take you up on our donut date. How does tomorrow morning at seven work for you?

Dash agreed, and they met at Ground Squirrel Bakery near their swim club. It was an open, airy, and full of retired folks kick-starting their day with coffee and conversation. The Ground Squirrel could have been a scene anywhere in America. Dash observed that none of the retired folks were sitting on their smartphones but engaging in conversation. Detective Evans was waiting for him in a corner table.

Dash looked at the scone on Evan's plate, "No donuts today?"

Detective Evans was in a good mood, "Good choice, Dash—this place is a real bakery, not a donut shop. Good view of the city too." The big picture windows had a view of the Salinas River to the West and the city. Great Oaks had no skyline, just oak-studded rolling hills with large stucco and brick buildings in the foreground, surrounded on all sides by vineyards.

"We're the lucky ones—we could be in Grand Rapids," Dash joked.

"Nothing's wrong with Grand Rapids. It's got civic pride, commerce, culture, breweries, art museums. I'd bet Grand Rapids even has a decent donut shop or two. All we've got is wineries, high priced restaurants, dive bars, horse shows, and a farm implement museum. The cost of living in Grand Rapids is half what it is here without the whiney Californians. Are you kidding? As soon as I retire, I'll have California in my rear-view mirror," Detective Evans said, polishing off his scone.

"Sure. On a day like today, where is better?" Dash looked outside at the bright blue skies and bucolic splendor of the Salinas River.

Detective Evans added milk and sugar to his coffee, took a large swallow, and got down to business.

"Who's the client paying you to investigate Claudia's murder?"

"Can't tell you that detective—maybe after I solve the crime, I'll tell you."

"Fair enough." Evans was not amused. "But that probably won't occur. If you want some reciprocity in the interim, you have only one card to play."

"Is that the only reason you wanted to have a coffee date?" Dash grinned, "Or did you have something else on your agenda?" Dash shifted his weight, peering over at the row of appetizing pastries that he could no longer eat. He did love a great Danish or croissant, but it didn't sit well on an empty stomach. He had no appetite for the mediocre coffee they served. He drank water.

Detective Evans ordered two cinnamon rolls to go, "Not now, but I want to keep the communication lines open with you. Amateurs and psychics have a way of stumbling across evidence and details that we may have missed."

"Flattering. I've never been compared to a psychic. We amateurs rely on intuition and good sense and often ignore the obvious because it doesn't hold our interest."

Detective FJ Evans allowed his cement jaw to finally break into a slight grin. "Bullshit. You boys just muck things up. What you call intuition, I call bullshit. What you call common sense, I call nonsense. What you call interesting—I call it a waste of time. I hope you got paid in advance," Evans got up from the table, self-bussing his plate and cup and proceeded to the door. Dash motioned for him to come back to the table and Detective Evans ambled back to the table.

Dash reached in his pocket, "I almost forgot—I brought you an Arturo Fuente Don Carlos Presidente," and handed him a wrapped cigar. FJ held the cigar between his thumb and forefinger like it was a precious coin.

"Thanks, Dash. You have impeccable taste in cigars. Women, not so much." FJ put the cigar in his pocket.

"One more thing—you said on the phone that Claudia's throat was cut. That sounds too ritualistic to be random."

The Detective sat back down, putting his bag of cinnamon rolls on the table. He lowered his voice.

"You're watching too much television. We've ruled out a serial killer because it was the only murder like that anywhere. It was more gruesome than ritualistic."

Detective Evans was done with the meeting and rose to his feet, heading for the door. He waved to Dash, who was left sitting, with his half-empty glass of water, and the check.

Dash peered down at the river where Claudia was found. He left the café and walked down a sidewalk to the bike path that ran along the dry river bank. There were several dirt trails off the bike path. He walked down an unruly cut through the thicket and immediately ran into a homeless encampment just a hundred yards from the bike trail. There were three men, all in their thirties, just rising and packing up for the day. One fellow lounged on a burgundy couch- the others had large garbage bags full of their belongings that they were attending to. He greeted them cautiously.

"Top of the morning to you—I wonder if I could ask you a question?" Dash asked.

The homeless men looked dazed and confused but not alarmed, "Can't you see we're busy."

Dash immediately knew that was code. He handed the speaker, a man in his thirties with oily black hair, a five-dollar bill. "Did any of you see the body of the girl down by the bridge at Twenty-Sixth Street?"

The speaker took the five-dollar bill and motioned that the other men needed a bill as well. Dash forked over two more five-dollar bills. They mumbled amongst themselves.

The speaker sheepishly answered, "Nah, we ain't seen anything. We heard about it—mostly from the cops. We heard she was pretty."

"Who told you she was pretty?"

"The Hamster," the speaker answered. The three homeless men started talking among themselves as if Dash wasn't even present. The interview was over.

Intuition told Dash that he had to find The Hamster. Good sense told him that he was probably also homeless. Curiosity led Dash to assume that The Hamster was on the move.

A hamster wouldn't last long in the wilds along the Salinas River.

Chapter Four:

THE HAMSTER

It was mid-day and already hot. Great Oaks is an ideal wine region because of the diurnal fluctuation, where temperatures fluctuate between forty and fifty degrees in a single day during the growing season. It also means that you stay inside or go to the coast mid-day and come out again in the evening. Dash would search for The Hamster in the evening when the temperature had dropped. He went home, wrote some notes, had lunch, and took a siesta.

Later, Dash put on some light hiking pants, a long sleeve shirt, leather walking shoes, and a cap. He took along a water bottle. He found parking along River Road near the Twenty-Sixth Street Bridge. It was after five—the sun was still unforgiving, and the temperature was still ninety degrees in the shade. One never gets used to extreme heat or cold. The planet is telling us that we'd better get used to it.

Dash followed a trail that ran along the base of the towering bridge above. The beautiful natural setting was blighted by the debris, furniture, shopping carts, and clothing spewed on the ground. Not a soul in sight. Dash wondered if it was a homeless holiday, or the homeless had moved on because of the heat. He decided to follow the dirt trail that shadowed River Road. He walked back towards the Thirtieth Street Bridge. Along the trail, he met a bearded man about fifty years old with sharp dark eyes. He, too, was searching for something.

Dash motioned to him, "Hello, I'm Dash—I'm not a cop—I'm looking for a man named The Hamster." The man would not make eye contact, and his expression was blank. Dash approached him wearily.

Dash repeated his question, "Do you know a fellow called The Hamster?"

The man stopped moving and gave a puzzled glance at Dash, "No, I'm looking for my son."

Dash knew that to be a lie. The man was looking for his belongings. "Ever heard of The Hamster from your son?"

The man gave Dash another furtive glance, "Heard the name—never seen 'em. Bye."

The man disappeared back into the heavy thicket. Dash continued on the trail. The absence of human and animal life was odd. No dogs, no squirrels, no rabbits, no feral cats - nothing. Dash walked past the Thirteenth Street Bridge to a public park that was located in the river bed. It probably flooded in the winter. There was one person sitting at a picnic table, and a mother and child on a swing set. Dash walked over to the man at the picnic table. The man was eating food from a Jack in the Box bag. The way he held it and devoured the food suggested to Dash that he found the bag. He was the oldest homeless person he'd seen. He looked to be in his sixties, longish grey hair, bent over frame and wrinkle lines that looked like they'd been carved into his dark tan face.

Dash sat across from him on the picnic table, "Mind if I sit here?"

The man gave him a long look and nodded. He continued eating.

"Where is everyone? I've been up and down the river looking for my son." Dash used the same line as the last homeless guy he'd met."

The man looked up from his lunch. His eyes were glassy. "How do you know he's down here?"

"This is where I found him last time." Dash tried to bullshit the man.

"You don't have a son. You look like a tourist or a cop. Why don't you find somewhere else to sit? I'm trying to enjoy my dinner."

"I'm not a cop or a tourist. I'm a private investigator. I'm looking for a man called The Hamster. Ever heard of him?" Dash asked.

"Sure, everybody's looking for him. Did he win the lottery? You got a check for him?"

"I have cash," Dash smiled, "a hundred dollars."

"He won't come out of hiding for less than two hundred dollars. Also, I need a fifty-dollar service fee."

Dash knew he was being played, "I just have six twenties on me. Would that work?" Dash pulled out the money and put it on the picnic table. The man looked at it for a minute, eating a French fry from the greasy bag. He ate another french fry, then picked up the money.

Dash was amused. "So where's this Hamster guy? How do I find him?"

The man at the picnic table ate the last of his french fries, examining the empty box before answering, "I could use some more french fries."

Dash looked around, and the closest fast-food restaurant was three miles away, "I could drive you, but you'll have to wait for a half-hour—I'm parked down by Twenty-Sixth."

The man at the picnic table crushed the greasy bag and threw it at a container. He missed. Dash got up and put it in the trash. The man got up and started to walk, "Let's go."

Dash followed, caught up to him. The old man walked fairly briskly, looking down at the trail. They walked several hundred feet without talking.

They came to the area where Dash's car was parked, and Dash pointed to the car. "It's the grey SUV on the road."

The man followed Dash up to the car, Dash opened the passenger door, and the man sat down. The man had a foul smell. Dash got in the car and turned to the old man.

"Do you have a preference for french fries?" Dash asked.

The man looked straight ahead as Dash turned on the engine. "McDonald's."

Dash drove him to the McDonalds at a large shopping center and got in the drive-thru lane. He drove to the ordering panel and looked over at the old man.

"Anything else besides fries?"

"Two orders of large fries and an apple pie."

Dash made the order, paid and handed the old man the food, and parked his car near the restaurant. "You took my money—I got you your fries. Now tell me where I can find The Hamster."

The man ate the french fries slowly as if each was his last morsel. "He's gone—he left the area after the police were on his ass. He found a body—they thought he knew something."

"Did he?" Dash lost his appetite watching the old man eat.

"Yeah, he saw the man who dropped off the body. I suppose you want the same information."

Dash looked at the old man hard, "What's your name—are you The Hamster?"

"Do I look like a hamster? No, my name is Frank. I've traveled with The Hamster. You won't be able to find him. He'll be back in the fall. He told me everything."

"Is that why you took the money?" Dash asked.

"I took the money because I need it. You need information—I needed french fries—you needed to know about The Hamster. We could go to the ATM and get more money."

Dash was flabbergasted by his demand, "Why?"

"Because I'm The Hamster."

Chapter Five:

ASK CHARLEY

Dash took The Hamster to the ATM and withdrew another two hundred dollars. He gave The Hamster another six twenties. He was happy. Dash wanted his money's worth. They sat in the bank parking lot and began to ask questions.

"Are you the person that found Claudia Bowers' body?" Dash asked The Hamster.

"No one ever said I found the body, but I saw it. My friend Charley found her. He has a weak stomach—he heaved everywhere. He came to me and asked what to do. I went and saw her. She was bled out like a lamb. She was a looker. Her face and hair were soaked in her own blood, but you could see her prettiness. Probably what got her killed."

"What do you mean by that?" Dash was disgusted with the appraisal.

"Saw her picture in the newspaper," The Hamster said without emotion.

Dash looked hard at the man with a furrowed brow and deep wrinkles. "What was she wearing?"

"Jeans, t-shirt, open-toed shoes with heels, a blue and white polka dot bra—her stomach was showing—she was hanging upside down tied to a tree branch. The coyotes hadn't touched her yet."

"Did they?"

"Yes, we left her alone thinking somebody would find her—we came back two days later. She was still there, but not pretty anymore. The coyotes had been at her hard. Charley barfed again."

"Did you call the police?" Dash shifted in his car seat, looking away from The Hamster.

"We went up to Wendy's next to the bridge—told the girl taking food orders—she called her manager. Guess that the manager called the police. We left Wendy's, but the police located us down at the same park you found me. They asked the same questions—got the same answers, but they didn't pay me."

"So, what do I get for my money?" Dash was firm.

"We saw the guy that put the rope out. We didn't tell the police—they didn't ask."

Dash smirked, "So, what did he look like?"

"He was wearing sunglasses. Younger than you, maybe forty. Had a gut, spikey blond hair, wore shorts and flip flops. Looked like he was going to the beach—he was trying to look young. Had a big tattoo on his arm, couldn't make it out."

"What do you mean, spikey hair?"

"You know how kids put goop on their hair to make it stand up."

Dash turned and looked at The Hamster, "You look under nourished-how fat was this guy?"

"Fatter than you and me, beer gut. He was breathing hard—like it was hard work walking a couple hundred yards through the brush. He was sweating—his shirt was wet."

"What color shirt?"

"Kinda' yellow with surfboards and palm trees on it—like the Hawaiian shirts—people used to give us them until they became valuable. People are now hoarding everything except the cheap shit."

Dash opened the windows again because The Hamster's body odor was permeating the car. Dash started the engine, "You got anything else for me?"

"Nah, but maybe Charley does, he's in San Miguel living with his sister. Don't ask me where—I don't know. She's Mexican like Charley."

Dash drove The Hamster back to the park where he found him. There was a parking lot next to the park, and it was getting late in the day. There was only one person, an elderly man, walking his dog. The Hamster got out of the car, touching the new money in his pocket. Dash was relieved to get him out of his car.

"Can I find you here tomorrow or the next day?" Dash asked out his car window.

The Hamster turned and looked at him, "Maybe, maybe not— bring money."

"One question—why do they call you The Hamster—you're tall and lanky?"

"There's not just one Hamster. We call a person who stores their stuff down here a hamster. Everybody on the river is a hamster. Get it?"

"So, did you tell me the truth about seeing the body and the man with the rope?"

"Fuck no, I didn't see anything—just heard the stories from Charley. His real name ain't Charley; you won't find him in the phone book."

"Do you know his real name?" Dash was losing patience.

"Pepe, maybe Pedro—I heard him answer to all those names. He's got a beard—he smokes Lucky Strikes—he's got a few teeth, squinty eyes. He's not pretty."

"Are you making all this up to get money?" Dash was skeptical.

"Maybe. Ask Charley." The Hamster walked away and sat on the same bench at the same picnic table. He pulled out a pack of cigarettes. Dash could tell they were Lucky Strikes.

Chapter Six:

TAYLOR THORNGATE

Dash was traveling a few hundred dollars lighter, thinking he'd been grifted. He knew no one in the mission town of San Miguel. Locating Charley or Pedro or Pepe or whatever the hell his name was going to be tough. Dash went home, showered, smoked a cigar, drank some good Port, and thought about Claudia. The Hamster had one thing right—she was pretty. It was her vitality, her quick wit, her fun-loving nature that made her pretty. The description of the man who dropped off the rope sounded far-fetched, like some kind of cartoon character. Dash thought he'd give a call to Taylor Thorngate, one of The Wine Sisters. She was a true sister to Claudia.

Taylor was not that receptive. Dash had used her to do some social media work for his wine brand—she had also helped with the wine label design. She was a talented graphic artist. She was bipolar in the truest sense. If you caught her in a manic phase, she'd knock your socks off with her creativity and energy. If you caught her on the downside, she'd be mean spirited and rude. Dash caught her on the downside. She didn't want to talk about Claudia—she had no interest in seeing Dash. Dash changed the subject and asked her if she would consider designing a poster for the Paderewski Piano Festival. Dash had volunteered to be on the advisory council to help out the tottering local cultural scene. She was intrigued and agreed to meet Dash at a hipster coffee house downtown in the morning.

Dash showed up early, ordered a cup of coffee and an almond bear claw, and waited. They roasted their own coffee, giving the place a nice aroma. He hadn't seen Taylor in three months, and that was the normal cycle. He'd run into her downtown or at a restaurant when she was a bright light. She would hug Dash and treat him like a long-lost friend. Other times, she'd ignore him, avoiding eye contact. Her behavior didn't bother Dash.

She arrived appearing to have just gotten out of bed. Her hair was pulled back in a harsh ponytail. She wore blue-rimmed glasses with thick lenses, leggings, and a hooded sweatshirt. She had put on minimal make-up: lipstick, eyeliner, and maybe a blush. Her look, though ill-conceived, was endearing.

Dash motioned to her, and she sat at the rough-hewn table on a wooden stool. She carried a notebook and a cup of coffee she gathered from the coffee bar.

"Good morning Taylor. I see you're ready to get to work. Are you familiar with the Paderewski Festival?" Dash asked.

Taylor had her face in the coffee mug, "Damn, I needed this. I can't even wake up without four cups of coffee. It's worse than an addiction," Taylor lifted her head and looked at Dash directly for the first time. "Paderewski, pianist, composer, first president of modern Poland and a wine grape grower right here in Great Oaks."

"Very good, this year marks the hundredth anniversary of his presidency in Poland, and we're making the festival grander," Dash beamed.

"Isn't it just a piano competition and recital—not much general interest?" Taylor resumed her coffee drinking getting up to refill her cup.

When she returned to her seat, Dash responded, "You're absolutely right. In the past, the festival has been just a piano competition on the Central Coast. This year we've expanded it to include dance, art, and small music ensembles. There'll be a large delegation from Poland arriving. It'll be the biggest event in Great Oaks, outside of the Mid State Fair and Pioneer Days."

Taylor broke into a slight smile, "When did you go to work for the Chamber of Commerce? I thought you were a half-ass wine grape grower and detective."

"I like to do a lot of things half-ass," Dash smiled, "I recently was hired on to look into Claudia's murder."

"I hope that's not the real reason I'm here. If it is, I'm outta' here." Taylor clenched her notebook.

"No, I'm here to discuss the design work, but we were both friends of Claudia—we have that in common. I'm sure you'd like her killer to be identified," Dash said, nursing his cup of coffee.

Taylor unclenched the grip on her notebook, "I've talked to the police several times—I don't think they have a clue. This was not random. Claudia even told me that she thought she was being stalked," Taylor paused, "Enough about Claudia—it's a real downer. What's the deadline for this design work?"

"Labor Day, September first, the festival is after Thanksgiving in early December. Do you need some more info to go on?" Dash asked.

"Are you the contact? Who do I submit the artwork to?" Taylor was warming her hands with the coffee cup.

Dash handed her a card for the festival manager. "Just submit to Jane's email," Dash pointed to the card, "on the card."

"Is there anything I need to know before submitting to this Jane woman?" Taylor asked.

"No, just be respectful—we're all volunteers, and it consumes a fair amount of time."

Taylor was aggravated, "You be respectful! I know you want the dirt on Claudia—you're not getting it from me. You think The Wine Sisters are all about gossip. You've got that wrong. Our sisterhood is just that—we only dish among ourselves. So, Dash, this vessel isn't pouring any juice out today."

Dash apologized, "You're partially right. I don't want gossip—I want to know the truth about Claudia."

Taylor got up to go, "Thanks for the Paderewski lead—I could do it with my eyes closed. You're not expecting a kick-back?" she laughed.

"Maybe a latte—if you get the festival gig," Dash said.

Taylor switched on her cordial side and shook hands with Dash, "That's a deal."

Taylor paused as if in deep thought, muttering under her breath before departing, "Claudia was sleeping with the enemy."

Chapter Seven:

THE ENEMY

Dash was left alone with his thoughts—a far too common occurrence. Dash was spending too much time alone, spending too much time in thought, not action. He could not let go of the conversation he had with Taylor—that begged the question—who was the enemy?

In Great Oaks, it was the battle of the billionaire wineries. There were the mindful-conservationists, who had the money to hand weed and hire goats, did not spray, built buffers around their vineyards of oak wildlands, had organic, sustainable grape harvests, recycled and reused their water, didn't use any single-use plastic items, and didn't allow their field workers to bring plastic water containers. The wineries bought them all thermos containers that the workers hated because of the extra weight.

Then there were the opportunists who preached the gospel of sustainability while clear-cutting ancient oaks, grabbing water rights, and hiring away the best winemakers while keeping their eye on the bottom line. If they had a wine that rated over ninety-five points in Wine Spectator magazine or won a prestigious gold medal or accolade, the consumers would overlook their farming practices to buy their wines. The consumer didn't care if the winery owner was environmentally conscious, as long as they produced a top-rated limited production Cabernet. They wanted a bottle for their wine cellar. It was like stamp collecting on steroids.

Napa Valley Cabernet Sauvignon brands like Screaming Eagle sell for over three thousand dollars a bottle. Ghost Horse, just under a thousand dollars. These are the benchmarks in the wine industry. The Central Coast is only one generation removed from Napa. The Cabernets from the region are now gaining ratings and recognition. With that recognition comes higher prices for a ton of fruit and a case of wine.

Dash knew from Bryson Jackson that Claudia was an activist, if not an outspoken advocate, for the oaks and sustainable farming practices. It would run counter to some of her biggest wine barrel clients. Were they the enemy? Dash knew the answer was probably not. Who was then the enemy that Taylor referred to? It would easier to find out who Claudia was sleeping with than to determine who the enemy was (an enemy of whom?)

These were the thoughts that drove Dash crazy. He decided to circle back to the Jacksons and go to their winery unannounced. Dash had cleaned up for his meeting with Taylor, wearing off white pressed slacks, a belt, new loafers, a blue striped long-sleeve shirt, and a coffee-colored fedora he'd picked up in Mexico. He looked like a country pimp driving an old Range Rover. It was Tuesday, and the winery tasting room traffic was dead. The Jacksons gave the tasting room staff Mondays and Tuesdays off. Jackie smiled broadly when Dash walked in.

"What's the occasion? She said, looking at his garb, "You going on a cruise?" Jackie chuckled.

"Nah, just doing some work for the Paderewski Festival. Have to look the part," he smiled.

"Can I get you a glass of wine or an umbrella drink?" Jackie grinned.

"Bryson is out doing some errands. Is there anything I can do for you?" Jackie was wearing a patterned dress. She was an anomaly in the wine country. Women wore jeans, leggings, and shorts—but rarely dresses. Jackie had a petit frame. She was a natural in a dress.

Dash thought his timing was fortuitous. "Actually, you may. I just spoke with a friend of Claudia's, and she mentioned that Claudia was sleeping with the enemy." Dash continued, "Does that make any sense to you?"

The normally bubbly and effervescent Jackie frowned, "Not really. Claudia had no enemies. She was well-liked in the wine industry, and she was highly regarded. She may have slept with some married men, but they pursued her. Not vice versa. It may sound strange to say, but she had a lot of integrity. I would trust her with my husband or my friends' husbands. She was not a predator."

"That was my take," Dash affirmed. "Sleeping with married men can gain you a lot of enemies and create some jealousies."

Jackie pondered, "I only know of one, Bill Lyons. He made no bones about the fact that they were in a relationship. His wife lived in the Bay Area—she never came around—it was like Claudia was his wife here. We introduced Bill to Claudia—he was smitten right away. She wouldn't date him for months. Bill never relented.

Dash accepted the bottled water that Jackie offered and was twisting off the cap. He took a long swallow. "Could Bill be the enemy?"

"No, not really. I can't think of anyone who doesn't like Bill. He's a regular stand-up guy. A charming fellow, a great businessman—just lonely. I think he's in a loveless marriage," Jackie said.

"What about her boyfriend, Gregg?" Dash asked.

"Gregg Perigold?" Dash nodded when Jackie said the name, "When they started dating, she immediately called it off with Bill. He was heartbroken, but he understood. They parted amicably. She was serious about Gregg, even though he was moving to London to study at the London School of Economics. She wouldn't date anyone once she was intimate with Gregg. She spent many nights here—just talking."

"You can't think of anyone else? Dash asked.

"No. Ask Taylor. That doesn't mean there weren't others, but if there were—she was very secretive of her private life. She didn't tell me," Jackie said.

Dash sensed he was on shaky grounds asking his client about Claudia's personal life, "Then who could possibly be an enemy?"

Jackie nervously wiped wine glasses behind the bar. She looked outside at the parking lot, hoping that some customers would arrive.

"You're going to have to ask Bryson—he should be back anytime."

Dash looked at his watch, still morning, "I'll guess I'll wait for a bit if you don't mind." Dash moved to a table taking his water with him, "What could Bryson add?"

Jackie grimaced, "Bryson recruited Claudia to help him with the Save the Oaks campaign. They made a great team. Not every landowner wants more regulations. Maybe he knows of someone who was upset by their campaign. We got a lot of good press because of it."

Just then, a group of eight wine tasters showed up filling up half the bar.

Dash shouted over the din, "Not all press is positive."

Chapter Eight:

BRYSON JACKSON

Dash listened to Jackie give her spiel about the Rhone varietal wines. She was well rehearsed but sincere and extremely proud of Red Fox Wines. It was in the low nineties outside; the tasters opted for lighter wines—a Viognier blend, a Picpoul Blanc, and the 2018 Rhone blend Rose. Bryson Jackson showed up just as the visitors were trying to decide whether to join the wine club or not. A wine club membership was worth about a thousand dollars a year in sales on average. The math was easy.

Bryson saw Dash and motioned for him to join him outside. He followed Bryson to the barrel room where it was cool—the aroma of barrel-aged wines was pleasantly seductive. They always brought the visitors to the barrel room on tours. Bryson had a small office inside the barrel room, and he pulled up a chair to the small work table for Dash to sit at.

"What's up, Dash. Any progress?" Bryson looked like he'd just come from a meeting with his bankers. He wore a pressed white shirt and navy slacks. His shoes didn't match his attire—crepe soles with dark brown oiled uppers. Winery shoes.

Dash answered with a question, "Which group was meeting?"

"It was our Save the Oaks monthly meeting. Can you believe we've raised over twenty thousand dollars? We're about to start an ad campaign."

Dash could read his pride, "I understand Claudia was a valuable member of the committee."

Bryson winced with the mention of her name, "Damn right. She was invaluable—she would not want us to lose momentum because of her death. We're forging ahead."

Dash asked, "Does your committee have any detractors or enemies?"

Bryson realized that he was being interrogated, "What are you getting at? Are you suggesting that Claudia's involvement got her killed? Not likely. We've been endorsed by the press, politicians, the wine alliance—even the Farm Bureau. The Perigolds wrote us a check. They've distanced themselves from the winemaker at Jasper Winery. He was responsible for the clear-cutting of fifteen hundred oak trees to build a reservoir."

"I read about it," Dash let Bryson ramble.

"The winemaker, Conrad Cook, wanted the reservoir for the planting of four hundred acres of Cabernet adjacent to the oaks," Bryson recited.

Dash paused to gather his thoughts, "Does this winemaker still work for them?"

Bryson smirked, "Yes, but he was moved to another winery they owned, on the east side."

Dash knew the east side of Great Oaks was generally hotter and considered less ideal for wine grapes than the cooler west side.

"What winery?" Dash asked.

Bryson got up, "You're good, Mr. Ramblar. You follow the bread crumbs. But they're only bread crumbs. The Perigolds didn't throw Conrad under the bus. They took the blame and made amends. Of course—the trees will not be replaced in two generations, but they're demonstrating corporate responsibility. It won't mollify the locals. Conrad works for Paint Horse Winery now."

Dash had another name, another suspect, "This isn't about oak trees, is it Bryson?"

Bryson looked at Dash hard. "Our committee is all about oak trees. I don't know where you are going with that question?"

Dash looked out through the glass at the hundreds of barrels stacked on metal frames to the ceiling, "Oaks were the victims—the motive was water. You need lots of water to make wine, no groundwater, no wine."

Bryson nodded in agreement, "Sir Conan Doyle would say 'a splendid deduction, Mr. Ramblar.'"

Dash was getting restless with the slow pace of the meeting, "A vibrant young woman is murdered. She was active in the committee. Claudia was dating a Perigold. I don't believe her death was random."

"I don't believe so," Bryson Jackson agreed.

"Her friend Taylor told me that she was sleeping with the enemy. You said she didn't have any enemies. Did you know who she was sleeping with?" Dash asked.

Steve's color rose, and he stumbled, "She was not Mother Teresa—she liked men—they liked her."

Dash walked past the pane of glass that separated the office from the barrel warehouse. "I can't continue unless you spill the beans. I'll give your money back, less expenses."

"You know about Bill Lyons. You know about the Perigold boy. The others weren't relationships—they were encounters. After she broke off with Bill, the Perigold boy was overseas. Claudia probably got lonely and bedded down a few in and out of the industry, but mostly in."

"Names," Dash was relentless. "I need their names even if it was a one-night stand."

"I heard rumors. She even boasted about picking up men at the local dive bar on Pine Street. She would not tell me their names—she let me guess," Bryson grinned.

Dash smiled, "This is a small town—people talk. I bet you have a good idea who they were. Don't worry—I won't betray your confidence."

Bryson took out a small pad of paper and jotted down four names. Dash recognized all the names. They were the who's who of the local wine industry: two winemakers, two winery owners.

Bryson handed him the note, "If my name is linked with the list, I'll have to kill you."

"You're forgetting one name," Dash asserted.

"You think she slept with Conrad, don't you?" Bryson asked.

"Maybe," Dash smiled, "He was the enemy. He ordered the clear-cutting of the oak trees. He was culpable."

Bryson was done with this exercise, "I don't commerce in gossip— these names are friends. I'm ashamed to have given you these names. Some of these men started their own rumors. They wanted to enhance their status as players. I don't think Claudia slept with any of them. She was a big talker—she went along with the gossip. She found it humorous that men would lie about their conquests."

Dash opened the office door and stepped out into the cool air of the barrel warehouse. He breathed deeply and looked back into the office where Bryson sat. "They didn't find it humorous."

Bryson was perplexed by Dash's statement, "It was just harmless chatter for God's sake —not anything serious. Men lie about their golf scores, about their income, about their acreage, about their female conquests, about everything to do with their egos. I'm not telling you anything you don't know. On second thought—give me that list back. I don't want to be associated with this parlor game, who slept with whom. Who gives a damn."

"The men on this list are suspects," Dash looked down at the list, "All except for one."

"Which one?" Bryson asked.

"The one not on the list," Dash slowly closed the door behind him, "Bryson Jackson."

Chapter Nine:

JASPER WINERY

Dash opened the car door on his grey Range Rover. Bryson Jackson followed right behind him. Dash knew that he would not let his comment go untethered.

Bryson was red-faced and perspiring, "Dash, don't speculate about my relationship with Claudia. I was a friend, confidant, and client—nothing more. Do you think if we were lovers, she'd have given me that list of men? She knew that she was living dangerously. She loved the game, the seduction, the romance, the intrigue, the deception, the knowledge that it gave her. She enjoyed living on the edge—it emboldened her. She was a truly modern woman."

The mid-day sun was beating down on them. Dash stepped into the shade of a sycamore tree at the front bumper of his car.

Bryson followed Dash, "I want you to continue your investigation. I don't want this conversation to get back to Jackie. She knew Claudia and I were close—she trusts me."

Dash put on his sunglasses while Bryson spoke, "You've already paid me. I've cashed the check. If the path goes full circle back to you, be aware that I have no qualms about notifying the police. I won't discuss your relationship with Claudia to anyone. Detective FJ Evans wants to know who you are—be mindful that you are on the radar."

Bryson clumsily shook Dash's hand, "Good hunting."

Dash drove off the Red Fox winery property on to the open road that ran from Highway 101 to the coast. Dozens of wineries big and small lined the road. Vineyards stretched up into the oak dotted hills. Swiss Italians had dairy farms along this road for over a century until the wine mania hit the area. Now those pastures where cows had resided were replaced by row upon row of wine grapes. The land had become valuable with this mono-crop of wine grapes. No other vegetation other than rows of grapes, trees, and decorative rose bushes filled the landscape. The golden hills were now green with Cabernet, Syrah, and Grenache grapes in pristine order. Some say the area looks like Tuscany or the Rhone region of France— they're mistaken. California vineyards are too orderly, too manicured, too sprayed to look like anything like the rambling vineyards in the old world. Nevertheless, the landscape was beautiful to behold. Dash drove west towards the coast to escape the heat of the day and take in the scenery. Driving had always been his form of meditation and contemplation. He'd roll down the windows, listening only to the sound of the wind, smelling the earth, and taking in the wonders of nature. When you're younger, the days of wonder are common. When we're older—the days of wonder are precious. Dash was in no hurry to get back home.

He found himself on Adelaide Road, which dead-ended at the base of the Santa Lucia Mountain Range, separating the wine region from the massive Hearst Ranch that stretched for thousands of acres along the coast. The last winery on the road was the legendary Jasper Winery. Dash drove down the long drive bounded by tall, slender Italian Cypress trees, then olive trees, and finally lavender. The winery was not ostentatious but modest in appearance, belying its wealth and reputation. Unlike the Spanish Revival and Italianesque styles that most wineries embraced, Jasper Winery had the bones of a New England farmhouse. The large building had a white plank exterior with green shutters, a large rectangular porch out back, and a cropped roofline. A California craftsman style house would have an overhanging roofline and a rounded wrap-around covered porch.

The interior of the winery was more impressive. The green marble countertops, the polished wood floors, stainless steel hardware on the drawers and cabinets, and little orderly islands of merchandise looked as though they could be in a Williams-Sonoma store. The wine bar was three-sided and could accommodate fifty visitors. It was near closing time, and the tasting room was nearly empty. They asked if he wanted a tasting menu. He said, "yes," and proceeded to try their legendary Bordeaux and Rhone varietal wines. The Bordeaux blend called "Pentangle" had scored a perfect one-hundred in Wine Spectator and was now a collector's wine. You had to join the Pentangle Wine Club to even buy the stuff. Dash preferred their Cabernet to the Pentangle. Their soft Rose was a pleasant surprise. The attractive woman in her forties doling out one-ounce tastes to the celebrants and aficionados was very knowledgeable, and Dash suspected she had longevity at Jasper.

"I am enjoying this Rosé—is it a Grenache?"

"Right you are. It's made in the Saignee method—the juice is bled from the grapes. The weight of the fruit and gravity is enough; it's not machine crushed; hence, the light color and delicate taste."

"Hell. My name is Dash," he introduced himself to the woman server, "I bought some grapes from Conrad Cook a few years back."

"Hello, I'm Ginger. You must be industry," she affirmed as she adjusted her glasses, "Conrad moved over to our Painted Horse property on the east side a few months ago."

"I didn't know that," Dash lied, "I have a small winery and needed some Grenache for my Rhone blend—Conrad was very gracious."

She became more attentive with the mention of Dash being a winery owner, "What's the name of your winery? I do have Conrad's number if you'd like to reach him."

"Blue Oak Vineyards—we do less than a thousand cases," Dash paused, "I'd love to get his number. He was in the center of all the controversy."

She smiled knowingly, "I'm glad that blew over—we got tired of hearing about how evil we were for cutting those trees. Look around the property—we maintain and plant hundreds of trees—it's not like we aren't good stewards of the land. Somebody made a bad decision—now everyone at Jasper is condemned for his actions," Ginger said.

Dash didn't want to talk about the oaks, "Conrad is quite the ladies' man. I think he cut quite a swath here on the west side—now he's working the east side."

Ginger pulled off her glasses, displaying her electric amber eyes. "Yes, did you see that in his press releases or from first-hand accounts?" Ginger smiled.

Dash returned the smile, "Rumors mostly—I heard that he was involved with Claudia Bowers, the barrel salesperson who was murdered."

Ginger frowned with the question, "Are you a detective? Conrad is an employee of this company. It is highly inappropriate for you to ask me about his personal life. If you are indeed a friend of his, you should know the answer without asking me. I'm sorry I told you anything about him."

Dash pulled out his private investigator's card and handed it to Ginger, "Yes, I'm investigating Claudia's death for someone in the industry. Conrad's name came up—I always follow a lead. I know this is not the time or place but if you do have any information to volunteer—call me."

Ginger put her glasses back on, picked up the card, read it, and put it in her skirt pocket. She excused herself so she could wait on other visitors. Dash walked outside as the tasting room closed. He walked around the property basking in the last of the afternoon sun and drinking gulps of the intoxicating coastal breeze. After a short stroll through the gardens and grounds, Dash walked to his car, where Ginger was waiting. She was wearing oversized sunglasses. She still had on the blouse and skirt she wore in the tasting room, but something about her was different. The contour of her long slender legs and torso was backlit by the afternoon sun. She had that breezy California look like the actress Diane Lane in "Under the Tuscan Sun."

"Mr. Ramblar—Dash—you made me very uncomfortable in the tasting room. I think you owe me an apology. I have some information that could be valuable to your investigation, but I won't divulge it here."

Dash was unsettled by her appearance and her statement, "I want to apologize for my rudeness... There's an outdoor nursery in Atascadero we could meet at—it's on Higuera Street, say eleven tomorrow? We won't be noticed there."

"You mean Eddie's Nursery? Sure, that works. I need to plant some perennials before winter."

Dash got in his car, rolled down the window, and said goodbye to Ginger.

"See you tomorrow at eleven at Eddie's Nursery in Atascadero," Dash re-confirmed.

"Yes, I'll be there and, no," Ginger laughed. "I'm saying no to your insinuation that I was among Conrad's conquests here at the winery. You got it backward. Conrad was among my conquests."

Chapter Ten:

GINGER RUTE

Dash loved shopping at nurseries for plants, trees, succulents, and porcelain pots. You can never overbuy or overspend. The same goes for cooking stores when buying cooking utensils and gadgets. Eddie's Nursery wasn't fancy or organized. The plants were scattered haphazardly around the two-acre property. The plants were in good shape, but you had to look for them. It was a bit of a scavenger hunt finding the plant or tree you wanted. New arrivals were mixed in with unsold inventory. Dash was looking for some perennials that were fast-growing and covered space, so he focused on sage and Ceanothus (California lilac). Dash had plenty of lavender, roses, geraniums, and rosemary. He was just biding time until Ginger arrived.

Ginger arrived nineteen minutes late, making no apology—she didn't need one. She wore tight torn jeans, a loose sleeveless blouse, canvas shoes, and her wavy auburn hair was pulled back in a messy bun. She wore the same big sunglasses and carried the same attitude as she did when he met her at Jasper Winery. She spotted Dash and walked over to him, surveying the plants as she walked. She picked up a pot loaded with pink geraniums.

"What do you think?' she asked Dash as she presented him with the geranium pot.

"Lovely, I'll take some cuttings from you next spring," Dash said.

Ginger looked alarmed. "You can buy your own damn cuttings—this plant has to survive the winter frosts first." Ginger shifted the conversation, "Did you find anything interesting?"

"I've been here a half an hour—I still don't know where anything is. I suppose the nursery gnomes will lead me to the plants that speak to me." Dash uttered.

Ginger smiled, "You're a bit odd, Mr. Ramblar. I haven't figured out whether I can trust you or not with my secrets. What are you looking for?"

Dash smiled back at Ginger, "Looking for a healthy Ceanothus and a reason why someone wanted Claudia dead."

"I believe the Ceanothuses are over there," Ginger pointed towards the shaded part of the nursery under some arching oaks. "As for Claudia— she was mixing a dangerous cocktail of politics, business, and sex. She should have kept them neat like a good whiskey."

Dash was amused, "How did you know about my cocktail preference?"

Ginger acted like she didn't hear the question walking towards a row of rose bushes. She found a yellow rose, "I've always liked yellow roses— kinda' of makes me miss home."

"Are you from Texas?" Dash asked.

"No, Whittier, where Nixon was from in Orange County," she set down her geranium pot and picked up the rose bush in a five-gallon pot, "I'll need your help carting these out of here."

"Sure, you didn't answer my question," Dash, "about Claudia."

"Conrad told me about her. She liked the sport of it, not so much the intimacy part."

Dash was taken aback, "That's not what I asked. I thought Conrad didn't kiss and tell."

"I had to beat it out of him, literally," Ginger laughed, "Conrad fell for her—big time, but then he fell for me. That ship has sailed," Ginger lifted her eyes away from the rose bush long enough for her to gaze at Dash, "Maybe, your ship will come in."

"I'm happy with a dinghy. A ship requires a lot more upkeep," Dash grinned.

"You're right. I'm too high maintenance for most men," Ginger smiled behind her big sunglasses.

Dash was not quite sure where the conversation was headed, "What else did Conrad tell you about Claudia?"

Ginger answered, "Conrad knew that he was being played by her—she was interested in the owners—not the winemakers. That's where she got into trouble. My owners weren't happy about her bonking their son, Gregg. They hired some people to look into her activities. They told Gregg that he was one buck in the herd. Gregg didn't care. She was traveling to London to see him. He was going to marry her."

Dash listened intently, "Sounds like she broke some hearts along the way."

"That's the fun in it," Ginger laughed. "Claudia didn't give a rat's ass about broken hearts. She was marrying an heir to billions leaving the thousand-airs to lick their wounds."

"They say to beware of a woman scorned, but how about men? We can be overwrought with jealousy and anger," Dash said.

"Enough to kill?" Ginger answered her own question, "Not these men—they have too much to lose. She was killed for different reasons."

Dash paused, "Yes, what reasons?"

"For sticking her cute nose in places where it didn't belong. It's one thing to get into their pants, another to get into their business. Never ask a cowboy how many cattle he has—never ask a winery owner how much money he's sunk into the winery or where he's getting his water."

"Is this about water?" Dash asked.

"You're not as bright as you look. It's always about water. No water—no wine," Ginger was done with the conversation. "Help me with this rose bush."

Dash walked behind her as she went to the outdoor check-out counter, which was on an old door atop a couple of wine barrels with an old cash register and an invoice pad.

Dash put the rose bush in Ginger's little Toyota pick-up truck, next to the geranium plant. Ginger got in her truck.

"Thanks for the help," Ginger started the engine to her truck, "Don't tell anyone we had this conversation. This is a small town. I don't want to end up upside down in the Salinas River, with my throat slit."

Chapter Eleven:

CONRAD COOK

Dash was unnerved by his meeting with Ginger. How did she know that Claudia was found upside down? Ginger had taken a risk speaking to him, when her livelihood came directly from the Perigold family winery, Jasper. Dash wanted to know who they hired to look into Claudia's background. He wanted to speak directly to Conrad Cook, the former winemaker of Jasper Winery, who now worked for the Perigold's other winery in the region, Paint Horse. Dash knew that Conrad would be reluctant to discuss Claudia.

Dash went home and decided to cook a nice meal for himself. Cooking got him out of his head and focused on a task that brought pleasure and gratification. He marinated some lamb chops in olive oil, garlic, and fresh rosemary. He made garlic mashed potatoes, roasted carrots, shallots, and sautéed spinach. He made a lemon tart with some Meyer lemons from his lemon tree. He sautéed the lamb chops and added some sweet vermouth, fresh cherries, and heavy cream to make a rich reduction sauce. The whole meal took two hours to make. He opened a bottle of a Paso

Diablo Tempranillo, a Spanish red varietal: smooth, rich, peppery pairing nicely with the lamb.

After the meal, he went outside to the redwood deck on his casita, formerly a little garden house, smoked a cigar, and sipped an aged Tawny Port. Dash did his best thinking when smoking a cigar. Time stood still. His thoughts were clear as the night sky. He wanted to like Ginger, but she came across a little crude and defensive. She used her sarcastic wit to keep Dash at bay and to guard against her vulnerability. What was she frightened of, and who was threatening her?

Dash suspected Conrad was a player, or thought of himself as a player. A winemaker in Great Oaks made you somewhat of a rock star. If he was half-way good looking and charming, he'd have his pick of the litter of the tasting room staff.

The following day after a lunch of pickled herring in white wine, hardtack, and cheese, Dash decided to go to Paint Horse Winery unannounced. The east side wineries were big and showy, and the quality of the wines varied from mediocre to decent. They were no better than the fruit, which was grown on rolling hills, exposed to the elements and the searing summer sun. The saving grace was the diurnal temperature fluctuation could vary as much as fifty degrees in a twenty-four-hour span. This factor, along with the calcareous limestone laden soil, makes for ideal growing conditions and reliably good fruit.

Paint Horse Winery sat on a hill above the main highway, a massive yellow building covered by a red tile roof attempting to imitate Tuscany but proving to be another monstrosity of bad taste. To be truly Tuscan, it had to have some antiquity, some flaws, some subtlety, some imperfect landscaping—less cement and asphalt. The tasting room was located in a smaller building in front of the winery. Dash walked in, smelling the familiar aroma of wine. Large bouquets of fresh flowers balanced out the acid stained cement floors, miles of polished wood counters, and merchandise racks. In the large tasting room, two employees were stationed behind the counter. There were only a handful of visitors tasting wines. The math in wineries never pencils out. You invest in a ten-million-dollar facility and lose twenty thousand dollars a month. It is purely an ego-driven industry. Only a few high-volume and high-end cult wineries make a profit. The others bleed money.

Paint Horse was in the last category, not big enough brand recognition or cache to break through the clutter—unlike its sister winery, Jasper, that had a large cult following. Surely, Paint Horse was Conrad Cook's Siberian exile. He had been the winemaker at a high-profile celebrated winery. Now he just schlepped bulk wines. Dash assumed that Conrad was in the winery and proceeded to climb the stairs to the main building. There was a small directional sign to the office around the side. He walked in, startling a young woman busy looking at social media on her smartphone.

He was told that Conrad was out back in the fermentation room, an enormous space with over twenty two-story stainless-steel vats. Conrad was walking around the vats with a tasting device, followed by an assistant winemaker who looked to be all of twenty. Conrad and his assistant both wore grey caps with the black and white horse head logo for Paint Horse Winery.

Dash greeted them, "Hello, sorry to bother you. I'm Dash Ramblar, a fellow winemaker—I'd like to meet the legendary Conrad Cook." Dash extended his hand to Conrad, who appeared to be flattered by his pronouncement. Conrad, a tall, sturdily built man about forty, was sporting a bit of belly fat and a sagging jawline compensated by growing a beard.

"A legend in my own mind," Conrad quipped, "Hello Dash, we're just tasting our 2018 wines. This vat is our Cabernet. Would you like to taste it?"

Dash nodded, and Conrad extended the wine thief to him, a small glass tube for extracting wine from barrels. Dash tasted the wine directly from the vat.

"A bit green but great promise," Dash lied, thinking it was dreary.

"Yes, we'll keep it here for another six months, then move the juice into French oak. Then we bottle the wine, keeping it in the bottle for another year before we release it. It's our flagship wine," Conrad said.

"Does it measure up to Jasper's Cabernet?" Dash declared, "You would know."

"Yes, I made my marks at Jasper—it was a great ride while it lasted," Conrad lamented.

Dash smiled, not knowing quite how to breach another topic, "I met your friend Ginger over at Jasper. She spoke highly of you and your reputation."

"How's she doing? I haven't spoken to her since I made the move. We used to talk every day at Jasper?" Conrad said, fearing that Dash may have been sent from Jasper to spy on him.

"She appears to be very happy at Jasper," Dash said.

"Can I show you around?" Conrad asked Dash, "I want to show you our reserve wines- we have a phenomenal Zinfandel that we're stoked about."

Dash followed him to another great room with fifty-foot ceilings. The room was temperature-controlled and contained hundreds of barrels on racks. The smell of oak and fermenting wine overwhelmed the nose. Conrad took him to a barrel that had chalk writing on it stating it was a 2016 Zinfandel. Conrad had some stemmed wine glasses handy, and he poured a taste for Dash and himself. Dash tasted it, realizing that Conrad had one winner.

"That's excellent. Is this American oak?" Dash asked.

"No, actually French Oak from a cooperage in Barcelona."

Dash began his inquiry, "What firm? Who's the rep?"

"Quercus Robur. They're in the process of hiring a new rep."

Dash paused and touched the oak barrel. "I think I knew the previous rep, Claudia Bowers, unfortunately, she was murdered."

Conrad took a hard look at Dash, "We all knew her, damn shame. I have to get back to work—is there anything else you'd like to see?"

Dash put down the wine glass, "Thanks, Conrad, for your hospitality. I had one question about Claudia."

Conrad looked at Dash in disbelief, "What is this about?"

"Rumor has it she was shagging some winemakers and winery owners, and may have stepped on some toes."

"That's not news or a rumor," Conrad's cheeks flushed above the beard line, "I don't know what you're asking. She was a sweet girl. You probably know that to be so—it's best not to talk about the deceased. I think you're snooping around for some information, which—you're not going to get from me." Conrad pointed to the exit door. "Show yourself out, Mr. Ramblar, or whatever your name is."

Dash turned and did his best Colombo impersonation, "One more thing, did the Perigolds know you were intimate with Claudia? I presume it was the reason you were buying her barrels."

Conrad angrily walked towards Dash, "That's bullshit. Don't impugn my integrity. We bought her barrels because they were good quality, and they were priced right. She was a true professional—not like you. Why don't you go fuck yourself—don't be showing up around here or at Jasper."

Dash exited the door. Conrad Cook's status moved from arrogant prick to suspect.

Chapter Twelve:

DYLAN DOTSON

Nothing is more precarious than opening your mouth. Speech is interpreted by the listener to be whatever they deem it to be. In the week following his conversations with Ginger Rute and Conrad Cook, life got interesting. Non-traceable phone call hang-ups, delivery trucks looking for fictitious people, and drones flying over the property. Dash was not prone to paranoia or intimidation, and he shrugged it off as petty intimidation. Dash knew he was on the radar. It was no coincidence when he had to take Bixby, his huge white Anatolian Shepherd, into the vet. He had found Bixby listless and without appetite. His nose was hot, and his breath was rancid. Bixby had been poisoned. Bixby was a large dog, weighing over one hundred and fifty pounds, fit and only five years old. He survived the poisoning. His Blue Merle Australian Shepherd, Barnaby, hadn't been poisoned—probably didn't eat the bait—he was a pickier eater than Bixby.

Dogs in a rural setting are freer and smarter than most domesticated dogs. They have more predators, including mountain lions, coyote packs, cattle, horses, and neighbors. The unwritten rule is that if your dog is on someone else's property, it's fair game. Some neighbors lay out poison for frequent unwanted guests.

Dash was angry. You can mess with him, but don't go poisoning his dogs. He checked with his neighbors, who denied the poisoning and hadn't seen Bixby. He believed them. Dash walked the perimeter of his property and near the gate at the top of his property. He saw a plastic container with an ounce of rancid hamburger meat left in it. Someone could have easily driven to his gate, walked down the driveway a few yards, and deposited the plastic food container. Bixby was prone to putting damn near everything in his mouth, including roadkill. He definitely was not a finicky eater. Dash picked up the container and put it in a ziplock bag, holding it away from his nose.

There were no other signs of human activity near the container. Dash took a long look around the driveway. He thought he saw a carcass, and he was right. It was a dead coyote. The coyote had apparently eaten the tainted hamburger. Dash covered the coyote carcass with leaves and brush and then headed back to his house. The front gate was near his mailbox; he walked over to it and collected the mail, bound in a rubber band, and walked down the driveway to his barn. Bixby was lying on his dog bed in the barn recuperating. He barely had enough energy to lift his head. Dash figured that Bixby was still not out of the woods. Dash's office was in the barn not far from where Bixby lay. He unbundled the mail. It was the normal mix of credit card offers, bills, and advertising fliers. There were no posted personal letters. One envelope had his name and address on a label like it had been part of a mass mailing. He opened the letter and found these words.

"Stay away from Jasper Winery and Ginger. Sorry about your dog."

Dash looked for a signature or return address—nothing.

Dash temporarily forgot about the investigation and was focused on Bixby's poisoning. The note confirmed his suspicion; the poisoning of his dog was related to his investigation. He contemplated a course of action.

He had a test done at the vet's office to determine the poison—it was found to be cyanide-laced bait for pocket gophers. You needed a permit from the county agriculture department to get it. It was no longer sold commercially at farm supply stores. Dash knew the county agriculture commissioner and called him to find out if he could get a list of growers that had a permit. He told the commissioner about the poisoning. He was sympathetic but unable to provide the list, but he would confirm a name if Dash provided it. Dash first asked about Conrad Cook, then inquired about Jasper Winery. The commissioner confirmed both were permitted. Then Dash asked whose name was associated with the permit at Jasper Winery. He reluctantly gave him the name of the vineyard and wine operations manager, Dylan Dotson.

Dash went online and found that Dylan Dotson owned his own vineyard management company employing dozens of field workers and supervisors. Jasper Winery was just one of many wineries that his company had been contracted to oversee. Dash put in a call to Dylan Dotson and got a recorded message. Dash left a message with the pretense of assessing his vineyard.

Dash got a call back right away from Dylan saying he'd come out to the ranch the next day. Dash was convinced that if he knew about the poisoning, he would've been reluctant to come by or question his referral by the Perigolds.

Dylan was a solid six foot two with a vice grip handshake, a full beard, Wrangler jeans, and a khaki work shirt. He wore a hat with the logo for DVM, Dotson Vineyard Management, on it. Dylan thought Dash was connected to the Perigolds, and he was cordial. He did have a surliness about him that he kept in check. Dash's intuition told him that this guy knew nothing about the poisoning of his dog. Dash's ten-acre vineyard was small potatoes for Dylan's operation, but he was willing to work with Dash in deference to the Perigolds. Dash didn't let on that he'd never met the Perigolds.

Dylan walked the vineyard rows with Dash and commented, "You maintain this yourself? I'd have to say that we couldn't do any better." Dylan lifted a trellised shoulder of vines and noted all the hanging fruit. "We could pick it for you." He lifted a spectrometer from his pocket and tested the grapes for sugar level."

"Who'd you send out to pick?" Dash asked.

"I'd normally send out my crew, but we're busy at Jasper Winery. I'd probably send out Hernando and his crew. They're working on the eastside for Paint Horse. Hernando's crew is first rate. I could call the Perigolds to see if they'd let Hernando take a day to pick your grapes."

Dash blocked the call, "Not necessary Rico, my ranch hand, and I can do the work with someday laborers."

Dylan was satisfied with the tour and jumped back in his truck, "Call me in January. We'll send out a crew to prune and rewire some of your trellises." Dylan left and sped up the road like he was late for another meeting.

One more name to navigate, and he was laser-focused on who poisoned Bixby. He couldn't walk past his big ailing Anatolian Shepherd without grimacing. Dylan Dotson and Hernando would both have access to cyanide-laced grain. Dash knew that Dylan was supervising picking crews at one of the many vineyards in the region that Jasper owned or leased. Dash called the winery and asked for the winemaker who replaced Conrad Cook. His name was Nathan Forrest.

"Nathan, this is John from Great Oaks Chevrolet. I got a call from Hernando about one of the trucks on his job. Do you know where his crew is right now?" Dash asked.

Nathan responded, "Sure, they're over on the east side at the Pomar Junction vineyard. They're picking Cabernet today and tomorrow."

Dash thanked Nathan and decided to go over to the vineyard even though it was fast approaching four and quitting time. It had rained the day before, and the crews were working overtime to pick the grapes before any mildew set in. Dash arrived, parking behind a line of trucks and big plastic bins full of grapes, a flat-bed truck with a forklift, and empty bins waiting to be offloaded. The crew numbered about twenty, yet it was easy for Dash to pick out Hernando. He was densely built with a thick neck and a buzzed haircut. He had a clipboard and was the only one not actively picking or sorting out grapes.

Dash walked over to him as Hernando was standing near the full bins.

"Hello, I'm John from Great Oaks Chevrolet—got a call about a truck out here on the job."

Hernando looked confused, "I didn't make a call—you can see I drive a Ford and most of the workers drive Jap trucks—you know Nissans and Toyotas. Who said they called?"

"I got the message from our receptionist at the dealership. She must have gotten the wrong name. Can I look at the trucks? There might be a Chevy here."

Hernando shrugged, "Go ahead—just don't bother the crews. We're on a tight schedule."

Dash walked along the line of trucks and peered into the truck beds. Hernando was right there wasn't a Chevy truck anywhere. He walked back to his Chevy truck and stopped to look in the bed of Hernando's black Ford truck. He saw what he was looking for a large plastic bucket of gopher bait secured to hooks welded to the bed of the truck. There was enough bait to cover a hundred acres.

Dash moved back to Hernando, who was now ignoring him, "You're right, no Chevys. You've got a lot of gopher bait in that truck bed. Enough to wipe out all the gophers on the east side."

Hernando lifted his head and sneered at him, "So, what's your point? Can't you see we've got a job to do?" Hernando returned to his clipboard as the forklift moved several full bins on to the flat-bed truck.

Dash responded in kind, "Be careful with that stuff. You could kill someone's dog by mistake."

Hernando put down his clipboard and walked towards Dash.

Dash smiled, "Yeah, if it's my dog, then there'd be hell to pay." Hernando gave Dash a long look, sizing him up for the first time, "What are you getting at Mister John? We know what we're doing with the bait. If we wanted to kill dogs, we've got that covered. You gotta' problem with that, mister car salesman?" Hernando encroached in Dash's space.

Hernando was angered, "Let's see your business card. I'm going to call the dealership and complain about you. We're trying to do a job, and you're talking about dogs. "

"I don't have a business card," Dash walked away.

"Then just who in the fuck are you?" Hernando blocked Dash's path to his truck.

"Like I said, if you have anything to do with poisoning my dog out on the westside, then you're in agua caliente."

Dylan stared at Dash and let him get in his truck, "Get the fuck away from here. If anyone sees you around here, the last thing you'll have to worry about is your dead dog."

PART TWO: VERAISON

Chapter Thirteen:

SAN MIGUEL

Dash took the warning and headed home. No one followed him, so he was in the clear, but they did know where he lived and where to put the poison for his dogs. The notion that when your home is trespassed upon you feel violated was true in spades for Dash. He thought about adding a layer of security by adding an electric gate with a code at the top of his driveway. He rebelliously said to himself, hell no! He was going to meet them head-on and exact retribution. You mess with a man's dog—you mess with him.

The next morning Dash received a phone call from Ginger, who was getting ready to go to work at Jasper Winery.

"Hey, Dash, sorry to call you at six in the morning, but I have a bone to pick with you."

"No problem, I just drank four cups of coffee, did fifty push-ups, fed the dogs—including the poisoned one. What bone?"

"Did you drive out to Pomar Junction to see Hernando?"

Dash was straight forward, "Yep, late yesterday afternoon. He's a strong suspect in the poisoning of Bixby, my Anatolian Shepherd."

"Sorry to hear about your dog, but you're putting me in harm's way," Ginger said.

"I was followed when I met with you at the nursery. I have been warned that meeting with you could jeopardize my job. The Perigolds don't like anyone prying into their business or harassing their employees. You're guilty on both counts. Please don't call me or try to reach me."

She hung up. If the coffee hadn't awakened Dash, the phone call was like pure adrenalin pumped into his veins. Ginger was the only inside informant at Jasper Winery, and without her, he was back to square one. The Hamster was his last source of information now, an unreliable french fries extortionist. He hadn't forgotten about the lead in San Miguel, a Hispanic man by the name of Charley, Pedro, or Pepe—the guy with a big beard, missing teeth, and a Lucky Strike smoker.

Drove up to San Miguel after he calmed down, Dash had an egg sandwich followed by a handful of Tums. San Miguel had a large ornate mission, Mission San Miguel Arcangel, founded in 1797, surrounded by a large walled enclosure. The mission was recently restored by the Hearst family, whose ranch is due west of the mission. San Miguel has a motel, a bar, a dollar store, a school, and not much more. It would be even poorer if the wine industry hadn't exploded around it. There were plenty of wine industry jobs for Hispanics. The large Hispanic population had settled in this north county town for years because of cheap rents, the mission church, and the spoken language, Spanish. San Miguel could easily be a village in Mexico.

Dash first went to the bar, and since it was morning, there were only a couple of customers and one tired bartender who probably worked twelve-hour shifts. The customers were drinking beer and speaking Spanish. Dash asked the bartender in English if he knew a Pedro or Pepe with a beard and missing teeth who smokes Lucky Strikes. The bartender misunderstood Dash, grabbed a pack of Lucky Strikes from the back bar, and put them in front of Dash. Dash figured he might need them for payola latter, so he laid down ten bucks and was surprised how little change he got back. Dash asked again, with the bartender telling him he didn't know a Pepe or Pedro with a beard. Most of his Hispanic customers don't have beards.

Dash then went over to the dollar store. A depressing place because everything for a buck, be it soda, chips, candy, packaged food, party favors, or kitchen utensils, all had one thing in common—poor quality. The clerk was a young Anglo from Atascadero. He was friendly and glad to be speaking English. Dash told him about Pedro or Pepe, and he said he knew the guy. He says he comes in daily for a pack of Lucky Strikes. Dash asked the obvious, "Had he been in today?"

The clerk said that he comes in around noon—it was just after eleven. Dash figured he'd wait in his car. Bored, he walked over to the Mission instead and did a self-tour. He wanted to take another look at the original murals inside the parish that were painted by the Indians designed by a Spaniard. The Mission was built for the sole purpose of converting the large population of Salinan Indians who habituated the area along the Salinas River to Catholicism. The walled grounds around the Mission were used for livestock, graves, outdoor cooking and dining, and safety. Walking around the Mission, Dash was transported to an earlier time, when life was more basic, more brutal, and shorter.

Dash sauntered back to the dollar store just before noon, waiting in his car for Pedro. About fifteen minutes past noon, a short Hispanic man with a full beard and a protruding belly walked into the dollar store. Dash got out of his parked car and walked inside the store. The clerk was selling the man cigarettes, and he nodded his head to give Dash the heads up. Dash waited for the man to leave the store, following him out the door. Dash took out his pack of cigarettes and offered to the man.

"I bought these cigarettes by mistake. I saw you buying Lucky Strikes, so I figured you'd take them off my hands."

The man took a step back and looked at Dash hard and then smiled as he took the cigarettes, "Thanks, Mister. You have a name?"

Dash smiled back, "Dash, what's yours?"

The man had already pulled a cigarette out of his pack and was lighting it, "The gringos call me Charley, my friends call me Pedro, my wife calls me Pepe and my children call me papa."

Dash smiled, knowing that The Hamster had given him the correct info. "I heard about you from a friend of mine, The Hamster."

Pedro's smile disappeared, "Don't bullshit me—you a cop? You ain't homeless, so you can't be friends with The Hamster."

Dash grinned, "I'm no cop, just a private detective trying to find the fat guy, in a Hawaiian shirt, spikey hair who hung up the girl in the river bed."

"The Hamster told you about him, huh?" Pedro started walking away from Dash.

Dash caught up to him, "Could you tell me what you saw?"

"I saw what the cops saw—a girl hung up on a tree with her innards eaten out. I didn't see no fat guy with spikey hair. I'm not homeless—I'm living with my kids. I don't want trouble—I don't want to go back to the River." He turned his back on Dash. "Forget you saw me."

"Tell me what you saw, and I'll buy you a carton of smokes. You won't have to come back here for weeks."

"Buy me two cartons, and I'll tell you what I saw." Pedro was still not committed to talking to Dash.

Dash grinned. He thought that Pedro and The Hamster went to the same school of negotiating.

"Sure, it's a deal. Follow me into the store, pick out the cartons you want, and I'll run my card."

Pedro picked up his steps—he knew an opportunity when it availed itself. He led Dash back into the store, telling the clerk to pull down two cartons of cigarettes—the gringo will be doing the buying. Dash paid and took holding the plastic bag of cigarettes until they got outside.

Dash held out the bag of cigarettes to Pedro, "Okay, what can you add to what I already know?"

Pedro eyed the cigarettes and paused, "First time I saw the fat guy with the spikey hair, he wasn't wearing no Hawaiian shirt. He was wearing a hoodie. So was his partner."

Dash interrupted, "You mean there were two of them scoping out the site?"

"Yeah, they weren't exactly scoping out the site—they was arguing. The partner was younger and more nervous."

"Describe him to me."

"Big guy, over two hundred pounds, looked like a lumberjack, unshaven—dark curly hair," Pedro was animated.

"Curly hair—I thought he had a hoodie on?"

"I could see his hair," Pedro exclaimed.

"What were they arguing about?"

"The spiky-haired guy was looking for a tree. The other guy just wanted to find a hole. I thought they were talking about a dog they run over or something—I didn't think they were talking about a woman. The one guy had a rope with him—his partner tried to get it from him. He didn't want any part of a rope. The older guy with the spikey hair won the fight. They left the rope. I went and looked at it after they left—I would've taken it—but I had no use for a rope. Anyway, it was dirty—oily—used." Pedro took a breath. "Now, give me the cigarettes."

Dash handed him the cigarettes, "One more question. How do you know both guys didn't bring the body? The Hamster said there was only one guy."

Pedro snatched the cigarettes with his left hand. He looked confused, clutching the cigarettes, "He came back—still had his hoodie on. It was dark, almost black—hung the rope up. He got hot and sweaty—took off his hoodie. Underneath was the shirt with palm trees on it, then he went and got the girl. It was dark, he didn't see me, but I saw him—shirt glowed in the dark, I swear. She was in a blanket, rolled up, she was unconscious. Then…"

"Then what?" Dash looked at him.

Pedro looked askance to make certain no one was listening to him, "Then he tied her feet up, lifted her upside down over the branch—then he…like some kinda' lamb slaughter."

"Lamb slaughter?" Dash was breathless.

"One movement across her throat—gushed out blood—it was awful—I puked—got the hell out of there. Came back later to cover my puke—that's when I saw what the coyotes had done."

"What did you see?" Dash persisted.

"Come on—you know—disgusting. I puked again in a different spot—had to cover both spots—afraid that they'd run a test on my puke."

Dash touched Pedro's arm, "I won't let them convict you. I know your story."

Pedro pushed Dash's arm away, "Sorry, mister, I don't trust no one—specially Gringos. Nothing personal, but when it comes down to the law—you know—stories change."

Pedro started to walk away, "Go back home to Great Oaks. I'm leaving this town—don't try to find me."

Dash waved a feeble goodbye, "Good luck. Enjoy the smokes."

Pedro turned back and stopped, "I don't need your luck."

He disappeared out of sight.

Chapter Fourteen:

FJ EVANS

Elated, Dash returned to his vineyard ranch. He had learned that there was a second accomplice in the murder of Claudia Bowers. He got a description of the second person of interest by Pedro described as a sturdily built man over six feet tall with dark curly hair and an unshaven face. Facial hair stubble is common among young men going for the lumberjack look with a plaid flannel shirt, jeans, and heavy work shoes with thick rubber soles. Pedro had described someone who fit Dylan Dotson's profile.

Dash's euphoria was met with reality when he waltzed inside the hacienda. His small house had been broken into. Every drawer, cabinet, and closet had been ransacked. Framed posters had been ripped from the walls, glass was everywhere, and even an old piggy bank had been broken. It wasn't the mess, not the intrusion. It was the notion that they, whoever they were, knew where he lived and could visit whenever they wished. Dash was no longer felt safe in his home.

Dash looked for his dogs. Bixby had hidden in the barn along with Barney. Bixby normally would have given up his life to protect the house, but since the poisoning, he was barely able to move. Barney was protecting

Bixby. Both dogs were feeling guilty about the intruders. Dash told the dogs they did the right thing and gave them a treat.

Dash went into his barn office, checked on his arsenal, his files, and his records, which hadn't been touched. He had purposely locked away his guns in the barn. 'Arsenal' was a misnomer because he had a shotgun, a twenty-two rifle with a scope for ground squirrels, a 9mm Glock Luger, and a semiautomatic Ruger snub-nose revolver. He retrieved the Glock out of locked storage and took it to his house, placing it in the drawer in the nightstand next to his bed. There's nothing like a Glock to make you feel secure in your home. The dogs had followed him back to the house.

The cleanup took about four hours, and he worked through dinner, only eating a can of sardines and crackers with a glass of Viognier to keep him going. He reckoned that they were after notebooks, files, or anything that may give a clue to his investigation. They even went through his trash, dumping it out on the kitchen floor. The used coffee grounds were a bitch to clean up.

Dash left a phone message for FJ Evans at his office, telling him that his dog had been poisoned and his house broken into. He also left a tease of sorts; he had a description of the murderers.

Naturally, FJ Evans called back first thing in the morning. He didn't ask about his dog or his house but went straight to the perpetrator descriptions. Dash said he'd have to come to his house to get that information.

FJ Evans arrived twenty minutes later in a new white Ford Explorer. The government plates were the only giveaway that it was an official vehicle. Dash met him at his car.

"Since when can the taxpayers afford leather in a cruiser?" Dash asked, looking at the buckskin leather seats.

"The dealer threw the leather in because he's a friend of mine. He still made a nice profit off the city. I noticed you're still driving that old piece of shit Range Rover—probably gets nine miles to the gallon."

Dash laughed, "No, eight. But the taxpayers didn't buy it."

FJ shook hands with Dash, and they headed for the house, "Let's see the damage."

"No damage, I spent the better part of the day cleaning it up, but you can see my dog Bixby who still isn't doing that great."

They went inside and were greeted by Barnaby, the Australian Shepherd. Bixby lay on his bed, motionless. Detective Evans was a dog lover. He bent over Bixby to touch his fur and offered him some encouragement.

Dash and FJ sat across from each other in big leather couches. The hacienda, as Dash called it, was a small house with red brick Saltillo tiles on the floor, knotty wood pine cabinets, rustic Mexican dark and tan wood tables, beds, and reclaimed wood bookshelves. There was an old saddle on a pine stand, a few cowboy hats and cowboy art hung throughout. It was decorated to look like an old bunkhouse: comfortable, sturdy, and sparse.

Dash liked having visitors. "Can I get you a drink?"

"Water's fine," Detective Evans settled into a couch, "Nice place you have here, Dash, looks like a mix between a cowboy flophouse and a Mexican brothel."

Dash laughed, "That's exactly the look I was after."

Dash grabbed a couple of waters in plastic bottles from the refrigerator, handed Detective Evans a bottle, and sat down.

Evans was not hesitant, "What've you got for me?"

"No pleasantries, no how're you doing, no how's business, no how's the harvest coming?" Dash grinned.

"Fuck you, Dash. The only reason I'm here is to get the information on the perps. Who's your source?"

"That's confidential. Suffice to say, he was an eyewitness to the murder, and more importantly, to the set-up, a day earlier."

"What do you mean set-up?"

"Two men surveyed the area, picked a spot, a tree, and left a rope behind the day before. A day later, one of the men delivered an unconscious body—then finished the job."

Detective Evans was all business, "Whoa, wait a minute. You're saying there were two men involved—only one of 'em showed up to murder the girl?"

"Precisely—my source saw the whole thing. He described what they looked like—in detail."

Detective Evans took a long swallow of the bottled water and leaned forward in the couch, "I will take down your description—eventually you're going to have to tell me the source, otherwise it's just rumor."

"That's impossible, I wouldn't know how to get a hold of him—he left town."

Detective Evans got agitated, "So, what the hell am I here for? If your source can't identify the killers in court, then your description only eliminates some suspects—maybe."

"Okay, two men, one heavy set guy with short spikey hair like a butch cut in your day with goop on it, except longer and the other guy, younger, beefier, tall with an unshaven face."

"Sounds like half the men in this town, except for old guys like me and intellectuals like you."

Dash smiled, "Thanks for the compliment. Intellectual—I didn't know you noticed."

"Look around, you've got books stacked everywhere—I don't see a television set anywhere, and the place is decorated with objets d'art. I know your type. You pretend to be a weekend cowboy, but actually you're a shut-in who likes to read and contemplate your navel."

Dash laughed, "Busted."

Detective Evans returned to the topic at hand, "Thanks for the descriptions, but until we narrow down some suspects—we have nothing.

The one takeaway from your friend's eye witness was that the murder was planned, pre-meditated."

"Exactly," Dash got up and opened the shades so the morning light could stream in, "They planned it, executed it—now they're covering their tracks. It's no mistake that once I started snooping around—my dog got poisoned—my house got trashed—and you showed up."

Detective Evans was not amused by his inclusion in the scenario, "I'm just doing my job. You, you're a paid dick—on commission—or per diem. You have no long game—just a short turnaround for profit. Do you trust your eyewitness, or do you think you were hoodwinked?"

"If you go back to the crime scene and look for two vomit traces. He says he vomited twice at the scene. It's his narrative. I believe him."

Detective Evans pushed himself out of the deep couch, "Thanks for the hospitality—the info may help. I'll send someone out to look for the vomit traces. There's only one problem. Everyone that went on the scene vomited."

Chapter Fifteen:

HERNANDO TORRES

Dash went out outside with the detective to his car. It was a beautiful morning, cool, crisp, blue skies, and the savory-sweet smell of autumn in the air. In California, there is a true Indian summer lingering well into November with bright warm days and brisk nights. On the Central Coast, many of the warmest days of the year fall after Labor Day; Thanksgiving Day can have temperatures in the eighties. They say the Central Coast has a true Southern Mediterranean climate, similar to Sicily or Northern Africa. Great Oaks lingers around thirty-five degrees latitude north, passing also through northern Algeria.

Dash had the whole day in front of him, but he wasn't motivated to do a damn thing, except have a nice lunch, take a siesta and contemplate his navel. That changed when a truck drove down his driveway. He recognized it as Hernando's black Ram pick-up. Dash didn't have time to arm himself or close the gates. Hernando drove right up to his hacienda, put on the parking brake, left the truck running, got out of the truck, and headed in Dash's direction. Dash could see there was another passenger in the truck.

Hernando appeared to be unarmed. Dash stood his ground.

"To what pleasure do I owe your visit?" Dash said sarcastically.

Hernando carried no expression and was not in the mood for polite conversation, "I saw the detective's Explorer at the top of the hill. Tell me what you told him."

Dash folded his arms, "No, I can't tell you. But you can tell me what you're doing here."

"Just a friendly visit," Hernando half laughed like he had a wad of tobacco in his jaw, "You've been busy since yesterday making the rounds. You don't have a clue who you're messing with."

Dash smiled at Hernando's tough-guy demeanor, "Tell me."

Hernando kicked some gravel in the driveway, "If you like your midget ranch, your vineyard, your peace and quiet—best you retire, grandpa. You're a bit old for this activity. You're on notice. We've got eyes and ears on you. That can't be too good for your health."

Dash smirked, "You drove down on my driveway, trespassed, telling me to retire-threatening me. I think you should leave now—tell the people that you work for that I'm not retiring, I won't be threatened, or cajoled so get back in your truck," Dash's jaw tightened, "I'm getting a restraining order and filing a report. It will be on your record."

Hernando's expression soured, "We can handle this here and now." Hernando motioned for the passenger to get out of the truck. The passenger was Dylan Dotson, the brawny twenty-something, built like a bouncer and with the same vacant look.

"I've previously had the honor." Dash grinned, "You two make a sorry pair."

Dylan dismissed all pleasantries walking towards Dash, kicking him in the shins with a steel-toed work boot causing Dash to double over. Hernando was about to land a punch Dash, on the top of the head, when Dash's Aussie, Barney (Barnaby), jumped on Hernando's chest, snarling and biting. Hernando grabbed Barney by his coat, throwing him to the ground. Within seconds Bixby appeared, silent and menacing, grabbing Hernando's partner Dylan by the leg. Bixby's size was intimidating; well over one hundred and fifty pounds—on his hind legs, he was over six feet tall. Hernando's frightened partner tried pulling away from Bixby, limping to the truck with Bixby in tow. Bixby released him when he opened the truck door howling from pain.

Bixby turned his attention on Hernando, shadowing him as he ran to the truck. Dylan slammed his truck door closed, yelling something inaudible at Dash from inside the cab. Dash went into the hacienda, retrieved his luger, and carried it outside. Hernando gave Dash a fist bump as he was pulling out of the driveway. Dash lifted his luger and took a shot at the rear bumper. The sound hastened the retreat of the truck as it sped up the driveway. Dash was heartened by his dog's defense, congratulated both, lowering himself to one knee embraced both dogs. Bixby was happy with just a pat, whereas Barney couldn't get enough adulation and affection. Bixby, who somehow revived for the assault, now retreated to his bed. Bixby would rest for another week before the detoxification was complete-returning to his old self.

Dash went into the hacienda accompanied by his dogs, and lifting a glass tumbler from the cabinet, poured two fingers of Whistle Pig Rye whiskey over a single ice cube. He only pulled out the Whistle Pig when he was celebrating or recalibrating an intense situation, like fending off two much thicker and younger thugs. Of course, the dogs were the difference-maker, so they both got a steak bone from the freezer.

Dash sat out on his patio watching the acorn woodpeckers, Western blue jays, mockingbirds, house sparrows, common flickers—all flitting around the massive blue oaks. This was all the entertainment Dash needed to relish the taste of a smooth and smoky whiskey.

After lunch, Dash called Detective FJ Evans.

"Hello Floyd, I just had some unwelcome visitors on the property. I thought you'd like to run a check on them."

"You again. First of all, don't call me Floyd; secondly, don't be calling me about trespassers—we've got a murdered girl, meth labs, ICE agents on our ass, and a shrinking city budget. You're the tough guy—why didn't you just kick their asses?"

"I let my dogs do the heavy lifting. I'm past my cage fighting prime. Since you won't ask, it was Hernando Torres and Dylan Dotson—they do contract work for the Perigolds."

"Good work if you can get it—so what's your beef with the Perigolds?" Detective Evans asked.

"Good question," Dash paused, "Why don't you drive over—I've opened a bottle of Whiskey Pig Rye—I've got a box of Macanudo Cigars, that needs to be broken into?"

"Pretty tempting," Detective Evans, "Okay, see you in ten."

Good on his word, Detective FJ Evans drove his new Ford Explorer into Dash's gravel driveway, parking in the same spot that Hernando had just a couple of hours previously. Dash was already buzzed from the rye whiskey.

Dash greeted Evans, "Hello, amigo, ready to tango?"

"You've been nipping at the whiskey, I can tell." Evans laughed.

They sat out on the backyard patio underneath the giant blue oaks, smoking cigars and drinking whiskey. Dash had brought out an ice bucket, some herring pickled in white wine, smoked salmon from Norway, crackers, and a bottle of aged tawny port for back-up. Dash figured that Evans would open up with a little whiskey, and he was right.

"What do you know about the Perigolds?" Dash asked.

"You could have looked them up online—you don't need me to tell you anything that isn't already public record." Detective Evans took a long drag on his Churchill length cigar. He was very content. "Nice patio you have here, Dash—very relaxing. The Perigolds can have their billions—all I need is a good cigar, a good nap, a good wife, good whiskey, and opera."

Dash was intrigued, "Opera?"

"My wife and I are both patrons of the San Francisco Opera. I contribute hundreds; they contribute millions," said FJ.

Dash laughed, "Billions, they didn't make billions in the wine industry?"

"No kidding, Jasper Winery is a write-off. They made their money in the Central Valley, almonds, pistachios, pomegranate juice, and water."

"Water?" Dash asked.

"Fuck, you're dumber than you look. The Perigolds locked all the water credits in the Central Valley, then comes the drought and the state of California buys the water back at a four hundred percent mark-up. They're trying to lock up the water rights in this area."

"We've got the water, the aquifer, enough for everyone." Dash poured another whiskey for FJ Evans and himself.

"You think?" FJ Evans looked serious, "They're trying to form a regional private water company. They want it on the ballot for god's sake. Their goal is the same as it was in the Central Valley—get the rights to the water, credits and so on, sell the water back to the city, the thirsty citizenry, the wineries, and growers when there's a shortage. We have water now. Double the population, add another four hundred wineries, plus irrigate row crops—you've got a shortage no time. I've read that the Perigolds consume more water than the city of Los Angeles. They're the biggest water users in the state. Now guess where their billions come from."

Dash smiled at his rhetorical question, "I know the ballot measure didn't pass—guess the populace smartened up."

"No, the citizens never smarten up. You can play them for suckers every time, especially the Perigolds. They know how to drop property values, manufacture a shortage, buy up land from desperate sellers, take their water credits, and sit on the land until a drought comes roaring back. Then they can name their price. Fortunately, other billionaires were against the water district. They ponied up the money to kill the ballot measure."

Dash stretched back in the chair, "Who were they, the other billionaires who saved the day?"

"Environmentalist—save the earth types—I don't much care for their politics—but they stopped the water heist cold. The vote was overwhelming, but don't think the Perigolds are done trying. They've got county supervisors on the payroll, planning commission officers bought and paid for, the Chamber of Commerce in their back pocket. Everyone is complicit; everyone has a price."

Dash took a long inhalation of cigar smoke. He lifted the cigar and looked at it against the sky.

"That's the problem with being in law enforcement. It gives one a dark view of the world. Guess they thought my price was too high, so they thought they could beat it out of me," Dash said smugly.

Detective FJ Evans roared with laughter, "You're kidding. They could give a shit about you. Weren't you listening? They've got everyone, in their back pocket, including the local rags, so why do you think they give a rat's ass about you? You're a single barnacle on the Titanic. Those thugs were just having fun with you. People don't like people prying into their business. I bet you asked him if he was banging Claudia."

"No, I didn't—maybe I should have," Dash smiled, "It's all about my investigation into Claudia's murder. She was engaged to Gregg Perigold. Don't you think they wonder about what I know and what I don't know?"

Evans pondered the question, washing it down with whiskey. "Perhaps. But don't let your head swell up. You're a small-town investigator with second-hand information in a town where everyone knows who farted."

Dash laughed out loud, "It must have been the truffle pate I had last night as an appetizer. Or was it the foie gras on my burger?"

Evans gave Dash an unscrupulous look. "Whatever, smart ass—your excess gas doesn't warrant a beat down. People get beat up in this town for stealing a parking space or looking twice at somebody's girlfriend. Guys like you are just fun to taunt."

Dash put out his cigar by crushing the ash hang into the stone ash-tray. "Sometimes a small obstacle blocking a large scheme gets the most attention. I'm that obstacle."

Chapter Sixteen:

GREGG PERIGOLD

Dash had a little buzz after Detective Evans left. Claudia Bowers' murder was deliberate, not random. Dash determined to keep peeling the onion until his eyes watered. What were the motives? If it was the big boys, then it was about keeping her quiet and out of view. If the motive was small ball, then it had to be about love, jealousy, lust, and vengeance. More than likely it was a combination of the two. Still, there was always the outlander, the one-night stand that got ugly, owed monies that brought retribution, or the worst motive—a mistaken wrong.

Gregg Perigold had returned to the Central Coast after his fiancée's death. He was rumored to already be back in the dating scene. Dash decided to find out for himself. He knew where Gregg liked to hang out when he was in town.

The Hotel Duval was a boutique hotel downtown off the square, designed to resemble a small Tuscan hotel, with a stone courtyard and fountain, iron balconies for each room looking down on the courtyard. The draw for Gregg Perigold, and other sojourners, was the outdoor bar that faced the street canopied by a large oak tree. A lively scene with live music, usually jazz or vocals, clever bartenders, featuring great local wines by the glass, and small bites. This is the locale where well-heeled singles mingle and savor the bouquets of the wines and eat olives while pretending to listen to the vocals.

Dash went to the bar three nights in a row running a bar tab, kibitzing with the bartenders, getting wine fatigue, have their ground lamb burger while trying to be discreet about his intentions. Dash had looked up Gregg's picture online, certain he'd recognize him. He did on Thursday evening. Gregg was sitting with a couple of toothsome thirty-year-olds, looking like a schoolboy in his jeans, t-shirt, sweater, and canvas shoes. By his cavalier style and his thick horn-rim glasses, you might guess he was a trust fund baby, an ivy-league educated alum, groomed to take over a multi-billion-dollar enterprise. Dash waited until Gregg came to the bar to order a bottle for his table.

"Hey Justin," Gregg said to the bartender, "do you have a good Albarino in stock?

"Sure, Gregg. Bodega de Edgar or Brecon—you choose," the bartender boasted.

"I'll take a bottle of the Brecon—I know their winemaker, Fredrick," Gregg stood by the bar waiting for Justin to decant the wine. It was Dash's opportunity.

"Good choice on the Albarino," Dash interjected, "Frederick knows his Spanish varietals.

Gregg took the bait, "You sound in the know—you're in the industry?"

"Mostly as a consumer but have a small vineyard on the westside. How about you?"

"Just getting involved. I've been studying abroad, but now I'm taking a crash course in harvesting at the family winery." Gregg underplayed the import of his family winery.

Dash let on that he knew him, "I'm a friend of Conrad's over at Paint Horse. He used to work at Jasper. Have you been under his tutelage?"

Gregg was taken aback at his recognition, "Have I met you before?"

"No, but I was friends of Claudia's. She kept pictures of you all over her apartment."

Gregg was visibly embarrassed and unnerved, "Let's not discuss Claudia—she was very dear to me, a great loss—I hope to move on." The bartender handed Gregg the chilled bottle.

"I'd shake your hand, but my hands are full," Gregg said as he tried to disengage from his conversation with Dash, "Your name?"

"Dash Ramblar, I'm a Private Investigator. Can I call you at the winery?"

Gregg's cheeks reddened, "Not sure. I was living in London—really don't have anything to add. Best to talk to her friends in Great Oaks."

Dash suspected that Gregg Perigold would ask around about him, eliminating a chance for a meeting anytime soon. Dash would take his advice, circling back to The Wine Sisters. Dash exited the bar, noticing Gregg was entertaining the same two women at a table. He was so engaged with them that he didn't see Dash passing through. Apparently, the mourning period was over. Dash walked on to the street, seeing that the weekly newspaper, The North County Gazette, with offices across the street. The lights were still on, after six, and he walked in the open door.

There were two people in the Gazette's office: one woman in advertising working late on copy, and a writer in the back of the office editing her story. He knew the writer, Mona Morgan, the food and wine writer for the Gazette. Dash stood at the front counter. The woman working on an ad looked up, "Can I help you?"

"I'd like to talk to Mona."

Mona lifted her head, peering at Dash, trying to determine if she knew him. She acknowledged Dash with a wave and came forward to the counter, "Have we met?"

Dash remembered, "Just once, at last year's roast of L'Adventure's winemaker, Michel." Dash extended his hand. "Dash Ramblar."

Mona returned his gesture, "Nice to see you again. What can I do for you, Mr. Ramblar?"

Dash looked at the advertising representative behind Mona, "Can we talk in private?"

Mona looked around and at the clock on the wall, 'I'm done here. Buy me a drink at the hotel bar across the street—we can talk there."

Dash nodded with a smile while she straightened up her desk, closed down her laptop computer, changed her shoes from running shoes to pumps, and gathered her purse. She looked like a wine writer. Her black hair was shoulder-length, her lovely walnut sheen was in her East Asian DNA. She wore thin tortoise rim glasses, a blue indigo dress that reached her knees, no stockings, and carried a short black leather jacket. She was in business casual attire and could go from the office to a cocktail party, by only changing her shoes. Dash noticed her sparkling dark eyes behind her lenses, a comely figure, slender ankles, and a slight overbite. Mona did not try to disguise her age by make-up or dress. She was in her fifties, accomplished and proud.

A woman who looks like this can be prickly or difficult for men. They are not easily swayed by male charm and bullshit. Dash preferred the intellectual challenge of rapport with a woman of substance, knowing vapid banter had no appeal.

Gregg Perigold was fully aware of the entrance of Dash and Mona. He looked befuddled as he tried to decipher who Mona was, not knowing where he'd met her, and what business she had with Dash. Dash chose to sit inside to avoid the stares of Gregg Perigold, who sat outside on the patio.

They sat at a cozy booth away from the din of the bar patrons. Dash was curious if she knew Gregg Perigold.

"Did you know Gregg Perigold?" Dash asked.

"I know of him, certainly. He was Claudia's fiancé and heir apparent to Jasper and Paint Horse locally. I've never met him officially. I really don't know anything about him other than what Claudia said."

The waiter came over, and they ordered two glasses of a Saxum Rhone blend. "I come here because it's the only place I know that sells Saxum by the glass," Mona said.

Dash was anxious to continue the conversation about Gregg Perigold, "I understand Gregg is staying on, not returning to London."

Mona took off her glasses and rubbed her eyes, "Sorry, long day. That's curious, we're in harvest, so it's a good time for Gregg to be here. He probably has no official role—just getting in everyone's way. I don't think he knows the first thing about viticulture."

Dash laughed, "That's a good thing. No one ever made big money with viticulture knowledge—he just has to invest wisely and not spend down the principle."

Mona looked at Dash, "So, are you in the industry or just a nosey guy?"

"Both, I'm a private investigator, and on the fringes of the industry," Dash winked, "So what makes you think I'm nosey?"

"First of all, men your age are not usually nosey—they think they know it all. They stop asking questions and listening. You don't fit the mold. You're a detective—I get that. You seem authentic, sorta' smart, and can afford to buy expensive wine."

"How do you know I can afford Saxum? I'm a private investigator, in a small city where everyone knows everyone's business. No one really needs a PI—so why would anyone hire me?"

Mona liked his answer and smirked, "Like being a wine writer. All the insiders know who's making the good stuff, but we direct the consumers to the better than average mead—drink free wine in return. There are so many brands, so many mediocre wines, so we try to un-clutter the field. Half the wine writers smoke or take drugs—and they're unable to taste anything. They talk to guys like you who tell us who is trending."

"I don't know what's trending—I do know that Jasper is a premium brand that can sell their wine for eighty-five bucks a bottle. You either have a premium niche, or you unload your wine at Costco. Like I said, it's a lousy business for most with the exception of the Perigolds."

Mona had already finished half her glass of Saxum, "Wine Spectator made this wine of the year, a couple of years ago—now they can't keep it in stock. Jasper is not Saxum, but close—the Perigolds don't give a rat's ass about profiting from wine, they make their money in other pursuits."

Dash savored the wine in his glass—it was that good. "What pursuits?' Dash asked a rhetorical question.

Mona took a long look at Dash, "Okay, be straight with me. I don't fall for the dumb ass act—you're investigating what and who?"

"I'm investigating Claudia's murder. I know you're a wine sister. You knew Claudia, and you might be privy to some inside information."

"Yes, I knew her—she wasn't a slut—if that's what you want to know. She was blessed with good DNA and a smart mouth—guys would fall over themselves taking a second look at her. She regaled us in her conquests. She made stuff up—she was hilarious. She'd tell us who had a good package, who was a dud, and who fell in love with her. The problem with a small town is that all the good-looking men are married, and the available ones are alcoholics or suffer from erectile dysfunction. What category are you in?"

Dash laughed, "The latter—but I'm not an alcoholic."

Mona ordered another glass of wine, and Dash ordered water—no ice.

Mona enjoyed Dash's attempt at self-deprecation. "Gregg Perigold—the Perigolds were not her problem. She pissed off some big players. They were local; they weren't in the industry. They don't drink in this bar."

Dash smiled, "Teamsters Union, the Portuguese mob, Wool Growers Association. I know, the Pickle Ball league? She said she played pickleball."

Mona ignored his humor, "She played pickleball, she went to dance classes in Atascadero, and she was an active conservationist: save the oaks, sustainability, water conservation—the whole gamut."

"You're not answering my question. Who were the big players she pissed off?"

Mona sipped her second glass of wine. "I could work you—get another couple of glasses of Saxum out of the deal. The truth be known, I heard all this second hand from Taylor Thorngate."

Dash was not deterred, "Don't be coy. You're basically a reporter. You've asked the same questions I've asked—maybe you didn't get an answer, but you got some morsel that you can share."

Mona reached across the table and touched Dash's hand, "I like you, you're funny. You're intuitive. I don't have a morsel—you're probably barking up the wrong tree."

"What precisely do you mean by that?"

"It's not about water. It's not about wine. It's not about the god damn oak trees. It's about fear and greed, the two biggest drivers of evil."

Chapter Seventeen:

MONA MORGAN

Dash offered to walk Mona to her car. Gregg Perigold and his female friends had left the bar for the evening. The music was winding down, and nightfall was pending. Mona's car was parked in the North County's Gazette's employee parking lot several blocks from the hotel, adjacent to the railroad tracks. The full moon provided all the light they needed to find her Honda Accord. All reporters had practical cars. They could not afford maintenance or repairs. Dash wished her well and thanked her for her time. She thanked him for the wine. It wasn't a date. It didn't end up like a date, yet it had the feel of the beginning of a wonderful friendship. There was that little spark of connection—like-minded souls stumbling along on the same journey. Dash and Mona were both intuitive, inquisitive, outliers confounded by life. They were observers on the outside, peering through the window on to the lives of normal people. Outliers were part of a tribe that recognized one another in a crowd. They were often the center of attention, but seemed awkwardly out of place, shooing the spotlight away.

"Good night, Dash. Good luck with your investigation," Mona said as she slipped into her car.

Dash waved as she left the parking lot. Restless, he decided to walk down to Fiftieth Street to get a better look at where Claudia was apprehended. Bars, restaurants, boutique hotels, gift shops, wine tasting venues were commonplace until he reached Thirtieth Street. The nightlife, the foot traffic, even the street lighting dimmed. Dash felt a chill in the air as he walked down Park Street and turned west on to Fiftieth Street. Midway up the block where Claudia had parked, was a vacant store, a real estate office across the street, and a Goodwill Store at the end of the block. Not a soul in sight, Dash found a stoop to a walkup office to sit on. He listened and waited. He laughed because the office was for an attorney. Dash didn't recognize the attorney's name. Dash looked at his iPhone for the time. It was eight-thirty. He figured he'd wait for a half-hour, and then head home. At five after nine, a slow-moving figure came up the street, dressed for winter. He had a hooded sweatshirt under a charcoal colored Carhartt twill work jacket. He wore tan work pants, work boots, and had a walking stick. He limped badly. The man with the walking stick didn't see Dash until he was right on him.

"What you doing on that stoop? That's my sleeping spot," The man with the limp asked.

Dash noticed the man had a bedroll. "I'm just holding it for you—making sure no else grabs it," Dash said with no sarcasm.

Dash got up and took another look at the man, "Damn it, you're The Hamster—what are you doing in town?"

The Hamster didn't recognize Dash at first, "I have my summer home and my winter home. This is my winter home. What's it to you, mister?"

"Don't you remember me? I bought you some french fries, and you told me about Claudia Bowers."

"Who?" The Hamster paused, "Did you ever find Charlie?"

"You mean Pedro, yes I did, up in San Miguel. He left town—started feeling some heat," Dash answered, moving off the stoop down to the sidewalk.

The Hamster pointed to his leg, "I wasn't limping last time I saw you, was I? Some asshole tried to break my legs. He told me to shut up about the girl. I don't know how he knew about you."

Dash looked around surreptitiously, "I swear every conversation in this town is broadcast. What did the guy who tried to break your leg look like?"

"Young, kinda' meaty, dark curly hair—like a guy that had a regular job."

"Do you think he beat you up for recreation or was told to?" Dash asked.

"Nah, he was paid. He said if I wanted to walk again, to keep my mouth shut."

Dash looked at the stoop after he'd gotten up, "You're not sleeping here tonight. Let me buy you a room somewhere."

The Hamster showed no emotion, "That's why I come down here—there's always a do-gooder, who puts me up in a motel. I can't remember that last time I slept here." The Hamster laughed out loud, startling Dash.

"You know where you're sitting, don't you?" Dash asked.

The Hamster looked around and read out loud, "Samuel F. Dotson, Attorney at Law."

Dash laughed, "You're an educated man, Hamster. This is the precise spot where Claudia Bowers was apprehended. Did you see it happen?"

The Hamster looked around to see if anyone besides Dash was listening, "Maybe, but it'll cost you a night at the hotel, not the motel. The Great Oaks Hotel has a complimentary breakfast."

Dash had to grin. He was being worked again by The Hamster. "Okay, the hotel on the square. What did you see?"

"Take a look around you, what do you see?" The Hamster was playing with him.

"A few parked cars, no human activity. A street that needs better lighting," Dash answered.

The Hamster raised his head and looked toward the second story of the real estate office. The office was not dark; it looked like there was some light in the windows. "They work late in that office, selling real estate, making after-hours calls—they can see the whole street from up there."

"What's your point?" Dash asked.

The Hamster got cranky with the question, "My point is—ask those folks up there—they see it all—I would know."

Dash knew he'd never get a straight story from The Hamster. "Are you telling me you didn't see a thing, but you think the real estate people upstairs may have seen something?"

"I don't see so good anymore. They do. I know they saw something."

Dash inquired, "How do you know?"

"Because I heard them come down the stairs, talking loudly. They waited for her. They parked on both sides of her, front and back—They kinda' of hemmed her in. She talked to them, and I saw her car drive away. They brought her car back without her in it."

"They?" Dash asked.

"No, it was just the driver, the other fella' was already gone with his ride."

"Do you remember their cars?"

"They weren't cars—they were pick-ups. Nobody drives cars in this town. It's all trucks."

"Do you remember color or makes of the pick-ups?"

The Hamster was getting restless, "Let's go to the hotel. I'm tired. I need a bath."

Dash opened the car door for The Hamster, putting his bedroll, walking stick, and pack in the back and helped him up into the Range

Rover. They drove silently to the hotel. Dash paid for his room while The Hamster sat in his car. Dash got the hotel room key, went back in his car, stalling before giving The Hamster the room key.

"Okay, Mister Hamster, I need some descriptions before I give you this key." Dash handed The Hamster the key, "Your information is safe with me—I'm not sharing it with anyone."

For the first time ever, The Hamster showed some emotion, "I'd like to tell you more. Those fellas' across the street, they'll kill me, dump me in the landfill if they knew. They weren't Fords, and they weren't Chevy trucks. Okay. They weren't skinny, they weren't short, and they didn't have long hair. They were younger than you. Their trucks were new, and they weren't white. Now give me the key—I need a long soaking bath."

Dash handed him the key, "You take care of yourself. Don't come back to the stoop. Stay at your summer home." Dash handed him his business card, "If you need a room, call."

The Hamster didn't say thank you or good-bye. He just left the parked car and headed for the hotel.

Dash went home, following The Hamster's lead, took a shower, a nip of whiskey, and headed to bed. He woke up the next day on Halloween. Dash was not crazy about Halloween. It represented the end of October, his favorite month, and the beginning of winter. Yet, it was going to be almost ninety degrees mid-day, so it didn't feel much like winter. It was a good day to stay on the ranch, avoiding the crowds of children trick or treating, the drunks, the cops, and the vandals. It was an ideal day to pick the grapes in the vineyard.

This was harvest time on the vineyard. The Zinfandel was at twenty-seven Brix sugar—ready to pick. The crew picked and de-stemmed the grapes in eight hours. Dash was always relieved when harvest was over. It meant that he could stop worrying about the hanging grapes: the birds eating the fruit, yellow jackets sucking the berries dry, the sugar level, the drip irrigation, and blight. The fruit was excellent, the tonnage not so great, because the vineyard had been radically pruned, the year before, to revital-ize the twenty-year-old vines.

Dash made it through Halloween without incident, but the next day proved otherwise. Dash got a call from Detective FJ Evans first thing in the morning.

"We found a homeless guy with his throat cut in a drainage ditch this morning. He had no identification. The only thing on his person was your card. Do you want to come down to the morgue and identify him?"

Dash was shaken; he knew it was The Hamster, "When did he die?"

"On Halloween night, he must have gone out trick or treating, and no one liked his costume."

Dash was still numb, "How did you know he was homeless?"

"He didn't smell—he was clean—he had a bedroll—a backpack—heavy clothes. He must have been in a shelter recently."

Dash didn't have to see the body to know who it was, "I can come by this morning."

"Meet you at the morgue at North County Hospital around eleven. Okay?"

"Sure," Dash ended the call and sat down. He had finished his nor-mal breakfast: soft boiled egg, a piece of raisin toast, a banana, a tanger-ine, cheese, and coffee. He didn't have the inclination to clean up or have another cup of coffee. He sat down, drank a full cup of water, contemplat-ing the last conversation he had with The Hamster.

The Hamster had apparently said too much, and it got him killed. He knew two beefy young men in Dodge, Toyota, or Nissan pick-ups had hemmed Claudia in her parking spot. They came from the real estate office across the street. One man drove her off in a car and returned without her.

Dash went to the morgue. It was in the basement of the hospital, temperature-controlled cold, bleak, sterile, and depressing. Bodies without life, souls, or spirit cataloged like books or dead files. Detective Evans seemed to relish the environment and the experience.

"It's showtime Dash—are you ready?"

Dash looked at Detective Evans in awe, "Without the music. Proceed."

The orderly drew back the plastic blanket that covered The Hamster. He looked younger than Dash remembered. He'd shaved. Dash realized that he was probably his age—early fifties. His hair was longish, mostly grey, with dark streaks. His neck wound was in a straight line that moved from his throat to his right ear, suggesting that a left-handed person made the cut in one backhand motion.

"Yes, that's him. I knew him as The Hamster. I have no idea what his real name is. He spent time at the River Park—I'm sure you've seen him before."

Detective Evans motioned for the orderly to cover up The Hamster and return the body to the drawer. "Sure, but he didn't loiter. He didn't appear drunk. He didn't urinate in public. He didn't commit any crimes. We had no reason to arrest him."

"The perfect citizen," Dash's voice broke. He was clearly overwrought."

Chapter Eighteen:

REX BECKETT

Dash was reeling from seeing The Hamster's corpse. He hardly knew the man, didn't entirely trust him, yet they connected on some level—as a fellow sojourner. On life's noble quest, we meet individuals who make us uncomfortable, as if they know us better than we know ourselves. Hamster and his ilk can smell the rancid lies because they've eschewed life's rat race, forcing us to re-examine who we are. The Hamster had that effect on Dash. The old saying "There but for the grace of God, go I" was how Dash felt meeting a homeless man about his same age who appeared content in his life, without a mortgage, home, vehicle, paycheck, or companions. The Hamster had no dog, no partners, just himself, a picnic bench, and some guile to survive off the grid. Dash would honor his memory by pinning his killer.

The Hamster did leave Dash some bread crumbs, or french fries, on a path to discovery. The real estate office on Fiftieth Street where two suspects came down from, according to his eye witness. Dash drove over there and surveyed the street. There were several real estate offices. A newer two-story brick building was on a corner. A stucco one-story structure was set back, and a large Victorian-style house was in the center of the block. The Victorian had stairs up to a wrap-around porch. It appeared to have three levels, with an insurance broker on the top floor. The Ranch and Farm Real Estate Brokerage firm occupied the bottom two stories. Dash went to the receptionist on the first floor. It was a typical real estate office with listings posted and videos of properties showing on several monitors. Dash looked at the photos of the agents. None were young men. Nearly all were women and a few retired men. None of the agents fit the description that The Hamster gave. From her photograph, the broker, Sara Hutchins, appeared to have the biggest hair. Dash said he was interested in listing his property and would like to speak to the broker. He was asked to wait a few minutes to see her. Dash looked closely at the listings. Many were ranch properties with a diagonal banner across the listings stating "reduced" in bold letters.

After a few sips of bad office coffee, he was led into her office. Sara was older than her professional photograph, which seemed to be true of every real estate agent he'd ever met. She had on tight blue jeans with embroidered artwork on the seat, a pressed white shirt, polished cowboy boots, and a bolo tie, and her hair cascaded down her shoulders. She looked like she just got back from the rodeo. She greeted Dash with a firm handshake and a genuine smile. He was a potential customer.

After a few pleasantries, Sara got down to business, "Tell me about your property."

Dash gave a description of acreage, vineyard production, structures, etc., and she followed with an obvious question.

"I'm assuming that you're on a well—how many gallons per minute does your well produce, and have you had any issues with the well?"

Dash knew that water is always a concern on the Central Coast, "The well is good, about four hundred and fifty feet down, gets about forty gallons per minute—we haven't had any interruptions even during the drought years."

Her response was interesting, "That's great—we're looking at proper-ties to list that have water issues. Investors are looking to pick up ranches that need deeper wells."

Dash stood up from her desk, "What investors? I thought investors would want a ranch with a good well."

Her expression became more strident, "We have agents who would be happy to list your property for potential residential buyers. My investors are looking to pick up distressed properties that they can flip."

"Just who are these investors?" Dash asked.

"You wouldn't know them—out of area folks primarily. The profile that they are seeking doesn't fit with your property. They want large par-cels—over fifty acres."

Dash thought her response was curious, "You're telling me that your investors want large parcels with well and water issues. What good is acre-age here without a good well?"

Sara smiled, "I don't question their motives—they're buying up a few parcels on the west side, but are aggressively buying properties on the east side."

Dash was confounded, "Where the wells have dried up?"

Sara was done with her conversation with Dash, "Can I introduce you to a residential agent?"

Dash got up out of the chair across from her desk, "Let me give it some thought." Dash picked up her card from a gold cardholder. "I'll call you when I'm ready to sell."

Dash went back to the lobby. He smiled at the young receptionist.

"What are the offices upstairs used for?" Dash asked as he looked at the interior staircase with a curved banister.

"Mostly our out of town visitors—we provide office space for them when they're in town. All our agents are on the main floor. Did you want to speak to anyone in particular?" She asked politely.

"Who are these out of town visitors who get the good office perks?" Dash asked.

"It changes. They're from all over the country. Do you have an appointment with any of them?"

Dash tried to manufacture a name and settled on, "The wine group from down south."

The receptionist lit up, "You mean Vino Veritas Group—Rex Beckett is here."

"Could you tell Mr. Beckett that I'm here to see him. I was hoping he'd be in today but failed to get an appointment." Dash danced verbally.

The receptionist called upstairs and got a positive response, "He wanted to know your full name."

"Dashiell Ramblar."

She repeated the name and called again to Mr. Beckett, who said Dash could come up. She pointed to the elevator, but Dash chose the stairs.

Dash saw the open door to a large office. The office was well appointed in wood, brass, and leather. It looked like the owner's office, not a visitor's digs. One wall was covered with large maps. The maps had parcel borders highlighted by red marker or blue marker pens. Dash guessed that half a dozen to a dozen parcels were marked. All the parcels were on the east side and formed a mosaic.

Mr. Rexford Beckett looked like a corporate guy. He wore a dark grey suit, a white shirt, no tie, black lace shoes—he was fit and tan. His salt and pepper hair belied his age. His left hand was professionally bandaged.

Beckett greeted Dash at the door and extended his right hand, "What can I do for you, Mr. Ramblar? Your name sounds familiar—I can't place you."

Dash changed the subject, "Looks like you had an accident."

Rex Beckett lifted his bandaged hand, "My dermatologist did her handy work—too much beach time in Orange County in my youth." Beckett smiled and rephrased his question, "What business are you in?"

"Sara said you might be interested in buying my ranch."

"Please refresh my memory, Mr. Ramblar, what ranch do you own?"

"No name, on the westside. It's planted in Zinfandel and Syrah."

"We're a wine conglomerate. We buy brands; we don't buy working vineyards. What's your brand?"

"No brand. I sell to different entities, winemakers, etc."

Mr. Beckett looked a bit confused, "I don't believe Sara mentioned your ranch. We don't normally buy on the west side, and we don't buy producing vineyards. We're interested in the dirt—not the grapes."

Dash was perplexed by Beckett, "Why is that?"

"The biggest aquifer on the West Coast is below us, down twenty-five hundred feet, from the ice age. We're lining up permits to access that water. Your vines are worthless without water."

Dash was following Beckett's line of thinking, "True, but there are no permits to access that aquifer. It's illegal to tap into it. If you do, they pour cement in your well."

Rex Beckett didn't find Dash funny. He walked to the door with the hope that Dash would follow. Dash picked up the get the hell out of my office gesture.

"Goodbye, Mr. Ramblar. I don't believe we have any business dealings. I'm sure Sara can direct you to a residential agent who can move your property."

Beckett closed the door behind Dash. Dash was met by Sara at the bottom of the stairs. She was displeased. "I didn't refer you to Mr. Beckett—I don't appreciate you misleading our receptionist."

Dash was less than cordial, "Do you know Claudia Bowers was apprehended across the street from this office by two men coming down your front stairs?"

Sara's face flushed, "Please leave the premises, or I'll have to call the police. You are way out of line. I don't know who you are, Mr. Ramblar, but I will find out soon enough and get a restraining order." She turned to the receptionist who looked mortified, "If Mr. Ramblar comes back—please call the police immediately. He is not allowed in this building."

Dash left the office, went to his car, turned on his car radio, played some Norah Jones to calm him, and drove home. It had been a while since he'd been thrown out of any establishment. It was like he was getting his "mojo" back. It went without saying that if you're thrown out of a place, you're either being a jerk or getting close to the truth. Dash was definitely getting close to the nub of the investigation. Neither Vino Veritas, Inc. nor any of the players Dash had met were concerned about wine or vineyard properties. They were laser-focused on one thing: the aquifer.

The harvest and crush at his vineyard went well. The sugar level, the tonnage, and the quality of the fruit were superb. The juice was now in the barrels, and a new vintage would not begin until next year with the pruning of the vineyard. Dash could focus entirely on the investigation. The obvious question is; What is the link between the aquifer and Claudia's death?

Dash circled back to Claudia's friend and fellow Wine Sister, Taylor Thorngate. Dash knew Taylor got the gig as the graphic designer for the Paderewski Festival. Reportedly, she had done an amazing job. She had turned the dour event into something fun and exciting, by simply changing the colors from black and grey to teal and cranberry, making Paderewski look younger with notes coming out of his bushy wild hair, and adding wine references throughout the artwork. Attendance was up to twenty percent, and she'd already been hired back for the next season. It was time to collect his adult beverage.

He was to meet Taylor downtown at a Spanish tapas restaurant called Alejandro's—it had a decent bar. They met at happy hour. By her brisk walk and gold-colored sweater and dark green jeans, Dash could tell she was in the manic phase of her malady.

"Let's sit over there where we can talk." Dash pointed to a table against the brick wall.

She ordered a dirty martini, and he ordered a mezcal concoction with some tapas plates, including calamari, stuffed chilies, and a polenta dish. They finished their drinks before the food arrived, so they ordered another round. After congratulations and toasting to the renewal of her contract with the festival, Dash tried to steer the conversation to Claudia.

"Last time we met, you said that Claudia was sleeping with the enemy. Naturally, I was intrigued by your statement. You don't have to give me names, but I would like to know what you meant by 'the enemy'?"

Taylor smiled coyly, "You won't give up, will you? I was referring to her indiscretions—she had no filter when it came to men."

Dash sipped his mezcal drink, which was sneaking up him. "How do you mean?"

"As much as I loved Claudia, she had a penchant for powerful, successful men. She didn't like to hang out with losers, wannabes, and pretenders. She wanted the real deal—men of substance. Consequently, they weren't all playing on the same team as her. They liked her obvious assets. They would patronize her politics, her save the planet philosophy. Once she found out that she was being played, she'd cut them off at the knees. They would give her a token check for a cause; then, when the vote came down with the city council, supervisors, planning commission, etc., it was obvious what side of the issue they were on. She was naïve but not dumb."

"You mean she'd break off the relationship?" Dash asked Taylor.

"More than that. She'd embarrass them in public, call them out and tell her Wine Sisters about their inadequacies in bed, etc. She was ruthless when she knew she'd been played."

"Would she confront their wives?" Dash demurred.

Taylor smiled broadly, "Didn't have to—Great Oaks is a small town. The Wine Sisters talk—the word would get back to the wives. The shit would hit the fan, and new BMWs and Land Rovers would show up in their driveways." She laughed at her little joke. She added with glee, "The men were pissed at Claudia."

"That can be dangerous." Dash ate some tentacles of the calamari that he dipped in aioli.

Taylor was younger and hungrier than Dash. She finished off the tapas. "That was delicious, she said and ignored Dash's statement. "I owe you a drink," she said, dropping a twenty on the table. Dash pushed it back to her.

"My treat," Dash wanted the answer, "You said she was being stalked?"

Taylor excused herself to go to the restroom. She returned still a little buzzed but nevertheless in a good mood, "I called Lyft for a ride home— will you wait with me outside for the driver?"

Dash nodded and followed her out the door.

"I will give you one name only. He's a developer from Orange County, Rex Beckett. They were lovers and became friends. She confided in him when she couldn't talk to anyone," Taylor steadied herself.

"Your ride is here," Dash said. He felt a little uneasy plying Taylor with alcohol and getting her to talk about her dead friend. It was the unsavory part of being a private investigator.

Chapter Nineteen:

VINO VERITAS

Dash took her lead and researched Rexford Beckett and Vino Veritas.
Vino Veritas was a holding company that produced no wine, had a large
portfolio of real estate valued in the hundreds of millions. Rex Beckett
was married, lived in Newport Beach, and his children attended USC, his
alma mater. Rex Beckett was the CEO of Vino Veritas. The company name
should have rightly been named Bandidas de Agua (water bandits).

Beckett was an A-Lister, belonged to several private and non-profit
boards, listed as a big alumni donor to USC, active in civic and cultural
pursuits. Vino Veritas was privately held, so profit and loss statements,
company officers, etc. weren't accessible on the internet. Dash called down
to the headquarters in Newport Beach attempting to get a prospectus or
a brochure, anything. The receptionist was polite and told him they had
no public information. The only information that Dash gleaned from the
conversation with the receptionist was that Rex Beckett was out of town at
a meeting with company partners.

Dash hung up and decided to do a little old-fashioned surveillance.
He drove to Fiftieth Street, where Beckett's office was located, and waited

across the street at a diagonal so his car could not be seen from the second story. It was after three in the afternoon, so he suspected that one of the cars in the employee parking lot was Rex Beckett's. Dash was correct. Shortly after three-thirty, Beckett came down the back stairs and got into a rented or leased black Cadillac Escalade. Dash followed the car to the airport road exit. Dash feared that he had missed the partner meetings and that Rex was headed for his private jet at the airport. The airport had no commercial flights. Fortunately, Dash's fears were allayed when Rex valet parked at the entrance to the Amalfi Resort. It was a massive hotel, spa, winery, resort and near the airport. Interestingly, Dash knew it belonged to a hotel group out of Orange County.

Dash parked his car in the parking lot, walked into the lobby of the hotel, and was greeted by the front desk receptionist. Dash said he was attending a Vino Veritas meeting, asking where it was being held in the hotel. They said it was occurring in the private dining room, the Zinfandel room. Dash asked for directions and followed the cavernous hallway until it opened up to the great courtyard. Greek and Roman statues encircled the courtyard. He found the single brass sign on heavy oak double doors, indicating that it was the Zinfandel Room. There was a bench just outside the door in the courtyard where Dash settled. He waited to see who was coming and going. He must have been late, as there was no activity. Then he realized that he was given the run-around. The actual meeting was occurring in the private bar at the back of the hotel near the outdoor pools. There were no patrons at the pool. Dash let himself into the pool and found a vantage point. The bar staff included one bartender and one busboy. There were half a dozen attendees to the meeting. Dash recognized most of the participants.

There was Rex Beckett, CEO of Vino Veritas. There was Gregg Perigold and his father Jason of Jasper Winery. There was Sara Hutchins, the broker from Town and Country Real Estate, Bill Lyons of Lyons Wine Estates, and one guest that Dash didn't recognize. He was a pudgy middle-aged man with navy slacks, a white shirt, and a navy blazer. The pudgy man was around fifty years old and was conversing with Rex Beckett. The participants were enjoying libation, hors d'oeuvres, and conversation. The meeting appeared to be casual. If there had been business, it would have been completed probably in the Zinfandel Room. The gathering seemed celebratory. Bill Lyons, who was critical of the Perigolds in public, appeared to be quite cozy and friendly with them in private. All the posturing about "Saving the Oaks" and "Saving the Aquifer" was probably a ruse. These men and their real estate holdings all needed plenty of water. Dash captured the busboy as he was headed out of the private room to the kitchen.

"Hello, young man. I'm with the group in the Zinfandel Room, and I can't recall the full name of the fellow in the navy blazer." Dash was very courteous to the busboy and gave him a ten-dollar bill.

The busboy looked at Dash strangely, "That's Sam Dotson. He's a local attorney." He answered formerly. The young man took the ten-dollar bill and smiled, "Everyone knows Mr. Dotson—he's a regular here."

Dash went to the hotel lobby, sat down, and googled Sam Dotson. His office was located on Fiftieth Street in Great Oaks. He was listed as a transactional attorney who also took DUI cases—the same Sam Dotson, whose entry stoop was inhabited by The Hamster. Dash didn't see the connection between these high rollers and a DUI attorney with an upstairs office in Great Oaks.

Perhaps more surprising was that Bill Lyons and the Perigolds were together. Bill Lyons was the former lover of Claudia Bowers. Lyons resided in Sausalito in the San Francisco Bay Area. Gregg Perigold was her fiancé at the time of death. Sex and money make strange bedfellows.

They would all appear to be suspects in Claudia's murder as members of the billionaire class; they would typically arrange a financial settlement with a part-time lover, rather than kill them when it was time to move on. Dash called his client, Bryson Jackson, telling him he wanted to connect a few dots. Jackson agreed, and Dash went over to Red Fox Winery, just before closing.

It was after five when Dash arrived at Red Fox; the skies were darkening, and a new front was coming in from the West- winter was nigh.

Bryson Jackson was in a jocular mood, slapping Dash on the shoulder and offering him a glass of Syrah. Dash accepted the glass of wine, and they settled at the bar—all of the patrons and staff had left for the evening. The Syrah wine is known for its deep plum color.

"I suppose you came because you have some information you want to share," Jackson said.

"Perhaps, as I mentioned on the phone—I wanted to connect some dots," Dash took a swallow of the Syrah, "Fermented plums never tasted this good," Dash continued. "I followed a suspect to the Amalfi Resort—I witnessed an unusual gathering: A local attorney, Sam Dotson, the Perigolds, Gregg and Jason, Bill Lyons, Sara Hutchins—a local real estate broker and a fellow from Orange County, Rex Beckett, the CEO of Vino Veritas. We can assume they knew Claudia, some intimately. They're rich and powerful. What else do they have in common?"

Bryson's mood became more somber, "You're partially correct. They've formed a group to finance the next water district. Together, their real estate holdings are over ten thousand acres in the Great Oaks region. I don't know Beckett personally, but his company's name keeps appearing on real estate transactions. They are buying up considerable acreage primarily on the east side of town."

"These properties, do they have dry wells and water issues in common?" Dash asked.

Bryson didn't ponder the question, "Precisely, the land is cheap."

"Won't the land be worth considerably more once there is water available?" Dash asked.

"Of course, but that's a long shot. Those wells on the east side are drying up left and right. They are drilling down over fifteen hundred feet right now—to no avail," Bryson answered.

"But at twenty-five hundred feet, Eureka!!" Dash exclaimed.

"That's the aquifer—it's illegal to drill into the aquifer." Bryson was enjoying the banter.

"Suppose that is the goal of the new water district—then you have a win-win for the billionaire's club. "Dash finished his glass of Syrah. Bryson poured him another. "What does this have to do with Claudia?"

Bryson looked annoyed, "Nothing. She had no political clout. She was above blackmail, and though she understood the aquifer stakes as well as any citizen, she was powerless to make a difference. The men and one woman in that room would only give lip service to her, or anyone, that deigned broach the subject with them."

Dash was not mollified, "You're underestimating Claudia. She was strong-willed, combative when she had to be—not easily dismissed, or played."

Bryson smiled, "She got to you too."

Dash and Bryson finished the bottle of Syrah and reminisced about Claudia. Dash left feeling that he and Bryson had connected in some way, though no dots had been connected. Dash drove the short distance home and greeted his dogs. Bixby was finally feeling better, so he rewarded him with a long walk, some cooked chicken and rice over his kibble. Barney trailed along on the walk and was given plain kibble.

The next day, Dash had a doctor's visit. The doctor recommended probiotics, apple cider vinegar, enzymes and Sauerkraut, and less whiskey. Dash was not impressed by his new diet.

He went home and lay down on the couch in his home office, mulling things over in his head. The investigation was wearing on him. He had not gotten over the murder of The Hamster and would never be over Claudia's murder. It seemed that every lead was a dead end. No one wanted to cooperate, and the case was becoming quite cold.

Dash had no real suspects, a few paramours, a few girlfriends, a fat blonde chap in a Hawaiian shirt, a couple of toughs, some high rollers in a political battle for water. He had no real expertise on the aquifer, other than it was verboten to drill it. He did not relate to greed and power. The murder of a young woman who slept with powerful men opposed to her political views wouldn't be targeted or murdered her for her activism. She had no real power and provided no risk to their machinations. She was an attractive woman, indiscreet in intimacy, a social-environmental activist, and a Wine Sister. It was time Dash knew more about The Wine Sisters. Sometimes, the most obvious connections are the most nefarious.

Dash got up from the couch and decided to have dinner at the Oliver Twist Organics restaurant where The Wine Sisters convened.

Chapter Twenty:

LAST TIME

Dash thought back to the last time he saw Claudia alive. He reminisced with the company of a good cigar and some decent aged Port. He had a couple of hours of winter daylight to enjoy; the midday sun in December is enough to warm the cartilage of weary bones. Dash had been training again for a triathlon and was on a strict regimen of swimming, cycling, and some running. His six-foot, one hundred eighty-five-pound frame was recognizable again, with a diminished waist. The cigars were not a good addition to the workouts, yet, a suitable antidote for abiding in the twenty-first century.

He recalled the day Claudia had called him at the last minute to attend an afternoon fundraiser at a local winery. It was mid-August, hot, and dry. Not ideal weather for drinking big reds, so Rosés and Sauvignon Blancs carried the day. There was a taco bar which sufficed for food. The auction items were awful: some mediocre wines, art, and crafts. The day could be described as a slow-moving disaster until Claudia told Dash that she wanted to move on from the fundraiser. They were near Tin City, so they went to a local brewpub, a big place with a beer garden. They opted to sit inside and enjoy some beer. Dash had a dark stout, and Claudia had a lager. They had a chance to catch up.

She talked about how she had fallen in love with Gregg, who now lived in London. She had met him in St. Helena in Sommelier school. They later connected in Great Oaks, and then he went to school at the London School of Economics. Her job allowed her to take two business trips to Europe; Gregg tagged along with her to Barcelona, Sardinia, and Lisbon. She enjoyed Dash's company because their relationship had evolved into a truly platonic friendship. It was a pleasant change for Dash—to have a platonic female friend, especially one so attractive, but he figured it was better to hang out with a beautiful woman than with some dude boasting about his halcyon years. At the time, Dash had also been in a similar situation, having a lover in Santa Cruz, which was over one hundred miles north of Great Oaks.

After a few beers, some live music, and another taco truck visit, they headed back to Claudia's house. She had some Silver Oak Napa Cabernet she wanted to try and, naturally, Dash was game. Claudia was a great hostess; she pulled some smoked salmon, capers, and crème fraîche out of the refrigerator, adding in some artisan cheeses, dry salami, pickled herring, and crackers to accompany the good wine. They took their glasses outside and looked at the night sky, enjoying the balmy night. Claudia convinced Dash to play Scrabble with her. Dash had only played it once when he was a teenager. He fancied himself a wordsmith, but Claudia knew how to work the board. She won. During the course of the game, she mentioned some things that Dash contemplated.

Dash had an X, a T, and a B plus two vowels. He was able to make the word Botox, which Claudia found hilarious. The word was in the Urban Dictionary. She admitted using Botox around her eyes and lips, which Dash thought unusual for a woman in her thirties. She refuted his claim telling him that all The Wine Sisters went to the same doctor for Botox injections.

The next thing she said was curious. She said not only did many of The Wine Sisters use the same doctor, but several of the sisters had also dated the same men. She said that is why she liked Gregg. He wasn't a player; he had dated no other women in town other than Claudia. Dash asked if any were jealous. "Not among the women, but among the men," She said. Dash wasn't prone to gossip, yet asked if he knew any of the men. She smiled coyly and said, "Some are notable, some are sleepers, some married, and some were players." "I was happy to get out of the small-town dating syndrome," she added. "It was getting too weird and a little dangerous."

Dash had asked what she meant by dangerous. She answered, "See these earrings? They're moonstone—not that precious, but beautiful. One man, in particular, gave all the women he slept with moonstone jewelry." She laughed. "We called ourselves the Moonies. When he found out, he was pissed. He threatened me to rip them from my ears," Claudia said.

"Did he try?" Dash asked.

"No, but I blocked his phone number and deleted him from my online social network. Others were just crazy, especially the married men. They thought they were getting away with adultery, but the joke was on them. We outed them."

Dash took a cautionary tone, "Wasn't that playing with fire?"

Claudia laughed, "Yes, but it served them right. The Wine Sisters are a true sisterhood. We out the scoundrels, make the players pay, and collect their jewelry."

After the Scrabble game and a day of drinking, Dash settled for spending the night on the couch. Claudia came out in her nightshirt, loosely hanging on her torso. Against the lamplight, he could see her wondrous figure. She was a goddess. She gave Dash another blanket, even though the night was still warm, telling him that it got cold about three in the morning. Dash thanked her and asked her if she felt safe, alone in this detached cabin, out in the country with former lovers knowing her whereabouts. Virtually the last thing that she ever said to Dash was prescient.

She said, "If something happens to me, the Moonies would know who did it. I confide everything with them even if it hurts them to hear it."

Dash held her close, comforting her. She would never let on that she felt alone and vulnerable. Dash knew the feeling well. Claudia kissed him and let her nightshirt fall from her shoulders. Their lovemaking was different now. After a year's hiatus, it was more tender, sweeter, and less frenetic.

The next morning, he left without waking her. He would never see her again.

Chapter Twenty-One:

AMANDA JACOBS

The Oliver Twist Organics restaurant was off Thirtieth Street just two blocks from where Claudia was apprehended. It was the first Thursday of the month, so there was the off chance The Wine Sisters were meeting this evening. Dash arrived during happy hour, ordered a Manhattan on the rocks. Dash had dressed for the evening. He wore a sky-blue sport coat, a French blue collared shirt, black slacks, black cowboy boots, and his signature Tom Ford blue-rimmed glasses. He could have been confused as a dude, a caballero, a tourist—someone certainly not from Great Oaks.

In Great Oaks, the tourists usually were underdressed or overdressed for this laid-back coastal town. When the locals went downtown, they wore their best jeans, their best jackets, their best boots, and their most colorful shirts. Tourists wore shorts, tee shirts, baggy jeans, and sneakers. The men wearing suits, ties, and tasseled loafers were also tourists or salesmen. The locals never wore shorts downtown, never wore ties, and wouldn't be caught dead with tassels on their loafers, even if they owned a pair.

Dash settled in at the end of the bar with his back to the door, allowing him to survey the entire restaurant. He spotted the owner, Brenda, a petite woman of sixty, standing at the hostess stand going over the reservations with the hostess. She had been recognized for her well-known and popular restaurant. Brenda had been single for years, having no intention of marrying, given that her net worth exceeded the combined worth of most of the available men in the area. She scanned the bar area and didn't recognize Dash.

The Wine Sisters rolled in at around six, mingling with Brenda at the far end of the bar. The only sisters that Dash knew hadn't appeared: Mona Morgan, the wine writer, Taylor Thorngate, the graphic artist. When they arrived together, a bit later, they were greeted by the other eight or so Wine Sisters who applauded the latecomers. They all went into the restaurant section, which was an enclosed outdoor patio. Dash had only a partial view of the group. He took out his notebook, jotting down the attendees.

Of those he didn't recognize was a petite blonde, who appeared to be in her fifties wearing a loose gold sweater that extended over the waist of her tight jeans. She looked like she had money by her jewelry and coiffed hair. A pretty young Asian woman appeared to be Thai or Filipino. She sported a large diamond ring and wore a plain navy dress. Her comfy plain wedge shoes suggested that she'd just gotten off work. A Rubenesque blonde was entertaining the wine writer, Mona Morgan. Mona's glasses and hourglass figure gave her an air of erudite sophistication. The jocularity of the zaftig woman and the attention given suggested her tales were juicy. The two appeared to be in their mid-forties. Almost all the women at the long table were laughing, and their conviviality was contagious.

There appeared to be only one woman at the table who was an outlier. She was a tall, striking brunette with apparent after-market work done on her face and body. Her dirty martini was keeping her company as she appeared a little ill at ease. She had come as a guest of Taylor Thorngate; she could have been a new member of the sisterhood. Dash was fascinated by her demeanor. In the small town of Great Oaks, she would stand out, more LA style and more glamorous. She wore a simple cobalt blue dress with a cinched belt at her waist, a slit up her leg on one side, and understated but expensive jewelry. She had the erect posture of good breeding, the high forehead of intelligence and the confidence of status. Taylor, who was at her side, turned her face towards the brunette, attempting to engage her in conversation. It worked. The tall brunette put down her drink and graciously smiled.

Dash weighed his options. Should he wait until they're ready to leave to introduce himself to The Wine Sisters, or should he wait and speak to Taylor about her friend, the brunette, sitting next to her? Dash was curious to meet them all. He nursed his drink and waited. Eventually, the bar filled up, and Dash was not alone. Brenda sat with The Wine Sisters but would get up occasionally to greet the customers. If she knew that Dash was at the bar, she didn't let on. They had been introduced a couple of times at wine industry events.

Around eight-thirty, the party broke up with The Wine Sisters leaving intermittently. Taylor and her friend were the last to leave, which gave Dash an opening. He walked over to the table, which was scattered with wine glasses and a few partially eaten plates of dessert.

"Based on the wreckage, it looks like you had quite a feast," Dash quipped.

Taylor was a little buzzed, taking a few seconds to recognize Dash, "Hey Dash, how are you? We Wine Sisters know how to pair delicious food with yummy wines. We're just leaving, but we'll stay and share a glass of wine with you."

Dash was surprised by Taylor's invitation. "Splendid, my name is Dash." Dash extended his hand to Taylor's mystery friend. I don't believe we've met."

"I'm Amanda Jacobs." She extended her hand, palm down, indicating that she didn't want to shake.

"A pleasure," Dash said as he held her hand lightly in his palm, noticing the large moonstone ring on her ring finger.

Dash sat down and opted for a Tudor Pinot Noir to round out the evening. Amanda stared at Dash.

"How do you know Taylor?" Amanda asked.

"We did a wine label together. Taylor did the artwork and the social media. She's very talented."

Taylor laughed, "What do you want, Dash? My rates have gone up, and you're notoriously slow to pay."

"I was about to ask Amanda the same question," Dash grinned.

Amanda blushed, "We go way back." Amanda grinned, "We just met at the last Wine Sisters dinner and have been hanging out. You know, two single women, on the prowl."

Dash swirled his wine glass savoring the fragrance and color of the dark Pinot Noir.

"I'm a single guy on the crawl. I do get around—surprised I haven't run into you before."

Amanda smiled at Dash's attempt at humor, "I'm in and out of relationships. It's been a roller coaster ride for the last nine months. It's good to be with The Wine Sisters—they motivate me to move on with my life."

Dash's curiosity was piqued, "Who's the lucky fellow?"

Amanda's brightness faded immediately, "I don't think you know him. He's an investor from out of the area. We spent most of our time in Palm Springs and Las Vegas. The good news is, he now frequents Great Oaks."

Dash needed to change the subject, "Palm Springs sounds inviting. The next few months here are cool and rainy. Maybe I'll take a trip in the spring."

"Taylor and I are talking about Cancun in February. Men aren't invited."

Dash laughed, "No worries. I'm not going anywhere until I complete Claudia's investigation."

Amanda looked confused, "What investigation? Are you a cop?"

Taylor, who had been drinking and listening, answered for Dash, "He pretends to be a private investigator—don't let him fool you. He's a true dilettante. He dabbles in wine, women, and detective work. His output is low, but I must say the quality of his work is high."

Dash smiled, "I take umbrage with that description—I think my work is average or just above."

Amanda and Taylor were quite buzzed. They were getting ready to depart. Taylor decided to go to the restroom one last time before she left the restaurant.

When Taylor was absent Dash addressed Amanda, "Can you think of anyone who would have wanted Claudia harmed?"

To Dash's amazement, she answered without hesitation, "Besides me, no one I can think of."

Dash followed, "What cause would you have?"

"That's personal. Suffice it to say that she was the reason for my break-up." Amanda blushed.

"What did she do?" Dash asked.

"She did nothing wrong. He did everything—he fancied her. She succumbed," Amanda said.

"Succumbing is not sufficient reason to get murdered," Dash declared.

"Come now, Dash, don't be naïve. We all know that she didn't get murdered for doing my boyfriend. She got murdered for not doing her due diligence."

Dash got up from the table as he saw Taylor heading back to the table to retrieve her coat.

"What due diligence?" Dash asked.

Amanda curtly smiled, "You get paid to determine that—I get compensated in free cocktails, dinner, and the occasional trip."

Chapter Twenty-Two:

DUE DILIGENCE

Due diligence usually refers to an investigation of a person or business prior to a transactional activity. Dash thought that perhaps Amanda used the expression improperly. If not, what transaction could she be referring to? The old expression "follow the money" can lead to convictions in criminal cases. People have been murdered for their life insurance, for inheritance claims, to circumvent a divorce settlement, or to eliminate a business partner.

Claudia Bowers was a barrel and wine bottle salesperson. She was employed by a company in Barcelona. She made an adequate living with her sales job, having the benefits of travel, entertainment, and free wine. Claudia would help her clients with harvest, wine tasting, and wine club parties in exchange for cases of wine. She lived modestly alone in a one-bedroom casita with her dog and cat. She leased her car, which she wrote off for tax purposes. Upon death, her total assets were less than thirty thousand dollars. She had a small savings account, an IRA account, and a pension with her company. She had no contractual agreements other than her rent agreement, and her credit card debt was minimal. She was very typical of a single woman in her thirties, divorced, living on her own. If not transactional, then what due diligence could Amanda be referring to?

She was engaged to a wealthy young man, Gregg Perigold. Prior to her engagement, she had possible affairs with Bill Lyons and Conrad Cook. Additional suspects included the vineyard manager, Dylan Dotson, and the developer Rex Beckett. Three of the suspects were wealthy: Gregg Perigold, Bill Lyons, and Rex Beckett. Dylan Dotson and Conrad Cook weren't wealthy. Given Claudia's liaisons, jealousy was the primary motive and, secondarily, blackmail.

Perhaps the Perigold family was investigating Claudia prior to her marriage to their son. It was time to circle back to the Perigolds. Dash called his mole or inside source at Jasper Winery, Ginger Rute, to find out about the Perigolds. He called her after work on her cell phone.

Ginger was not happy with the call, "We had an agreement. You said you wouldn't involve me in the investigation. The holidays are coming, and I can't afford to lose my job."

Dash apologized, 'I'm sorry. One simple question—when do expect the Perigolds to be back in town?"

Ginger hesitated, "They'll join Gregg here for the first two weeks of December, they then head to the Caribbean for Christmas and New Year's. They have a home on Harbor Island."

"Thanks, Ginger. Can I buy you a cocktail to celebrate the holidays?"

Her voice sweetened, "That would be nice." She then hung up.

Dash deducted that Gregg Perigold was still in the area. He had a short window of time to see him. Dash wasn't sure what he wanted to know, but sometimes exploratory questioning turns up gems.

After his first encounter with Gregg Perigold, Dash never got a call. Gregg knew that Dash was a private investigator and wanted nothing to do with the investigation. Dash had to concoct a story to get Gregg to the table.

Dash called Gregg at the winery and asked him a simple question.

"If I could tell you who killed Claudia—would you be interested in meeting?"

Gregg's answer showed he had discipline, "Yes, and no. Of course, I'd like to know who killed Claudia. Why is it necessary to meet?"

Dash responded, "I don't like talking over the phone or texting. I'd prefer to meet you in person. Also, you're the only one who can confirm my hunches."

Gregg laughed, "In other words, you don't have the slightest clue who murdered Claudia, but you want to cross-examine me to get some leads. I'm not doing your leg work for you. You're going to have to do the heavy lifting. If I can provide you some information that will lead you to that conclusion—then I'll answer your question, but not in person."

Dash was prepared, "Did Claudia know about your dealings with Vino Veritas?"

Gregg was caught off guard, "What does Vino Veritas have to do with anything? In answer to your question, No. We never discussed Vino Veritas—it never came up."

Dash knew that was a lie based on Gregg's emphatic response, "Just a word of warning, Gregg. These players from Orange County play hardball. They're using your family money to secure the region's water rights."

Gregg chuckled, "Don't worry about us. We play a special brand of hardball. We always win."

Dash kept him on the phone, "Claudia's murderers were paid."

Gregg took a deep breath, "Plural? There was more than one murderer? Paid? Are you saying—hers was a murder for hire?"

Dash knew he'd piqued Gregg's interest, "Yes, and yes. Your parents were doing a background check on Claudia. They knew about her political proclivities—they didn't purport with your family's values. She presented a problem for your family."

"What are you implying? Of course, they did a background check on her. Her values aligned with mine, but not with my parents. That's not uncommon for parents and children to hold different views. They never told me that I shouldn't marry her. They were happy that I was finally settling down."

Dash couldn't let Gregg's comment pass. "I've seen you about town—you obviously haven't settled down."

Dash could sense Gregg's anger, "Stay out of my business and my family's. Do we have to get a restraining order?" Gregg's tone changed. "If you do indeed find the suspects in Claudia's murder, I would surely meet with you. In the interim, please don't contact me or my parents. I'm still wounded from Claudia's passing. We are taking a short holiday in two weeks, so if anything comes up, please text me. You have my number."

Gregg hung up without saying goodbye.

Chapter Twenty-Three:

RELEASE PARTY

Dash went home to his vineyard. He decided to attend to his own affairs for a change. He scheduled a wine release party for mid-November for his 2016 Vintage Zinfandel. He invited Mona, the wine writer, The Wine Sisters, Bryson and Jackie Jackson, and some neighbors. He also invited Ginger. It was to be an afternoon affair, seafood, and vegetarian paellas that Dash prepared. His secret was simple. He opened four bottles of white wine the day before. He dropped some saffron threads in each open bottle, letting them sit in the sun. The white wine would become infused with saffron and be used to plump up the Bomba rice as it cooked. He would have the party in the rustic barn with repurposed redwood and tin. He hired a singer and an accompanist to play old-time rock n' roll music. He invited about forty people thinking twenty-five would show. Thirty-five people showed, including a few uninvited guests.

The party was on a Saturday afternoon. The weather cooperated, and by two, the barn was full of guests mingling and sampling the 2016 Zinfandel. The music was good, the wine better than expected. The paellas were a big hit with the guests. Ginger came alone. Mona came without her husband. Several of The Wine Sisters brought dates. Taylor Thorngate came with Conrad Cook, who alternated from being charming to having a surly demeanor in an instant, depending on who was in front of him. He was thicker around the middle than Dash recalled, wore a baseball hat with a popular local beer logo on it, contrarian for a winemaker who was attending a wine event.

"Hello, Taylor. Thanks for the coming to the release party," Dash said, attempting to be cordial to her and her uninvited guest.

Conrad looked at Taylor, "You didn't tell me that this dude was the host."

Taylor smiled, "Get yourself a beer—Dash won't bite you."

Conrad agreed, looking towards the bar, "Good idea, I could use a beer."

Dash walked away from them, sensing that Taylor was in her familiar dark mood. He saw Conrad standing alone later with a beer bottle in his hand, pouting.

Amanda Jacobs arrived with a surprise date, developer Rex Beckett.

Rex Beckett couldn't place Dash, the fellow he tossed out of his office. Rex behaved gracious and friendly, as though he'd met Dash at a soiree or a polo event. Beckett wore a scarf and sport coat, with a wool turtle neck sweater underneath. He expected the barn to be cold. It wasn't warm.

"I understand you live in Orange County. What brings you to town?" Dash asked.

"Real estate deals and Amanda." Beckett nudged Amanda, who was the same height as Beckett in cowboy boots. Amanda was dressed just the opposite. She was ravishing in tight Western jeans, pearl button plaid shirt, and a lightweight jean jacket. Hatless, her black hair cascaded down to her shoulders. A large Moonstone pendant hung from her neck matching the ring Dash had seen at The Wine Sisters dinner.

Dash smiled at Amanda, "She's reason enough." Dash shook hands with Rex Beckett and hugged Amanda. Amanda and Rex Beckett made a bee-line for Bryson and Jackie Jackson. Dash could tell that Jackie was more than enamored of Rex Beckett, whose debonair looks and style were in direct contrast to her husband's crude behavior and appearance.

Dash walked away, confused. He couldn't comprehend that Rex Beckett didn't recall the events in his Great Oaks real estate office just days ago. The only thing that Dash could figure was that he was scoping out his property—now interested in acquiring it. Amanda was very attentive to Beckett, clinging to him like a high school girl. Dash had to assume that Claudia was the love interest that got between Amanda and Beckett.

Dash looked around the big space in the barn. The wine-infused guests were dancing and laughing, and the party was getting more raucous by the minute. As the afternoon went on, the guests got more buzzed, and the din in the room elevated. Dash was mindful of the liability for drunk drivers, so he got assurances from the departing guests that they had a designated driver or had hired an Uber to get a ride home.

Bryson and Jackie Jackson were the only couple dancing to the music. Dash had never seen Bryson so intoxicated. When they got off the dance floor, Jackie had to hold him up for balance. He came over to Dash, slightly slurring his words.

"Great party, old boy—they're some real lookers here." Bryson surveyed the room and pointed with his half-full wine glass. He then noticed that Jackie was giving him the stink eye, so he edited his statement, "But I brought the best of show, a real thoroughbred, wouldn't you say?" He nudged Dash.

Dash kissed Jackie on the cheek. "I'd have to agree with you, Bryson."

Bryson started waving his wine glass and sloshing some wine around, "I better put this down, or I'll be wearing it," Bryson put his glass down on a nearby table.

"I can't believe you invited Conrad Cook. He's a complete asshole. He was nasty to Claudia when she wouldn't date him," Bryson Jackson said haltingly.

"I didn't invite him—he was a plus one with Taylor, whom I did invite. I thought Conrad and Claudia were an item at one time?" Dash asked.

"For a nanosecond. She found out early on that he was a real jerk. He told her that if she wanted to do business with Jasper Winery, she'd have to sleep with him."

Dash exploited Bryson's loose lips, "She didn't need him—she was seeing the owner's son."

"That came later. Then she had him fired or transferred. He was really pissed," Bryson said as spittle accompanied the word pissed.

Dash followed up, "How pissed?"

"He bad-mouthed her all over town, calling her a bitch and worse. He would have continued, but he wanted to keep his job at Paint Horse. She said he was stalking her. She even got a restraining order on him."

Bryson looked over at Taylor and Conrad, "That guy is unbelievable. He confirms that cliche—nice guys finish last—and real jerks get all the lookers."

Jackie had heard enough. She took Bryson's arm in hers, "I think it's time you went home."

They started to move away from Dash, "Thanks again for the invitation. My husband can drink his wine all day and never get drunk. He has three glasses of wine at a party, and he's wasted."

Bryson slurred his words, "I'm not wasted—I'm just inappropriate."

Dash consoled his client, "No problem. I don't think anyone heard you." Dash picked up a keyring off the floor next to Bryson. "Did you drop your keys?"

Bryson held them up to his eyes, "Nope, not mine." Jackie escorted Bryson out of the barn door and into his vehicle. Dash followed, making sure that Jackie was driving. Bryson was being obstinate, demanding to drive his car home, but Jackie prevailed.

Dash walked back in the barn party room. He looked at the keys and read the Dodge logo. They were truck keys plus half a dozen other keys. Dash went back outside and noticed that there was only one truck in the parking lot, a big three-quarter-ton truck with a raised body and extra searchlights on the cab and the front bumper. It was a redneck wagon. The only one who fit that description at the party was Taylor's date, Conrad Cook.

Dash went over to where Conrad and Taylor were fully engaged with Ginger.

Dash's presence was not welcomed, "Hi, Dash, don't you have other guests to attend to?" Conrad asked.

"Yes, a room full. Would you happen to know whose keys these are?" Dash held up the keys.

Conrad changed his tune, 'I'll be damned. Where did you find 'em?"

"Over there on the floor—must have fallen out of your pocket," Dash said, pointing to the floor.

"I was probably fishing for my pocket knife. Conrad pulled out a long slender pocket knife with his left hand, "Good thing I didn't drop this. It's more of a machete than a knife." Conrad laughed and took the keys from Dash. Conrad didn't thank Dash but picked up the conversation with Taylor and Ginger. Dash went back outside to catch some fresh air and look at the sky full of stars.

Why did Taylor Thorngate bring Conrad Cook to the party? Was she that tone deft to know that her best friend Claudia couldn't stand the guy? Conrad attempted to be cordial to Dash but didn't pretend that they were friends. Conrad avoided contact with Dash throughout the remainder of the evening. Ginger came over to Dash alone and touched his shoulder.

"Nice party—thanks for the invitation," Ginger smiled warmly.

"Surprised you hung out with Taylor and Conrad. I thought you were on the outs."

Ginger winked at Dash, "Trying to being politically correct. Conrad misses working at Jasper. I know what he misses, besides me. He's lost power, prestige and feels alienated. I'm his only link within the winery."

Ginger was quite alluring. She had on snug leggings that elongated her legs. Her shape was flattered by a tight leather jacket zipped open to the waist. Her reddish hair was down, accented by bright red lipstick and eyeliner that emboldened her green eyes.

Dash smiled, "I can only guess."

Ginger came close to Dash and whispered in his ear.

"I don't feel safe around him," She said.

Dash assumed she meant Conrad, and he asked, "Then why humor him?"

She looked around the room, "I didn't mean Conrad." Then she left his side.

Dash shivered as the early evening got cooler. He was so busy hosting he'd forgotten to drink or eat anything other than water. Mona Morgan came over to Dash and asked him to dance.

"I started taking dancing lessons with Claudia a year ago. I'm a little rusty. I need to practice the nightclub two-step," she said.

Dash looked around the room and saw that all The Wine Sisters were dancing with their dates. Dash capitulated, "Okay, but you'll have to lead. I don't know the night club two-step from a Viennese Waltz."

Mona grabbed Dash by the arm and lead him out on to the floor where the blue tooth receiver was blaring Queen; it was difficult music to dance to. Dash was, by now, well lubricated and managed to cut a few moves with Mona.

Dash said to her, "Where's your husband tonight?"

"He's not much of a partier—he thinks The Wine Sisters are evil," Mona answered.

"Are they?"

"Of course not," she laughed, "We gossip, we cavort, we complain about men, laugh about their little blue pills, but mostly we're harmless," Mona chuckled.

The party winded down. The Wine Sisters had the most fun and were the last to leave. Dash let his dogs roam. They happily picked through the left behind trash. Dash turned off the lights and music and headed for the comfort of his bed.

Walking the few hundred yards to his house, he felt the chill of the evening. An unpleasant coldness surrounded him, shrouding the euphoria that was present just an hour ago. Dash had the haunting notion that the perpetrator or an accomplice in the murder of Claudia Bowers had been present at his wine release party.

Chapter Twenty-Four:

YULE TIME

Dash generally celebrated the winter solstice in reflection and rest. He endured the holiday season, avoided the New Year's Eve festivities, finally breathing a sigh of relief when Valentine's Day displays disappeared. To Dash, the holiday season was a gauntlet of persistent reciprocity and obligation. He partook in gift-giving, holiday parties, visits with the relatives, etc. while cursing the blustery short days, the long cold nights, the surfeit of sweets, the overconsumption of alcohol, and the reoccurring nightmares that heralded the morning wakeup.

The nightmare that stood out was the enhancement of the description that The Hamster gave of Claudia hanging head down with her throat cut, bled out, ravaged by coyotes, in the swath of the dry Salinas River arroyo. He thought of Hamster, whose similar fate stubbornly stuck in his craw, in his nightmares. The Hamster appeared as the oracle, not the victim. Ginger's admission of fear also plagued the fatigued Dash Ramblar, who awoke daily tired and cranky. He would stay that way until the month of April arrived, and bud break occurred in the vineyard.

Dash's agreement with his client, Bryson Jackson, would terminate at year's end. He had a few obligatory suspects, a congregation of motives, and little else. Bryson Jackson did not contact him after Dash's wine release party, so it was up to Dash to take the initiative. He called Bryson and set up a meeting, carrying a sign-off sheet releasing liability and detailing his findings, which were obscure at best.

Bryson's reaction was surprising. "I want you to stay on course," Bryson said after a few pleasantries. "I know you are digging the right trench because the blowback is getting stronger."

"From whom?" Dash queried.

"From the wine industry, from local politicians, from my friends and the police," Bryson Jackson answered.

Dash was intrigued, "How do you know? They don't know you're my client—your name has never come up. You're under the radar, my friend."

Even though they were alone in a private room, Bryson brought his face closer to Dash's ears and whispered, "Taylor told me. She says that she overheard a conversation that implicated you. She says that you should be wary, and to watch your back."

Dash laughed, "I'm delighted that one of The Wine Sisters thinks I'm a threat. I know they're connected. Their currency is gossip, and their hobby is manufacturing it. I know men also deal in rumor, are often more malicious in intent, more heinous in action, but they lack one weapon."

Bryson sat back, enthralled, "Which is?"

"Pillow talk. Men reveal themselves after intercourse. That's when they're the most vulnerable, most apt to spill the beans, about their machinations and criminal intentions. I suspect that Taylor Thorngate got her information from a lover, not from one of The Wine Sisters. You saw her date, Conrad Cook, at the wine release party."

"Conrad does winemaking consulting work for me, and most of the wineries in the area."

Dash drilled a little deeper, "He's been demoted by Jasper Winery—his stock is definitely down."

"That's possible. Conrad Cook still does a lot of freelance consulting for a lot of folks in the industry. Oftentimes he's the only person around that they could confine in. I get some of the juiciest info from him. He knows who's doing who, who's getting divorced, who's going bankrupt. Shit, he even knows about business transactions months before they become public."

"If he's talking about you—could be a liability," Dash said in a measured tone.

Bryson grinned, "Yes, he is. Two can play the game. Say you wanted to spread some false information, he's your man. If you mention a competitor, they'll hear about what you said the same day. Frankly, he's invaluable."

Dash was not convinced. "Assuming Conrad Cook indirectly threatened me through Taylor Thorngate, how do you know? You haven't told Conrad about the investigation?"

"I suppose I could have said some things, nothing pertinent, nothing about Claudia. He asked if I knew you. I said we were friends. I never mentioned the investigation."

"If that's the case, why would Taylor Thorngate convey veiled threats and turn up the heat on me without you telling her that we're connected?" Dash asked.

Bryson paused, "Taylor was good friends with Claudia. Taylor knew I was fond of Claudia. She also knew that I was extremely upset by her death. She probably connected the dots. You were snooping around town, asking questions, and I was keeping quiet. She knew that was not my nature, so I suspect she put us in the same box. If it weren't for Claudia's death, none of this would be happening. It's put everyone on alert, especially Taylor. She feels especially vulnerable."

"So, who am I? The good guy, or the interloper who is stirring up the pot?" Dash asked.

Bryson reached in his pocket and pulled out a check for ten thousand dollars. "This is for another sixty days. I know, it's below your asking rate, but Jackie and I are looking for closure."

"I understand why you need closure, but Jackie? Are you sure she's signing off on this expenditure?" Dash asked. "This investigation has altered my plans. I usually go to Mexico in January—or get the flu. Nothing usually ever happens in January, but I can't imagine letting this case get any colder."

"You could go down to Cabo for the weekend?" Bryson Jackson asked.

Dash tightened his jaw. "Claudia's killers won't be getting a vacation either."

They walked together back to the tasting room, which was crowded with customers buying wine for the holidays. Jackie was at the tasting room bar, along with two other servers. They were selling wine by the caseload. Another male employee was carrying wine to the various cars in the parking lot.

"She doesn't need to sign off on it. This is our winery. My investment firm is writing the checks."

Dash understood that Bryson's interest in Claudia's death was personal.

Bryson accompanied Dash to the parking lot and his silver Range Rover. Dash thought about the conversation they'd had and paused.

"One question. When Conrad Cook came to my release party with Taylor, he was wearing a knit watch cap. I assumed he was hiding his baldness. I've never seen him without a hat. Is that the case?"

Bryson almost doubled over laughing, "Conrad Cook, shit, he's got tons of hair. He puts product on his hair that makes it stand straight up."

"What color is his hair?"

Steve laughed again, "He dyes it blonde—doesn't match his dark eyebrows."

At home, Dash went online and found Conrad Cook's Facebook page. He was friends with dozens of people in the wine industry, lots of single women, and almost all of The Wine Sisters. He was listed as a wine-maker consultant, single, a high school graduate in 91' making him around 38 years old. He was a resident of Great Oaks, having lived in the area for his entire life. Several photos showed him with various haircuts from shaved to over the ear dark hair to his recent blonde spiked hair. He looked to be a good twenty pounds overweight. Most of his posts were of him on vacation, drinking surrounded by bikini-clad girls, or with his bud-dies drinking at clubs. His Facebook profile didn't mention any ex-wives or children. A google search confirmed that. From Dash's assessment, he had a typical profile of someone with little education or responsibility. He appeared to be well-liked, social, and law-abiding—not the profile of a murderer. The only surprise was several posts of him in a local group dance lesson. He didn't have a dancer's body, but that didn't seem to prevent him from attending. Perhaps, he was smart enough to know that dance groups were a good place to meet women.

Conrad Cook did fit the description, however, of the one that The Hamster gave of the man who dropped off Claudia's unconscious body. He'd witnessed Conrad coldly killing her in a left-handed way with one long fluid knife movement across her throat. Conrad was belligerent towards Dash but was well known to The Wine Sisters. He had accom-panied Claudia's best friend, Taylor Thorngate, to Dash's release party. To Dash, he was now a prime suspect. What would be his motive?

Dash mulled it over while taking his dogs for a walk. Bixby now mended, enjoyed a romp with Barney, who had the heart of a puppy. They walked up the road to take in the expansive views of the hillsides and win-ery estates. Dash was in the heart of the wine country where only the occa-sional pasture broke up the battalions of vineyard rows stretching for miles in every direction. Mono crop agriculture, the planting of a single crop with the elimination of all others, was not what nature intended, but it was a pleasurable sight to behold.

Dash decided to attend one of the dance classes that was offered by the Wine Country Dance Studio. He thought it rather ironic that he'd attend a dance class for an investigation when his former girlfriend could never get him on the dance floor. Dash got to the class five minutes early, paid twenty bucks, and waited as the attendees started to show up.

Dash was surprised at the range of ages, body types, and gender. Surprisingly, there were ten women and nine men in attendance, with the male instructor taking up the slack. The lesson was the East Coast Swing, which was relatively easy for the heavy-footed Dash. He realized it was a beginner class, but many of the attendees were quite accomplished and helpful. Some of the females detected that he was a beginner and led. Others helped him lead. Mona Morgan was not at the class, which gave Dash the opportunity to do some queries after class.

The instructors, one male and one female, would show the group a dance step, then ask the dancers to rotate clockwise, from one partner to the next. Dash got a chance to rotate three times through all the female participants. When the class ended, he was finally getting the hang of East Coast Swing. He liked the movement of the dance steps, the pass-throughs, to the lilt of the music.

"It looked like you were having fun out there. Are you considering continuing the classes?" the female instructor asked.

Dash was coy, "Yes, I'll probably come again." The instructor stood close to him so she could hear him above the loud chatter and music in the background.

The instructor had exotic features complemented by dark hair and eyes. She had a dancer's ageless body—slender and lithe. She danced with expressive arms and hands. Dash found her very alluring. She was reason enough to take more dance lessons.

"I like East Coast Swing. I think I can become proficient," Dash laughed. He changed the topic quickly, catching the instructor off guard.

"Did you know my friend, Claudia? She suggested I come here for months. Then she was gone."

The instructor turned ashen at the mention of Claudia's name. "We were becoming best friends. She loved to dance. She was a natural, quite lovely, as you know. The men loved having her as a partner."

Dash was sensitive to her emotions. "I miss her, too."

The instructor touched Dash's arm, "What a horrible ending. She was a risk-taker. I mean, she befriended everyone, without question. We do get some predators here."

"What do you mean?"

"You know, men looking to hook up with lonely women who may have money."

"She was neither," Dash added, she lived modestly."

"It didn't stop them."

"Anyone in particular?" Dash was unabashed.

"A couple of creeps. I've asked them not to return. A fellow named Conrad. Another fellow named Dylan. Both young guys with beer guts, bad attitudes, lousy dancers, but intent on taking her home."

"Did either succeed?"

"No, they tried. They had that millennial sense of entitlement that turned everybody off, including Claudia. She was the only reason they showed."

Chapter Twenty-Five:

BILL LYONS

It was that manic time between Thanksgiving and New Year's. It's thirty-plus days that are usually lost in the twilight zone. There is little human production other than commerce, retail, and grocery. All other pursuits wane as the energy of the season overtakes the sobriety of the moment. Dash cashed the ten-thousand-dollar check from Bryson Jackson, working diligently during the holiday period, despite the obstacles. It was difficult reaching anyone or anyone getting back to him. They had lives, and Dash was concentrating on those who had their lives taken from them.

Dash was a notorious list maker, so he wrote down on four sheets of paper the various groups: The Wine Sisters: Mona Morgan, Taylor Thorngate, Amanda Jacobs, and the late Claudia Bowers. The Jasper Wine Group: Gregg Perigold, Conrad Cook, Ginger Rute, and the vineyard contractors, Dylan Dotson and Hernando Torres. **Claudia's** supposed lovers: Bill Lyons, Gregg Perigold, and Rex Beckett, all associated with Vino Veritas and, headed by Rex Beckett, aggressively acquiring large vineyard acreage vineyard to procure water rights. It was interesting to Dash how so many names intersected. Or was it more to do with big-monied fish in a very small pond?

There had been no other incursions or interruptions at the ranch. He hadn't heard from any of The Wine Sisters or from Ginger. Dash was invited to soirees and holiday parties, but he went solo. Though Claudia had been dead only four months, her name never came up. The holidays have a way of glossing over the trauma of the year. Dash avoided direct contact with The Wine Sisters, Jasper Winery workers, the Wine Country Dance Studio, and the real estate developers, knowing he may run into them. He did go to a holiday party that the Jacksons had at their private home. He had his first encounter with Claudia's ex-lover, Bill Lyons, owner of Lyons Wine Estates, the biggest wine producers in the region.

Dash had never been to the Jacksons home and was surprised how opulent it was. It was designed to look like an Italian villa. The windows and ironwork were imported from Milan. The tile was from Naples, and the art was inspired by the Florence masters. He suspected the Jacksons were wealthy, but this house was way over the top. He learned that Bryson Jackson not only was a former hedge fund director but had also started a mailbox company that became a national franchise with huge residuals. The party took place in the lower level fronting the back terrace, pools, and gardens. The pergola had large wine cordons around the perimeter for summer shade. There were still grapes hanging from the cordons in December. Everyone congregated at the bar. It was a large room with reclaimed brick walls, rustic timber, and tile floors covered with woven rugs. A door behind the bar led to the wine cave housing hundreds of dusty bottles. The ceiling was arched brick like the Mexican boveda ceilings that Dash had seen in San Miguel de Allende. A large game room was just outside the bar with a pool table, several poker tables, and a lounge with overstuffed leather chairs anchored by a huge screen television that was showing the classic movie *La Dolce Vita* on a black and white video loop for a colorful party. The food was plentiful. There were pates and pickles, cheeses and breads, various olives including Calabrese olives from their own orchard, and small pizzas from their own pizza oven as well as gelatos and Italian pastries.

Vintners brought their own estate wines, winemakers brought their favorite wines, and other guests brought spirits. Despite all the wine industry attendees, it was whiskey, mezcal, vodka, and cognac that was the beverage of choice. The party began with complimentary champagne or Bloody Marys. The men followed with aged whiskeys while the women went to martinis. The men dressed casually, wearing only expensive shoes and watches to belie their class, whereas the women wore shiny blouses, beaded sweaters, and quirky jewelry—their individual statements. Some wore numerous gold and silver loops on the arms, some large turquoise medallions; others wore charm bracelets, all sporting large diamond rings and holiday-inspired earrings. The guests were in their forties and most fifties. Unlike Los Angeles and Orange County, the wives were partners, not trophies. There were a lot of second marriages that had held. It was a conservative crowd politically and culturally. Dash was age-appropriate and dressed appropriately wearing a pullover lavender sweater and grey slacks, conservative in appearance, inferior in wealth to some less in debt than others. Yet, he felt he was the outlier, the revolutionary, the misfit, the stranger, the reprobate. Everyone was polite, kind, generous, civil, and prosperous. It almost made Dash nauseous.

Bill Lyons looked younger than expected, also in his late forties or early fifties. He was over six feet, slender, with black hair that he wore long, tortoise rim glasses that even made him look younger. He wore a navy blazer with gold buttons, khaki slacks, and a pressed white on white shirt that made him look like he'd just come from a polo match. His wife looked a good ten years older than Bill, full-figured, with sweeping blonde hair. She looked like a former debutante who had married well.

Bill Lyons strayed over and casually introduced himself to Dash.

"I'm Bill Lyons. I don't think I've had the pleasure," he said, extending his hand.

Dash shook his hand. "Dash Ramblar. The Jacksons are certainly adept at hosting a holiday party," Dash said awkwardly.

"Can I get you a refill?" Bill asked, "Mine's a bit drawn out." Bill looked at his empty wine glass.

"Only if you're drinking some of your own estate cabernet." Dash handed him his wine glass.

Bill was pleased with his answer. He quickly retrieved two glass of red wine and handed Dash a glass. "It's my personal favorite. We call it a Claret—a blend, all estate-grown fruit."

Dash tasted the wine and smiled. "Claret, eh, a tip to your British forebears, or just trying to fool the experts?"

Bill Lyons was enjoying the banter, "Neither. My parents took me to Europe when I was a teenager—a Claret was the first wine I tried—I loved it. It's a tribute to that style. "

Dash held the wine up to the light. "Aren't Clarets a lighter wine? This has cherry and plum notes."

"Quite right, Mr. Ramblar. All the reds from this region have dark fruit. This is a blend of Cabernet Sauvignon, Merlot, Petit Verdot, and Cabernet Franc. I believe 60/30/10/10 by percentage."

"Marvelous body and subtle complexity." Dash swirled the wine, getting the wine fingers to crawl down the glass. He was anxious to change the subject. "I've met Rex Beckett. He says that you belong to a vineyard acquisition group together."

"We're trying. The price of real estate, especially farmland, is escalating so fast. The Harvard University fund is a big player along with the usual suspects: The Gallo Family, Constellation Wine Group, and now Silicon Valley types. They're flooding the market with all-cash deals. Did Rex discuss being an investor, or are you a seller?"

"Neither, I just find it curious. There's a glut of wine grapes, especially Cabernet, coupled with a severe water shortage, all counter-intuitive to the land rush, driving up the price," Dash said with his best poker face.

Bill Lyons was not going to divulge anything to a stranger, "Our group has a different business model. We're looking at the bigger development picture, just not wine grapes. We're convinced the land values in this area will continue to rise, so we just want to be well-positioned."

Dash thought he was listening to the reading of a prospectus. "Don't be coy, Bill. We all know it's about water rights and credits."

Bill smiled, "That's one scenario." Bill was getting restless. Dash thought he'd better be direct.

"Bryson Jackson has told me that you were friends with Claudia Bowers."

Bill Lyon's face reddened, "Why, yes. Why did her name come up?"

Dash was direct, "I'm investigating Claudia's murder? Your name has been suggested by several people as a former paramour."

Bill resumed his composure and was civil. "That was a private matter between us. Can I ask—who hired you?"

"That's confidential. Do you have any notion of who would have wanted her dead?" Dash pressed.

Bill looked around at the holiday party with music, food, drink, and conviviality, and smirked, "A rather bizarre question, given that we are both guests at a party. I think I will take my leave. I can't say it's been a pleasure. In answer to your question—Claudia was loved, not hated. Merry Christmas."

Bill Lyons moved defensively back to his wife, who was conversing with another couple. Dash had gotten nowhere with Bill Lyons. He didn't deny that he was her lover, nor did he threaten him. Dash felt that Bill Lyons had to be on the suspect list, but near the bottom.

Dash looked around at the party-goers hoping to recognize a friendly face. He saw Mona and her husband conversing outside on the patio. Dash joined them. Mona was very pleased to see Dash.

Mona smiled in the bright December sun, "I can never get enough sun; it must be my East Indian complexion. So nice to see you Dash, I hope you're wrapping up your investigation."

Dash smiled and shook hands with her husband, "No, quite the opposite. It's taken on a life of its own. I'm just here for the gossip and free booze."

Mona touched his arm. "You're so coy. You just like hanging out with crazy rich white people. I was invited to add a wee bit of color to the festivities." Her Caucasian husband didn't find her humorous.

Dash nodded, "You're here because you can make or break a winery with one Wine Spectator mention. I suspect your glass in never empty."

Mona looked down at her glass, "I'm drinking Bryson's wine tonight—it's politically correct. Everyone wants me to try the wine they brought, but I'm here to enjoy, not work."

Mona's husband wandered off to the buffet that covered the long kitchen island. Dash stood closer to her. "I had some of Bill's Claret. It was very drinkable," Dash said, smiling.

"Who said large wineries can't make a great wine?" Mona's dark oval eyes beamed on Dash. "Did you ask him about Claudia?"

"Yes, probably a mistake. It was a real conversation ender. He is still obviously hurting. How long have they been broken up?"

Mona laughed, "You're pathetic. It's been at least two years. He's already moved on to new ground."

Dash took the tease. "Let me guess, a Wine Sister?"

"Right you are, Taylor Thorngate. She doesn't let any moss grow," Mona laughed at her slightly naughty suggestion.

"Isn't that dangerous?" Dash asked.

Mona whispered in his ear, "Only if she gets caught."

Chapter Twenty-Six:

HOLIDAY GIFTS

The holidays came and went. The winter rains came in torrents soaking the parched ground and filling reservoirs. Dash didn't have much of a Christmas gift list, so he went down to the homeless encampments on the Salinas River plain and handed out bottles of whiskey. They were very appreciative. They said they were tired of church groups giving them blankets, old jackets, and hand me downs. They said the two things that made them happiest were new socks and whiskey. The ground was soaked, the river was flowing, the birds were nesting, and the first buds were showing on the scrubby trees.

Dash got a chance to talk to some old—timers in one homeless encampment under the bridge abutments. It was not far from where Claudia's body was found.

"Any of you fellas know The Hamster?" Dash asked.

They all laughed and smiled. "Hell yes," one grizzled and grey man said. "He loved french fries and Coca Cola—not much of a drinker."

"Was he a loner?" Dash asked.

"He had a Mexican friend, Pedro, but mostly kept to himself. Somebody said he was homeless by choice, that he had rentals in Orange County and money in the bank," the grizzled man laughed, "You gonna' hand out his inheritance checks to us now?"

Dash showed his empty hands, "Never heard he had money. He was always hitting me up."

Everyone laughed in agreement, "The only thing that made us wonder about him… he'd disappear for the wet months and head south to Mexico with Pedro. Somebody said they rented a beach house with servant girls to make their beds and do their laundry."

This was all new information to Dash. He wanted to believe that The Hamster was more than a hapless homeless guy who died broke and alone.

Dash had to ask, "This is near where the girl's body was dumped — any of you see anything?"

The tone changed, "Thanks again for the whiskey, mister, but we got nothing to add. The police have been down here a hundred times, tromping the ground and asking us the same questions over and over again."

"Have you seen anyone peculiar or odd other than the police?" Dash queried a restless group.

"We get tourists who pay us to show 'em where her body was found. Sometimes it's a regular circus around here. It ain't private property here—people just show up—ask questions. The other day some fat guys showed up and rifled through our things."

Dash was curious, "Did they say what they were looking for?"

The old grizzled guy who'd been talking gave Dash a peculiar look, "Damned if we know—these guys were looking for something—didn't tell us what. They said, 'Keep your mouths shut.' That's all they had to say. "

"Did they take anything?" Dash asked.

"Only our rope."

Dash pulled out a twenty-dollar bill and gave it to the geezer. "What rope?"

"We use rope to tie up our bedrolls. They just took it all."

Dash asked, "The girl's body was tied up—could it have been the same rope?"

The geezer looked at Dash like he was crazy, "How would we know? We just pick up whatever rope is lying around. We don't steal it—rope comes in handy in the campground."

"Could you describe the fat guys?" Dash asked, pulling out another twenty-dollar bill.

"One guy was average height, with a big beer gut, the other guy was a little taller and in a little better shape. They were young—maybe forty or younger. They had work clothes on, work boots, and heavy farm jackets— like they just come from work. They just took the rope. They had baseball caps on, so I couldn't tell you if they had hair or not."

"Do you see what they were driving?" Dash asked.

"No, but they musta' come in a big diesel truck. I heard them leave. It was loud."

Dash left the encampment when it started to rain. The campers pulled out a big plastic tarp hanging it over their bedding and clothes. They were already drinking the whiskey and laughing. They had a little battery-operated heater, company, hooch, and a makeshift roof over their head. It could be worse.

Dash was restless. He liked thinking that The Hamster took a vacation to Mexico every year and that he had money in the bank. Dash left the river and headed home. He found a text message from Ginger on his cell phone. "Meet me a Sadie's at seven."

Wedged between a beauty salon and quick mart store that sold beer, lottery tickets, and cigarettes, Sadie's was a local dive bar for alcoholics. It was pitch-black outside, and a big winter storm front was blowing through.

Dash got to Sadie's early and talked to the bartender. The place had been around for twenty years and was in its third owner. The bartender said drinkers couldn't afford all the fancy bars downtown with twelve-dollar mixed drinks. Ginger arrived in a rain parka, stretch pants, and a bulky sweater underneath her parka. Her hazel eyes were shining, and she had a toothy smile.

She ordered a Maker's up (Maker's Mark bourbon) and let Dash pay for it.

Dash had three layers on but didn't take any of them off in the bar. "What brings you out on this miserable night, besides my charming company?" Dash asked.

Ginger took off her parka and slung it over the back of her barstool. "We've got a problem, Mr. Ramblar. It seems you were asking Bill Lyons some dumb questions. Word is out that you're barking up the wrong tree, peeing on the city hydrants, when you should be hunkering down in your kennel."

Dash always marveled at what a small town he lived in, "So, I don't think Bill Lyons told you. Perhaps it was Taylor, or somebody else?"

Ginger looked around at the empty bar directing her voice away from the bartender, "It doesn't matter, except I'm perceived as your friend, which puts me in an uncomfortable position. I'd like to get to know you, but under the circumstances, it's a non-starter. That's not why I wanted to meet. I was given a message to relay to you. She pulled out a blank envelope with writing on it. It said, 'Ginger, tell your friend to butt out, or you'll end up in the river, upside down."

"Where did you get this?" Dash asked.

"At work, somebody stuffed it through the door crack in my employee locker."

Ginger had ordered another drink before Dash had even touched his. She was facing her anxiety with an old remedy. Dash listened to her go on about work and pressures. He had heard enough.

"I have a three-bedroom house. You're welcome to take a bedroom tonight. I don't think it's safe for you to go home," Dash said.

Ginger didn't hesitate, "Okay, I keep an overnight bag in my car."

The gravel road to the ranch house was bumpy after days of rain. Dash got a roaring fire going in the fireplace, put on some music, and brought out some good sipping rum. Ginger took off her bulky sweater. She had a Patagonia synthetic ski top on that didn't disguise her contour. She let her auburn hair down, laid back in the overstuffed loveseat, and patted the cushion. Dash joined her on the loveseat.

His heart was racing. Ginger was one of a kind. The notion she carried an overnight bag with her and that she probably had a bedroll in her truck was impressive. Dash had to check himself.

Dash thought that when love comes around, he's never been ready. It happens so fast and without warning. He was not anxious to go down that rabbit hole again. His last relationship was a real roller coaster ride, and when it collapsed, it was heartbreaking.

His daughter, Amber, was grown. She lived in Los Angeles, worked as an RN, and only contacted Dash when she wanted him to do a background check on a boyfriend. It usually meant she was looking for an exit tragedy. She would never do a background check on a new beau—it would poison the relationship. Dash called Amber weekly on Sunday nights. He wanted to hear her voice to know that she was okay. His empire, small as it is, would all be hers one day.

Dash had no desire for marriage, as independence trumped commitment. Dash rarely traveled abroad, never went on a cruise ship, nor on any trip that came with an itinerary. He liked the option that he could decide on a Sunday to fly to Puerta Vallarta on Thursday without consulting anyone, except the dog sitter. The snow conditions looked good for Lake Tahoe—he might head up to North Star or Heavenly for the weekend.

All these thoughts went out the window sitting next to the toothsome Ginger. She was smart, beautiful, alluring, and grounded. They discussed relationships. She spoke in generalities, not dissing any former lovers. She said, "I like to have fun. I like company; I like adventure. I like men who don't need me. I like my independence; I'm not starting a new family."

Dash was thinking to himself that she was the perfect match. He followed, "You're preaching to the choir. I have to be honest. I think you could become habit-forming. What if a man becomes addicted to you, falls in love, needs you?"

"That would be his problem," Ginger laughed, kissing him lightly on the lips, lingering, then dragging her lips across his face.

Dash was taken aback. He responded with another kiss, putting his arms around her, then touching her face when he stopped kissing her. She relaxed, letting him touch her. He touched her lithe legs, moving his hands to her hips, brushing his arms against her breasts. She responded by kissing him, more wet, more tongue. Their breathing became noticeable, their kissing continued, until she rested her hand on his lap. She touched him through his pants. He pulled away from her, stretching his arms along the top of the loveseat. He opened the two top buttons of his shirt. Ginger unbuttoned the other five buttons on his shirt. She played with his chest as he played with her hair.

In an earlier time, they would have consummated the relationship within minutes, but now older, they relished the moment. Slowly, they undressed one another, kissing between each movement, then when they were down to their essentials, got up off the couch, and walked into the bedroom, hand in hand.

Ginger disappeared into the bathroom as Dash patiently waited. She appeared in the doorway in a chemise. Where she got it, he had no idea. The light through the chemise presented a stunning silhouette. She came to bed. They continued at their slow pace, exploring each other's bodies. Dash lingered at a shoulder bone, a space in her neck, her belly button—applying coconut oil to her back—massaging her slowly. Their breath picked up again. They both loved the intimacy which they admitted they missed. Ginger fell asleep in his arms. She had been overtired, anxious. Now she was satiated.

The next morning, Dash brought coffee to her from his French press, along with buttered cinnamon toast, a quarter of tangerine, and a creamer. She passed the eye test. She looked marvelous in the morning, without makeup, sitting up on the pillows with the chemise back on.

"What do you have to say for yourself, Mr. Ramblar?" Ginger asked from the bed.

"I'd have to say that I'm one lucky cowpuncher. When I offered my house, I never in my wildest dreams...."

"Don't go there, Dash. You knew full well what your mission was—seduce a femme fatale and then play dumb in the morning," Ginger said.

Dash laughed, "You're no femme fatale, and I'm no Don Juan. I realized that this moment might never come again, so I savored it."

"You're right about one thing. This moment may never come again," Ginger teased.

After she got up and dressed, Dash drove her back to her car parked near Sadie's Bar. It was not a pretty sight. Someone had slashed her tires and broken her side mirrors. Ginger cried and shook in Dash's arms. She didn't lose her grit.

"Somebody's 'gonna' pay for this," Ginger wiped away her tears. "I won't back down. Maybe I'll go public with you, Dash. Fuck 'em."

Dash had her car towed and drove her home. She still had her old Japanese pick-up truck. Her shift at the winery didn't start until noon, so she had time to get ready for work. She kissed Dash goodbye. Dash knew what they had was more than coincidence and circumstance. It was a real connection. He could tell from the gleam in her eyes that she felt the same way. Only time would tell.

Feeling uneasy, Dash called Detective Evans at the police department and told him about the threat Ginger received and her car damage. Detective Evans was not impressed.

"You're bad news, Dash. Everywhere you go, trouble follows you. Now, you've got this poor woman mixed up with you. What's her name?"

"Ginger Rute."

"Sounds like a stripper's name. Does she need a restraining order? Does she even know who's stalking her?"

"She doesn't know. We assume it's somebody at Jasper Winery where she works. It could be one of their contract workers. I'm only mentioning this to give you a head's up, in case something occurs."

Detective Evans tried to end the call, "Okay, I got it. Now, just stay at home on your computer. Avoid people, places, and public gatherings. You're toxic."

"Okay. It's been almost five months. Any updates on Claudia's murder?" Dash asked.

Detective Evans replied, "Maybe. Maybe not. It's none of your business. If I find out anything of merit, I'll pass it along. Otherwise, Happy Lunar New Year."

Dash answered, "Whatever, Happy New Year to you, Floyd—I mean FJ," Dash said sarcastically.

Dash called Ginger to see if she was doing okay and back to work. She said nothing out of the ordinary had occurred. It was the slow season in the winery business: cold, wet, and overcast most days. The short Mediterranean winter seemed to linger with February being wetter than normal. Everyone was looking forward to an early spring. Dash had Ginger on his mind.

It was quiet. Dash felt it was the calm before the storm. He was prescient, not psychic, and knew that Claudia's murder case was about to be back on the front page.

Chapter Twenty-Seven:

CITY COUNCIL

The Great Oaks city chambers were always full for the Tuesday night City Council meetings. They were held in the large auditorium in the new library building. There were a dozen items on the agenda, along with an open forum, public feedback, and reports from the planning department, the police department, the city works department, and a report from the mayor, Pete Ligotti. The meetings were broadcast on local radio, and print beat reporters had to cover it. The weekly meetings were a snooze-fest, a sure cure for insomnia.

The one item that stood out was a pre-approval for a six-hundred-unit housing project east of town, on the large five hundred-acre Santa Rosa Ranch. Rexford Beckett, the spokesperson for the developers, Vino Veritas, was listed as a presenter.

It was apparent to all in attendance that the fix was in. The development would add to the city's tax revenue base, spur more business growth, and ensure that the city was on an upward growth projectile. The planning department spokesperson gave a lengthy defense of the project, citing its environmental impact and traffic impact reports. The development included expansion of the main arterial road that passed by the development, along with a new road to the development. There were smiles everywhere; Rex Beckett was treated like a favorite son.

One measure not on the docket; the Estrella Water District formation. Following the presentation of Vino Veritas housing development, which met with unanimous resolution and the city's blessing, Rex Beckett brought up the formation of a new water district.

Ostensibly, the new water district was conceived to provide adequate water for the needs of some new fifteen hundred residents of the development. This was a ruse, as the district would have dominion over some forty square miles, enveloping the entire east side of Great Oaks, plus a major portion of the unincorporated land east of the city limits.

Rex Beckett said to the city council, "This water district would not only ensure deliverable water to this development, paving the way for future developments, within the city limits and beyond. It would hamper any attempts by outside groups, including the State of California, to interfere, levy taxes, or divert our waters away from the new district. This water district would protect, secure, and conserve our water for generations."

The speech was met with applause from the audience. It was strategic that Dash Ramblar was there. He watched the proceedings and was struck how well the developer from Orange County was received. It didn't take long for Dash to see the connection. Bill Lyons and Gregg Perigold, both winery luminaries in the region, spoke on behalf of the new water district. This was a power play in its most blatant display. The city councilmen supported the concept of the new water district and drafted an endorsement on the spot. It would have to go to a vote, but with big money behind it and endorsements from the politicos, it could be automatic. Dash tried to assimilate what he witnessed.

Did this correlate with Claudia's murder? Or was it a coincidence that within six months of her murder, a water district proposal was before the city council? She knew all the players, having been intimate with two of them. She knew their machinations and opposed them. She was just a barrel salesperson, knowing their plans could destroy the many small family wineries and artisanal winemakers, who could not afford a steep rise in the cost of water. The water district would secure the rights to the water then resell the water to the users at a premium. The land grab would continue, and the big operations would expand by buying up the smaller players who were teetering on bankruptcy.

Vino Veritas could buy up land for pennies on the dollar, secure more water credits, and monopolize the region by building more developments and making their principals rich beyond their dreams. Dash sat dumbfounded how simple a plan it was, and how easy it would be to implement.

As the meeting ended, Bill Lyons and Rex Beckett recognized Dash. They ignored him, continuing to self-congratulate one another and converse. Dash approached them.

"Hello, gentlemen. I was curious how you slipped in the Estrella Water District before the city council. It wasn't even on the agenda," Dash said.

"I don't know what your problem is, Mr. Ramblar, but suffice to say, you have a unique talent in making any encounter awkward," Rex Beckett said.

"That was my intent." Dash grinned.

"Go back to your hovel and pretend that you aren't a damn fool," Rex Beckett sneered.

Dash stood tall, "Yes, I'm foolish enough to give a damn. You've finally met your match."

Rex Beckett had heard enough, "If you're so smart, Mr. Ramblar, how come you're not rich."

Dash grinned, "This is rich. You think that the good folks in Great Oaks are too asleep to know precisely what you're up to. Water has always been" front of mind "on the Central Coast. They will drag themselves away watching motorsports and pro wrestling in their Barcaloungers, to squash your agenda."

Beckett was not impressed. "Are you done?" He and Bill Lyons promptly walked away.

Dash turned and headed out of the meeting. He walked to his car, which was parked a couple of blocks away. He let the moist air wash his face and fill his lungs. He knew that behind all the bravado, there was a conspiracy. A conspiracy that he would upend.

He believed that the residents of Great Oaks would never approve of a water district plan that gives power to the few. They would have to silence more than just Claudia Bowers. They'd have to silence an army of nay-sayers.

Dash was not an activist or politically minded. He believed in the code of honor, be it the Cowboy Code, Chivalric Knights Code, or the Seamen's Code. He felt it was his duty to right wrongs and to bring daylight on the wrongdoers. If he made a few bucks along the way, met a willing partner, had a sumptuous meal, a good glass of claret, and slept well at night, what more reward was needed?

He drove home from the meeting, fully intending to expose Vino Veritas and its investors. By the time he arrived home, his aspirations had expired, and all he wanted was a good night's sleep. Tomorrow, he'd just settle for making someone uncomfortable. Those plans would also expire.

Chapter Twenty-Eight:

MONA MORGAN

Dash's mid-winter sleep was interrupted at eight by a call. It was Mona Morgan, the Gazette wine writer and Wine Sister, on the phone. Before Dash could get his eyes open, Mona was going off about the City Council meeting. She couldn't believe the gall of Vino Veritas, "They're going to shove their water district down our throats." Mona kept talking over Dash, who was trying desperately to get his coffee maker revved up. He fumbled with the buttons on the coffee maker consul. When he heard that sweet sound of coffee brewing, he started tuning into Mona.

"Would you like to meet?" Dash asked.

Mona was still talking about the damn Orange County developers when she finally came around to Dash's question. "Sure, how about coffee in an hour, at Dog Brew."

Dash said yes and got himself ready. He drank two cups of coffee in five minutes and put Barney on a leash. He knew they were dog friendly, and Barney needed a break from nursing Bixby back to health. Barney jumped in the back of the old Range Rover, and they headed for town.

Dash arrived to see Mona already sitting at a table, talking on her cell phone, drinking coffee, and taking notes. Dash could never multi-task like women. She waved him over, and he gathered Barney. Barney had been to Dog Brew before, and it was his favorite haunt. Barney liked the smell of coffee, pastries, humans, and other dogs.

When Barney tried to greet Mona, she ignored him. She wasn't a dog person. Dash got up and ordered a cappuccino and avocado toast. Mona got off her phone, and Dash returned to the table where Barney was enjoying his view.

"I see you brought your dog," Mona said with a slight sneer.

"Yeah, I've been an absentee pet owner of late," Dash looked to see if anyone was eavesdropping on their conversation. "I was at the meeting last night. It was alarming."

"Alarming? It was a shit show," Mona said, "I'm writing an article today lambasting the project and the water district. The new district will kill off the last small wineries which are hanging on by a thread anyway."

"Claudia predicted it," Mona continued, "She knew this fellow, Rex Bennett, and of course she knew Bill Lyons and the Perigolds. She told me to keep my ear to the ground. Claudia said that it was the beginning of the takeover."

"The takeover?" Dash asked.

"What we discussed, the aquifer. Claudia was my best source. She knew everything about the wine industry, not just here, but Napa/Sonoma, everywhere in California and in Europe. She was a great resource. She had her nose to the grindstone and her ears to the ground," Mona replied.

Dash didn't need his cappuccino to be energized, "Okay, I understand. What did she know that could be damaging to the developers and ultimately to herself?"

Mona slowed down, "She had a short fling with Rex Bennett, the CEO of Vino Veritas, and he laid out their plans for Great Oaks in detail to Claudia. She broke it off and became more active in the Save the Oaks campaign. Rex reluctantly went back to his old girlfriend, Amanda, a new Wine Sister."

"Was Claudia your only source?" Dash asked.

"Funny you should ask. I just heard from Taylor Thorngate, another Wine Sister, who's taken up with another Claudia reject, Bill Lyons, and she confirms what Claudia conjectured."

Dash moved in closer to Mona, "Which was what?"

"Aren't you listening? The seizure and utilization of the aquifer. It's a simple plan. You buy up all the ranches and vineyards where their wells have gone dry at bargain-basement prices, then access a new unlimited water supply, and bam, the property values go through the roof. "

Dash laughed, "I know you grew up in India, educated in England, but did ever hear the expression 'bam'?"

"I read everything I could get my hands growing up on in Mumbai, including comic books, where I learned to use onomatopoeias."

"You're quite amusing," Dashy smiled, "The aquifer is now illegal to tap—hell its down ten thousand feet below the Salinas River bed. It would take a lot of capital to access it. Brad has targeted the big money players in Great Oaks. I don't see it stopping, even if Claudia was still alive."

"You're partially right. The machinations of the billionaire class can't be stopped by activists or civic-minded do-gooders. Claudia was eliciting the aid of other billionaires who were environmentally conscious."

"Sounds like an oxymoron, environmentally conscious billionaires. I know there are few, but here in Great Oaks?" Dash asked.

"Damn right. One Swiss billionaire who has a winery here enjoined other big landowners to get on board, opposing the new water district," Mona was animated.

"Killing Claudia wouldn't have made a difference. If that was the case, Taylor Thorngate would also be in danger."

Mona's face turned ashen, "She's in real danger. I spoke with her last night. She has been threatened to keep her mouth shut, and not to talk to me or you. That's why I called you. Both our names were brought up by..."

Dash broke in, "By whom?"

"She wouldn't say. Taylor had a bad break-up with Bill Lyons and went to Conrad Cook on the rebound. She's in deep," Mona said. She excused herself and went to the restroom.

Dash surmised all this before, but he was still reluctant to harbor a notion of motive. The big money playboys don't murder their lovers because they talk. They have them murdered if they betray them to their enemies. Bam.

Chapter Twenty-Nine:

DOG PARK

The rain had been unrelenting. Storm fronts were backed up into the Pacific awaiting to come ashore like container ships queued up at anchor, awaiting a berth. The rain would come down in sheets, then drizzle; then there'd be a short respite before the next wave. One day out of seven, the sun would shine. They had planned the abduction on a clear day, according to the weather app, on their smartphones.

She had been clubbed with a weighted and padded short metal shaft, a makeshift Billy club. They must have known her schedule. She had gone to the dog park on Vineyard Drive at five in the evening just before dusk, on the only sunny day of the week. Her dog, Chloe, was a small dachshund who loved her daily visit to the dog park, which had been recently interrupted by the rain. Chloe was getting up in the years, but she still managed a spurt of energy for their visit to the park. Chloe had her group of familiar canine friends who'd sniff, wrestle, and drink from a common water bowl. Chloe chose other senior dogs to play with, letting the younger dogs romp amongst themselves. Today, there was only one other dog, Chester, an aging Spaniel.

When the play period ended, Taylor put a little leash on Chloe, walked with her to the car, and lifted her into her car bed. As the sky darkened and raindrops commenced. She said goodbye to Chester's mom, an elderly woman, also a regular.

There was a large four-by-four truck next to her car, with a lifted chassis. These vehicles were common on ranches and favored by faux cowboys and rednecks.

Taylor had the passenger door open, which faced the truck, and was wiping off Chloe with a towel when she received the blow to the back of her head. She slumped down. Chloe was confused by the weight of her owner. The two men hastily put her limp body in the back seat of the truck. One man got into her Nissan Sentra, using Taylor's keys, still in her hands, and drove away. The other man got in his truck, and started up the big Diesel engine, and pulled slowly out of the parking lot, which had only one other car.

The elderly woman, sitting alone in the dog park, with her dog Chester had no idea that anything peculiar occurred in the parking lot, which was obscured by a high fence line, hedges, and trees. The only thing that she noted was that Chloe's owner didn't honk when she left the parking lot as she normally did. The elderly woman raised her head and saw Chloe's Nissan Sentra and a big truck leave together.

The driver drove the Nissan Sentra to the apartment complex where Taylor lived, parked the car, let Chloe out. Chloe walked down the path to the apartment and waited patiently to be let in. The house key was on her vehicle key chain. He let Chloe into the house. He returned to the parked Nissan Sentra, leaving the keys in the front seat. He walked to his truck, which was parked on the street a hundred and fifty yards from the apartment complex. He saw no one as he walked, as most people were already in for the evening. In the distance, he could hear a dog barking.

The man who drove the truck parked on River Road, adjacent to the mile-wide Salinas River bed. The Salinas River is an ancient waterway that empties into the Pacific over one hundred miles north of Great Oaks. Sections of the river are dotted with oil rigs pumping around the clock. The Salinas River bed is miles of tangled underbrush, sycamore, scrub oaks, and elderberry.

As he had done with Claudia, he carried Taylor along a dark path to a pre-determined spot and put her body on the ground. She was barely conscious. He tied her ankles with a rope than hoisted her body over a tree limb doubled up with her head facing down. He surveyed the area. No movement, no sound, nothing. He took a long breath. He was winded, sweating, and he wiped his brow with a teal-colored bandana. Adrenalin was pumping through his veins, and he finished the job. He took out a long slender knife from his jacket and ran it along her throat. At first, a thin red line appeared, then torrents of blood rushed down her face, into her hair, and into the ground. The ground was wet and muddy—the rain had subsided and was now just a cooling mist, refreshing the killer's brow.

The rain had cleared, and the stars shone in the dark. There was no moon visible. The killer fumbled with a flashlight as he left the scene, making certain to leave no debris and tracks. His boots were wrapped in plastic and tied at the ankles. He walked back to the truck in silence, paused to make certain that the silent night was just that. On the path near the road, his teal bandana fell out of his coat pocket on to the ground. There was not even a rustle in the trees nor an animal scurrying in the bush. The air smelled of wetness and decay. He turned off his flashlight, jumped into his truck, and headed home.

A sparkling day greeted Dash, and he was invigorated. The sun was unabashed, the hills were a psychedelic green, and the birds were on the wing. The Central Coast is particularly resplendent after a winter storm front moves through the area. Dash looked again at his list of suspects, motives, and the groupings that intersected. It was old school. It didn't account for a one-off or spurned lover. Dash could not let go of the fact that Claudia's life and death were conspiratorial. Her murder was planned, carried out, and the tracks were being covered.

Dash had little time to ponder his notes before he got a Monday morning call from Detective Evans.

"Dash, I thought I'd give you a heads up. This morning a body was discovered in the river bed in the same manner as Claudia's. Fortunately, the body had not been savaged by coyotes. The corpse was recognizable, and we were able to make a positive identification. We have not notified next of kin, so I can't give you her name.

Dash was alarmed, "If it was a she, then I know who it was."

"I'm not going to play a guessing game with you, Dash. Leave it alone," Detective Evans continued. "I'll call you when I can give you more details."

Dash interrupted Detective Evans's salutation, "It was Taylor Thorngate."

Detective Evans was taken aback, "Keep it to yourself." He then abruptly hung up.

Chapter Thirty:

PRESIDENT'S DAY

Dash felt like he had failed Taylor. All the time he had feared for Ginger's safety, he harbored a nagging suspicion that Taylor was in the crosshairs. She was Claudia's closest friend. She had done work for Jasper Winery, she had dated Conrad, and was involved with Bill Lyons. Taylor's scenario and murder mirrored Claudia's, with the same vile result.

Dash was dismayed by his gut reaction. He mourned her loss, contemplating her final hours, reflecting on how she met her end. He was upset, angry, but mostly energized. Unlike the murder of Claudia Bowers, where he was brought into the investigation late in the game, having to piece together the events with a paucity of evidence, Taylor's murder was fresh. Not even twenty-four hours old. Dash knew the players, the suspects, the victims, and was familiar with the murder site. He was confident that the proximity, the close time frame, would allow him to get within striking distance of the truth.

Dash ran through his mind all the interactions, conversations, and observations he could muster regarding Taylor Thorngate.

She was a close friend of Claudia's, the youngest members of The Wine Sisters. Dash had last seen Taylor with Conrad Cook at the wine release party. Taylor had planned to go to Cancun with Amanda. In his meeting with Taylor at the coffeehouse, Taylor had said that Claudia was sleeping with the enemy. Taylor didn't believe that Claudia's murder was a coincidence. Unfortunately, Dash never had the opportunity to ask Taylor who the enemy was?

Dash called Amanda, who had recently befriended Taylor.

"Hello, this Dash Ramblar."

Amanda sounded a little groggy, "What's this about? You know I'm seeing someone, so that eliminates that option," Amanda asserted.

"It's about Taylor Thorngate," Dash said flatly.

"What about her? I assume you could call her directly. Weren't you a client of hers?" Amanda asked.

"She's gone missing. I thought you might know something," Dash remained coy.

"That girl, she's a free spirit. The only thing she ever cared about was her dog, Chloe. She's probably at the dog park. She goes at five usually, but sometimes earlier," Amanda said.

"When was the last time you saw her?" Dash asked.

"Yesterday, for lunch. She was telling me about her new boyfriend."

"Conrad?" Dash asked, "They were together at my wine release party?"

"No, he was just a fling. She found Mr. Right," Amanda said in a sing—song voice.

"Mr. Right. She had high standards—who could measure up?" Dash asked.

"Let her tell you his name. It's not good karma to spill the beans—I don't want to jinx the romance," Amanda said.

"I think I know. Bill Lyons." Dash took a wild stab.

Amanda hung up before he got an affirmation.

Dash suspected that Taylor Thorngate had been seeing Bill Lyons, who was youthful, rich, handsome, and whose wife lived two hundred miles away. Bill's influence and contacts in the wine industry were unparalleled. Claudia and Taylor were both vendors to the wine industry: Claudia sold barrels, corks, and labels, whereas Taylor sold graphic design and social media expertise. Bill Lyons could easily boost their recognition and business. Lyons Wine Estates alone could feather the nest of both victims.

Dash had known Claudia better than he knew Taylor. He was confident that Claudia was motivated by emotion, not avarice. The two main suspects in Claudia's and Taylor's murders were the same. In detective 101 class, the primary suspects are the lovers, boyfriends, and exes, or current husbands. There was the erstwhile boyfriend, Conrad, and the major love interest, Bill Lyons. Dash decided to drive out to the Lyons Wine Estates executive offices. It was a Monday, Presidents Day. He took a chance that the corporate offices were open on the bank holiday. He also took a wild guess that Bill Lyons would be in town for the long weekend. He was right.

The executive offices were down a paved road surrounded by vineyards. The crushing pad, the barrel warehouses, the tasting room were all close to the main highway. On the paved road, you passed by the hospitality center and the production facilities to get to the executive offices. The offices were built to look like a large ranch house with a sloping roof and a small tower cupola at the apex of the roof lines. The front porch and deck extended the entire frontage of the building, which was deceptively large with a grand reception area, a staircase to the second floor, elevators, and a buzz of activity expected of a million case plus wine operation. Several salespeople waited in the reception area. Dash expressed his interest in seeing Bill Lyons, telling the receptionist that he was the new barrel salesperson for Quercus Robur, the Spanish barrel makers, Claudia's former company. Bill Lyons agreed to meet with him.

Bill Lyons was dressed like a CEO. He had a pressed button-down blue shirt, no tie, dark blue slacks, loafers, and was wearing an Apple watch. His black hair was combed back, he was clean-shaven, and he had carried an air of smug prosperity seen in the confines of a country club.

Bill recognized Dash right away, but couldn't place him, and went to a file regarding the French oak barrel order for the upcoming year. "We have ordered two hundred and fifty new French oak barrels to be delivered before harvest. Are there any issues with the order?"

Dash disguised his real purpose for the meeting. "None whatsoever, I just wanted the opportunity to meet with you. As you know, I've replaced Claudia Bowers at Quercus Robur. She was much admired in the industry. I've read her notes, your client history, and I'm current on your recent activity."

Bill Lyons displayed no emotion, "She was a good salesperson. I liked her."

Dash was sitting across from Bill Lyons. There was a large window that overlooked acres of dormant vines soon to be pruned back, and oak tree-dotted hillsides in the distance. The office was spartan and reflected an agricultural endeavor. There was a large trophy case that had awards from different wine competitions, a signed letter from President George W. Bush regarding Lyons wines served at a state dinner, and an oil painting that depicted field workers, harvesting wine grapes. The only exceptions were an expensive-looking rug on the hardwood floors and a large wine rack within a temperature-controlled windowed cooler. The wines were all estate-bottled wines. An overhead fan moved slowly. The office had the smell of prosperity—clean with vanilla and mahogany notes.

Dash moved uncomfortably in his chair. "I may have some unwelcome news for you, unfortunately."

Bill Lyons looked at Dash with alarm. "Regarding wine barrels?"

"No, regarding Taylor Thorngate. Detective FJ Evans of the Great Oaks police department said that they have positively identified her as the female victim found in the Salinas River Bed this morning.

Bill's face turned ashen. "What! How would you have this information? Just who are you again?"

"We've met before at a party. I'm Dash Ramblar, private investigator. I'm aware of your past relationship with Claudia Bowers and your current relationship with the deceased, Taylor Thorngate."

Bill Lyons had the look of a man who had lost a big sale rather than a friend. He looked perplexed and confused. "We were just friends. She was working on our social media."

"Were you just friends with Claudia?" Dash asked.

'You're here under false pretenses making wild accusations. You're very foolhardy, Mr. Ramblar." He clicked on his intercom. "Send security up, now."

"Not necessary," Dash said as he lifted himself out of the leather chair.

Bill Lyons pushed his hands against his desk and rose up out of his chair. He walked to the door and opened it. "It's time you left."

"I can't leave until you answer this question. Do you have any idea why these women were murdered? Your association with them could be the reason—not mere coincidence."

"That is a private matter. I can't think of any reason that they were murdered. You knew them both. Perhaps, you're the link." Bill Lyons laughed at his own feeble attempt at cleverness.

Dash exited the door. "I will relay the conversation I had with you to Detective Evans."

Bill Lyons chuckled out loud, "Go ahead—I have my people downtown."

Security guards arrived as Dash was exiting. They escorted him to his car without uttering a word.

Dash left with a recurring empty sensation. He was met with road-blocks everywhere by the same powerful people. It took ten minutes to depart the hundreds of acres of Lyons vineyards and facilities on the east side, heading back to Great Oaks. Dash continued on the east side of the Salinas River dry riverbed along River Road and the scene of Taylor's murder.

He found the exact location of her murder by the number of squad cars parked in one vicinity. The body had been dumped at the northern end of Great Oaks, two miles north of where Claudia's body was found, in the discordant undergrowth of the Salinas River Bed, and five miles from downtown. The foul wild smell of the river bed was undisguised by the bright sunlight on a chilly February day, made colder by homicide detectives scouring the scene.

Dash parked his car and walked underneath the yellow tape that blocked the pathway down to the river. He walked only a few feet and saw a teal bandana lying on the ground. He lifted it up with his pocketknife and placed it in a ziplock plastic bag. It was dry, indicating that it was recently discarded. Dash lifted it to his nose, smelling it. It smelled like cigar smoke. Whoever owned this bandana smoked cigars or was around the cigar culture. Dash put the bandana in his pocket and walked down to the forensics team that was scouring the crime scene.

"Can we help you?" a uniformed officer asked.

Dash responded cheerfully, "No, this path is where I usually walk my dog. Any problems?"

"Yes," the uniformed officer half Dash's age replied. "Didn't you see the yellow tape?

"Yes, just curious," Dash apologized.

"This is a homicide investigation. The trail is closed for now."

A plainclothes detective overhearing the conversation asked Dash. "Did you happen to see or hear anything yesterday?"

"No, I didn't walk my dog yesterday. I was planting starts in my greenhouse," Dash answered truthfully.

"Then, we'll have to ask you to leave the area," the plainclothes officer said.

Dash quickly perused the scene, noticing that a portion of the rope was still attached to the tree. It had been cut at the limb. Dash assumed the rope was now evidence. It had been used to attach Taylor to the limb. He headed back into town.

Baxter's Cigar Shop was on Main Street in a pathetic little strip mall. The Cigar Shop occupied the biggest space retail space, a large walk-in humidor, a lounge with a pool table, televisions, and a small kitchen. Dash frequented Baxter's on occasion, and he knew the clerk working.

"Hey, Dash, what can I get you today?" The clerk asked.

"Thanks, Bob, I just need a little information." Dash pulled out a ziplock plastic bag containing a teal bandana out of his pocket and showed it to Bob. "Does this look familiar?"

Bob thought Dash was kidding. "Is this a riddle?"

"No, I found it, and it was lousy with cigar smoke in the Salinas riverbed. Do any of your customers carry bandanas?"

Bob looked at him oddly, "Maybe none, maybe all of them. I can't recall seeing that bandana."

"You'll read about it. A local woman was found in the Salinas River bed yesterday," Dash said.

"That's a regular dumping ground for bodies. Homeless people drown in the river in the winter, and bodies show up in the spring. You won't catch me anywhere near that place," Bob said, shaking his head.

A stream of customers starting arriving for their afternoon cigar. They went into the walk-in humidor, picked out a cigar or box of cigars, and went to Bob to check out. Dash busied himself by checking out the merchandise and pricing. Unfortunately for California cigar retailers, the state tax makes it far more affordable to buy them online from Florida, where there is no tax. Dash picked up a couple of Arturo Fuente's 858 Madura cigars. He liked the coffee and chocolate notes. As it approached five, the customers filed in to hang out in the private lounge to watch television, drink whiskey, and smoke. Dash wandered into the lounge and immediately recognized Conrad Cook. He looked like the cartoon character that The Hamster had described. His bleached blonde hair stood up in a buzz cut. He wore a faded Hawaiian shirt and had tattoos on his naked arms. Conrad also recognized Dash.

Conrad snarled at Dash, "They let anybody in here. Are you still playing amateur detective?"

Dash noticed that Conrad looked fatigued, and the spare tire around his waist was more pronounced as it pushed the lower button on his shirt out.

"Yes, I'm a customer," Dash lifted his pack of cigars. "I thought you'd be here. I found a bandana that might be yours." Dash pulled out the bag with the teal bandana and showed it to Conrad.

Conrad gave Dash a death stare, "Where did you dig that up? I wipe my snot on my assistant winemakers. Why would I need a handkerchief?"

"It's a bandana. You could tie up your girlfriends to the bedposts with it," Dash mused.

Conrad was not amused, "Do you want to step outside, old man, and I can rearrange your nose on your ugly mug?"

"You didn't answer my question. Is this yours?" Dash asked again.

Conrad didn't wait. He put down his cigar, walked over to Dash, and pushed him back to the door. He punched Dash in the gut. Dash had covered his face, expecting a blow. Dash was stunned by the blow to his lower extremities but recovered quickly enough to tackle Conrad at the knees, where a fat guy like Conrad was most vulnerable. Several other patrons tried to break them up. Conrad was furious. He charged again at Dash, flailing away with his closed fists. The patrons pulled Conrad off Dash, who walked outside through the door. Conrad attempted to follow, but a couple of patrons blocked his exit. Within minutes, the city police showed up.

An officer took Dash aside, "I understand you started a commotion. You're not a member of the cigar lounge. You were trespassing, and you started a fight. Would you like to comment?"

"Possibly. I came to the store to purchase some cigars and saw a friend of mine named Conrad Cook. I asked him about his former murdered girlfriend. He didn't like it and charged me. End of story."

The officer looked closely at Dash, realizing he was sober and lucid and appeared to be some twenty years older than Conrad, who was now talking to another officer.

"We'll let you go home. The shop said they wouldn't press charges because you're a customer, but you've been denied lounge privileges for now."

Dash pulled out the two-pack of cigars he intended to buy and handed the officer forty dollars. "This is for the cigars. Let Bob keep the change." Dash left a little roughed up and headed home.

Conrad Cook just moved to the top of Dash's suspect list. The Hamster had identified Conrad as the accomplice in the murder of Claudia Bowers. It was only hearsay now since The Hamster was dead. Conrad was the type who bullied their way to the top, believing that laws didn't apply to them and he could get away with murder. Dash feared that he might be right.

Chapter Thirty-One:

TEAL BANDANA

Dash felt emboldened. Soon the musty winter smell of dirt would turn sweet. Spring was just around the corner. The fruit trees were budding and flowering, and the freezing overnight temperatures waned. The suspects were lining up like tin soldiers, but there were several problems. There were no credible witnesses, no motives, and the only pieces of evidence were rope fragments, a teal bandana, a Hawaiian shirt, and some Moonstone jewelry—hardly anything to build a case on. Dash pondered his options. He was certain that Dylan Dotson, Hernando Torres, and Conrad Cook were linked and involved in the actual crime. Other than Conrad, who had been dumped by Claudia, there was no motive, unless they were hired killers. Dash believed that if he followed the money, he'd find the puppet master. Elementary, Sherlock Holmes might say, except that he was only one man without forensics experience or access to banking information. He was stifled. Dash decided to meet with Detective FJ Evans to somehow triangulate the suspects.

To Dash's surprise, Detective Evans was anxious to meet with him. He had a very cold case with no one in custody, and now, another murder of a young woman. The heat was on, from every corner. The specter of a brutal killer still on the loose gripped the city and county. A special task force was created, and the FBI was brought in for their expertise. No one now believed that Claudia's murder was a crime of opportunity. A killer was in their midst with an insatiable blood lust.

Dash met with Detective Evans at the Squirrel Hill Bakery. Detective Evans was in a foul mood, even though his retirement was within range.

The two sat across from one another in a secluded part of the bakery. The morning rush had ended, and it was ten in the morning, so the place was practically empty.

"Hell, everyone is up in arms. We've got the Feds involved, the mayor, the supervisors. The heat has been turned up. Everyone's trying to cover their asses while looking for a fall guy. Central casting has determined that I'm perfect for that role," Detective Evans said.

"You're forgetting a third victim: The Hamster. He was a witness," Dash added.

"No one cares about a homeless guy killed on a stoop. I know you think he was linked to Claudia's murder, but I think he just played you for free french fries." Detective Evans tried to inject humor into the sordid affair.

Dash held firm, "It was The Hamster who determined that there were two perps who drove trucks. He described what they wore, their body types, and their approximate ages. He also determined that they cased the location a day prior to the murders and that they left behind the rope. He saw the suspects come out of the Ranch and Farm Real Estate office at night and saw one of them drive off with Claudia. He also had his throat cut in a similar manner to Claudia. Now, I'm a witness once removed."

Detective Evans had out his notebook and scribbled down everything Dash said, "Okay, you said on the phone—you've matched the identities, given to you by The Hamster, with the suspects."

Dash took a deep breath, "All the suspects work directly for, or are contracted by, Jasper Wines. Both of the victims did work for Jasper Wines. Conrad Cook, who has spiky blond hair, a bit of a gut, and probably has a Hawaiian shirt or two in his closet, was part of the tandem that cased the murder site, leaving only a teal bandana as evidence. Conrad carries a long slender knife and is left-handed. Dylan Dotson is fitter, taller, and he now has a full beard. When Claudia was murdered, he just had some stubble. Dylan carries a long slender knife, and I believe he was the actual killer. Hernando Torres, I believe poisoned my dog, and might be an accessory."

Detective Evans was fixated on the narrative, "But your witness is dead, and our only case is built on hearsay—yours—which isn't worth a damn—most likely hyperbole." Detective Evans sat back in his chair.

"Hyperbole! I've never heard you use a four-syllable word before," Dash said as he tightened his grip on his coffee mug.

Detective Evans ignored Dash's comment.

Dash put down his coffee mug, pulling out a plastic ziplock bag with the teal bandana in it, "I found this at the crime scene. You boys must have missed it. It smells like cigar smoke, and I believe it was owned by Conrad Cook, who smokes cigars daily and goes to the Cigar lounge every day after work."

Detective Evans lifted the bag, "Can I take this for testing?"

"Sure." Dash handed the plastic bag to Detective Evans. "Unfortunately, my fingerprints may show up in the tests. I'm willing to testify as to where and when I found it."

"Fuck it. We still don't have a motive or any real evidence. We have a long way to prove anything. I can bring the suspects in for questioning, but I can't hold them." Detective Evans droned on.

"I have an idea," Dash said with sudden clarity. "Bring in Hernando Torres for questioning. I don't believe he was involved in the murders, but he might implicate Conrad and Dylan unwittingly. There's a chance he saw or overheard something. I bet Hernando has a family he supports and can't risk going to jail. When you ask him about poisoning my dog, I'd like to be present."

Detective Evans took time to write down his notes before lifting his head and responding to Dash, "Okay, I'll bring Hernando in for questioning. You won't be present for the questioning, but I'll let him see you when he enters the police station, so he knows that you're the culprit. We'll pick him up tomorrow at work. I don't want to alarm his family."

Dash was impressed with Evans' decency. "I don't think he'll admit to the poisoning. I think he'll act like he has no idea what you're talking about. Attempting to poison a dog, who survived the poisoning, is not a major crime. I suggest you link it to the girl's murders, by suggesting that they were killed like lambs."

Detective Evans frowned, "I don't know him, but he's a labor supervisor for Jasper, which suggests he's a bright guy, bi-lingual, and knows his rights. We won't be able to corner him."

Dash agreed, "The only card you have is to suggest that Jasper Wine is hypersensitive to any bad publicity—suggesting this could jeopardize his labor contract with Jasper."

Detective Evans was not opposed to playing hardball, but he didn't appreciate Dash's approach. "We're not in the business of threatening hard-working people because someone believes their dog may have been poisoned by them. I'm not going to mention Jasper Winery or the murders. Your witness, The Hamster, never mentioned a Hispanic male. Hernando may have poisoned your dog, but the damn dog is still eating and shitting. Hopefully, he divulges something about your suspects."

Dash and Detective Evans finished their meeting. Detective Evans told Dash he'd notify him when Hernando Torres comes to the police station for questioning. In the interim, Detective Evans said he'd expand his investigation to include Dylan Dotson and Conrad Cook.

Dash remained at the bakery and stayed on for lunch. He had been wanting to try their Reuben sandwich. Dash had been disappointed by the versions he'd tried on the Central Coast. Without good pastrami, real sauerkraut, and non-processed cheese, it would be an abject failure. He asked the bakery where they got their pastrami. He canceled his order when he found out the supplier was Farmer John, an LA firm. A bakery should stick to making scones.

Dash was prone to dreaming. He contemplated opening a real New York-style delicatessen. The only other food he craved that he couldn't get on the Central Coast was good Chinese. There were plenty of decent Thai, Vietnamese, and Sushi restaurants. Dash realized then he had a reality check. He didn't have the energy, money, or time to invest in a delicatessen. He went back to thinking about the investigation he was currently employed doing. This mind lapse had more to do with his frustration with the investigation than his stomach. He had divulged all his information to the good detective. Now he had to sit on his hands and wait.

He didn't wait long. The next morning, Detective Evans called and said Hernando would be coming in at noon, during his lunch break. Dash arrived at eleven thirty and waited in the lobby of the Great Oaks Police Department building. The lobby was cold and smelled of Lysol. Hernando paid little attention to Dash, other than giving him a sneer. Hernando wore jeans, a tan Dickies work shirt, and lace-up work boots. He was short but solidly built. His head was shaved. Dash remained in the lobby Hernando was questioned.

As the detective presumed, Hernando denied any knowledge of the dog's poisoning. He said that Dash came to the job site with a bullshit story about being a truck salesman and later went to his house to tell him to stay away from the Jasper Wine vineyards.

Detective Evans listened intently, then seized the opportunity when the name Jasper came up.

"Why do you think Dash is hanging around Jasper job sites and not at other wine operations?"

"He's got a girlfriend at Jasper. He's been nosing around the winery. People don't like him," Hernando said without emotion.

"Why do you think he's nosing around the winery?" Detective Evans asked again.

Hernando paused. "I don't know. Could have something to do with Gregg Perigold's fiancée, Claudia, who got herself killed."

"Who's fiancée?" Detective Evans asked.

"You know, the Perigold kid," Hernando answered.

"What's that have to do with Dash Ramblar?" Detective Evans asked.

Hernando didn't like where the questions were headed. "I told you. I don't know. I'm a contract laborer for Jasper. I hear everything second hand—I don't give a rat's ass about Dash. All I care about is my work. I didn't poison his dogs—I got better things to do." Hernando started to get out of his chair, "I have to go back to work."

"One more question, Mr. Torres. "Did you know that Conrad used to date Claudia?"

Hernando looked at him strangely, "That's news to me. He dropped her name when he drank. I knew Gregg dated her, but not Conrad."

"What did Conrad say about her?"

Hernando smiled, "He said she was hot. Conrad said he had a chance with her, but he blew it. She dissed him."

"How do you know that?" Detective Evans asked.

"He was all sad at work—called her a crazy bitch. That's what men say when they've been dumped." Hernando exited the room and walked past Dash.

Hernando sneered at Dash one more time. "You're next, asshole."

Dash met with Detective Evans, who looked bushed.

"As I expected, he denied everything. We have no reason not to believe him. I think he poisoned your dog on orders. I think he considers it part of his job, not a crime."

"Exactly," Dash quipped. "I think Dylan and Conrad are acting on orders too. So who the hell is giving those orders

Detective Evans countered, "Men don't commit murders for hire. That's Hollywood crap. These murders were planned, ritualistic, and gruesome. Hypothetically, If you're hired to do a murder, you're going to do the easiest, cleanest, and most efficient manner. These murders were messy, even though they did leave the crime scene pristine."

Dash listened patiently. "Then you're saying I'm barking up the wrong tree with the wrong suspects? Conrad and Dylan have ample motivations: job security, babes, and beer money. "

"Like us. Come on, Dash, knock it off—admit that your narrative doesn't jive with reality," Detective Evans sneered.

Dash laughed, "'Jive? I haven't heard that expression in thirty years. Maybe you're right, but those two fit the description that The Hamster gave me—got him killed for doing it. The only other witness I have is Pedro in San Miquel, who said he was leaving town. My guess is he's still buying cigarettes at the dollar store around mid-day." Dash looked at his watch. It was eleven in the morning.

"I'm heading up to San Miguel. Do you want to come along for the ride?" Dash asked.

"I need to get out of town. We'll take my car—it's city business," Detective Evans sighed.

Chapter Thirty-Two:

LUCIANO PAVAROTTI

Dash and Detective Evans drove up to San Miguel on an overcast late February day. The only signs of spring were the wild mustard flowers, the lush green hillsides, and the shorter shadows. Otherwise, it was a cool winter's day.

Dash looked over at Detective Evans. Detective Evans looked older; his belly hung over his belt like water over a dam, and his double chin looked more like a triple chin.

Detective Evans smiled, "We just got our season tickets."

"For the Dodgers?" Dash asked.

"No, I don't care to watch sports—The San Francisco Opera is for me," Detective Evans said smugly.

"It beats listening to karaoke at the Pine Street Saloon," Dash said. Detective Evans ignored his attempt at humor.

"We've had them for years. I got hooked thirty years ago when I saw Pavarotti perform. A friend of mine was an usher at the Opera House and saw the operas for free. He got Karen and me an ushering gig, and we've been going ever since. Opera's unique—the performers have this rare gift…" Detective Evans paused, "Am I boring you, Dash?"

"Not at all. I love music, any music. I have to say that opera is better live—I don't listen to recordings," Dash replied. "Karen and I listen to operatic music almost every evening. It soothes the savage heart."

"I envy your marriage. It sounds like you and Karen share many interests," Dash said.

Detective Evans chuckled, "The grass is always greener. You envy my life; I envy yours. I'm at the age that it's too late to change horses or direction. I've become comfortable, but that doesn't mean I'm content. I have a bucket list that'll never be filled."

Dash lamented, "A bucket list is overrated. Most are tourist traps: The Great Pyramids, the leaning tower of Pisa, the Great Wall of China, etc. You take a few photos, buy the t-shirt and go home to friends who could care less."

"My bucket list is a little different. We want to see all the great opera houses in the world," Detective Evans beamed.

"That's admirable," Dash said. "You still have time."

They arrived in San Miguel and got to the Dollar Store at ten minutes before noon. Dash walked inside while Detective Evans stayed in his car. The same Anglo clerk, Cyle, was behind the register ringing up pre-lunch sales of beer, prepared sandwiches, sodas, and cigarettes. There was a short queue of working men and women. The store wasn't a deli, but it sold food of scant nutritional value.

Dash waited until Cyle was done at the register. "Remember me? I was here before looking for the Hispanic guy who buys Lucky Strikes. Have you seen him lately?"

"Funny you should ask—he was gone for about a month—then he showed up again yesterday," Cyle said.

Dash bought a carton of Lucky Strikes, went back outside, and gave Detective Evans the thumbs up. Dash lingered in the parking lot as Detective Evans remained in the unmarked squad car with the nice heated leather seats.

Right on cue, Pedro showed up, almost unrecognizable to Dash: clean-shaven, his hair had been chopped off, and was wearing cowboy boots, jeans, and a pearl button cowboy shirt. Like The Hamster had said, Pedro's eyes were narrow, almond-shaped. When Pedro saw Dash approach him, he turned away. Dash caught up to him.

"Don't worry, Pedro. You're not in trouble," Dash assured him.

"Bullshit, gringo. My friend, The Hamster, gets his throat cut and all you can say is you're sorry. Typical gringo lies. They hurt you bad, and all they can say is I'm sorry," Pedro said.

Dash handed Pedro the carton of cigarettes. "Yes, I'm sorry about The Hamster. I saw him the day before he was killed. I put him up in a hotel. You are now the only witness I have to the murder of Claudia," He pauses, "Now another woman has been murdered. Do you know anything about that?"

Pedro took the cigarettes. "You loco, senor. I have been in Oregon for the last month. I know nothin'—I'm not a witness to nothin'. Sorry, gringo."

Dash was undeterred, "Name is Dash—you said there were two men, both young, both stocky, one with facial hair, and one with spiky blonde hair and a Hawaiian shirt."

Pedro looked at him and laughed out loud, "Did I tell you that, or did The Hamster? We just made that shit up. There were two guys both covered up in hoodies. We couldn't see their hair or their faces. All I know is one guy was in good shape. We told you about two fat guys because The Hamster needed french fries, and I needed cigarettes. Everyone around here is fat, so we figured it would keep you busy."

"So you're saying that one fit guy and one fat guy in hooded sweat-shirts did the deed? Or, are you making that up too?" Dash stood back and waited.

Pedro was uncomfortable with the conversation, moving closer to Dash, putting his mouth near Dash's left ear. "I ain't gonna' testify. The one fit guy is tall, older, and the other guy is younger, stronger, heavier, but not fat. Both gringos. Both serious. They were on a mission. They will kill me, you, anybody. They don't fuck around. Look what they did to those girls—to The Hamster." He walked away from Dash.

Pedro lifted the carton of cigarettes and smiled, "Gracias, senor."

Dash went back to the squad car and spoke to Detective Evans, "There's your witness. Better pick him up, or you may never see him again. Book him for stealing my cigarettes."

Detective Evans drove around the corner and saw Pedro jump into an old blue Chrysler mini-van. A woman was driving. Detective Evans let them pull away before he turned on his police lights and siren. The van pulled over, Detective Evans went to the van, handcuffed Pedro, and brought him back to the squad car.

Pedro looked angrily at Dash. "You motherfucker, I ain't talkin' to him or you."

Detective Evans drove Pedro and Dash back to the station. He booked Pedro on petty theft and an outstanding warrant for a DUI. Pedro had no bail money, so he went to jail. Dash went home.

Detective Evans called Dash the next day, "Your friend Pedro isn't talking to anyone. He missed his court date for the outstanding DUI, so we can hold him for that, but he's not telling me what you told me about the suspects. He says he made it all up, so he could get some cigarettes. By the way, he has a passport. He's Filipino, not Mexican. His last name is Mendoza."

"Hold on to him. I think I can get him to talk." Dash said.

"Do you speak Filipino?" Detective Evans chortled.

"No, but he and The Hamster vacationed every winter in Mexico on The Hamster's dime. Check his passport to see when and where he went. I don't believe he was in Oregon—I think he was somewhere else. Find out if he inherited The Hamster's money."

"What's that got to do with anything?" Detective Evans followed with a definitive answer. "No, you're grasping at straws. He's already changed his story once about the suspects' identities. He's not a reliable witness. You can question him after we release him on bail."

"When's that going to happen?" Dash asked.

"Today, Pedro posted bail. He must have inherited some money because he had a certified check."

Dash ended the call. He decided to abandon reason, follow instincts, and go for broke. Had Pedro really changed his story, or had he revised it for another reason? Had Conrad gotten to him? He was the primary suspect. Why was he deleted from Pedro's description? How did Pedro know about The Hamster's murder? It was never printed. Was a police report issued? Dash knew the answer. Pedro had been threatened. He inherited The Hamster's money, went on vacation, and was sworn to secrecy by Conrad or one of his henchmen.

Now he had to just prove it.

Dash looked at his watch. It was past lunchtime. He made a grilled cheese sandwich with two kinds of cheese, sharp cheddar and pepper jack, and kosher dill slices on sourdough. It was lazy, comfort food. He decided to go to the dog park and do a little reconnaissance. He got Chloe, put a leash on her, and helped her jump in the back seat of his old range rover.

The parking lot was getting full. It was the after-work crowd. The dog park was below the parking lot, surrounded by boxwoods and trees. The trees were deciduous, still leafless in February. The large bark-covered park was split between a small dog area and a larger big dog area.

Dash knew that Chloe, Taylor's dog, was small and probably stayed in the small dog area, which was closer to the parking lot. Several women were gathered on benches on a cement walkway surrounded by dogs playing on the chips. It was social hour for the dogs and the women.

Dash let Barney out in the big dog side of the dog park to play, opened the gate that led to the small dog portion of the park, and walked up to the women.

They stopped talking to listen. "Hello, my name is Dash. I was a friend of Taylor Thorngate's. Did any of you know her?"

"We were just talking about her. The news says she was killed by a serial killer,"

Dash was taken aback, "A serial killer? I hope not. When was the last time anyone here saw her?"

Another woman, slightly younger, with dyed red hair, wearing a heavy sweatshirt that said on the front, "Dogs and wine make everything fine," spoke up. "I saw her two days ago about this time."

Dash was surprised, "That was the day she was abducted."

"I don't know about that," she continued. "It was getting dark. We were the only two people at the park."

"Did you see anyone, hear anything?"

The red-haired woman smiled, "Are you a cop?"

Dash laughed, "No, I don't think a cop would have a little dachshund like Chloe.." He motioned to the little dog who happily came right to him. I'm keeping Chloe until I can find her a suitable home.

"I was her friend and client. Her disappearance and her murder make no sense." Dash lowered his head.

"Well," the red-haired woman said, "I saw her leave. I saw a big truck and her car leave the parking lot at the same time. She didn't honk her horn."

"What?" Dash asked.

"She would always, always, honk her horn when she left the parking lot. It was her way of saying goodbye, and that she was okay," the red-haired woman said.

"Did you see or hear anything else? What color was the truck?" Dash asked again.

The woman thought for a moment, "Well, I thought it was odd that a big truck would pull out of the parking lot so fast. The parking lot was empty, no cars except for Taylor's, no need to rush. I walk my dog here. It would normally be dangerous to drive so fast, but I guess they thought it was okay because no one was here. The truck was grey, dark grey. Taylor drove her car out afterward. She was driving fast too, which is unlike her. She was a careful driver. She told me that she had bad night vision, and it was especially bad at dusk," she paused, "

"That's very kind of you to keep Chloe. We miss Chloe—maybe you can bring her by more often—she has many friends here."

Dash left with one bit of information. A confirmation that the big lifted-chassis truck was dark grey just like Conrad's. Dash was now certain that Conrad was a participant. He called Bryson Jackson.

"This is Dash. We've got to meet".

Chapter Thirty-Three:

RED FOX

Dash went to the Red Fox Winery early the next day, before the tasting room was open. Bryson Jackson met Dash alone. His wife, Jackie, was still at home. Bryson began the conversation without Dash having an opportunity to convey his new information.

"Dash, thanks for coming over. I know you have a month left on our current contract, but I need to end it now. You can keep the retainer. I feel, since Taylor Thorngate was murdered, this case has gotten too big for one man. I've read that the FBI is now involved. They're consulting with the serial killer team at headquarters. If I believed that Claudia's murder was a singular event, I'd continue, but it looks like the whole thing has blown up."

Dash drank the cappuccino that Bryson had made for him, trying not to act surprised, "There is no doubt that Taylor's murder complicates matters. And yes, I know about the Feds involvement from my sources. It's notable that her murder and its links to Claudia's murder have drawn me closer to the truth. I believe that Conrad Cook has a major role in both murders. I have found evidence of his presence at the murder site, and a confirmation of his vehicle at the point where Taylor was apprehended."

Bryson responded as if he wasn't listening to Dash, "I have it on good authority that Conrad Cook has a bullet-proof alibi. He's no longer a suspect. I've also heard you got into a fight with Conrad at a cigar shop. You've been harassing Jasper contract employees. Jason Perigold, the owner of Jasper Winery, called me. Somehow, he knew that you and I were connected. He told me that they're issuing a restraining order against you at the winery. You lied to get access to his employees. He's not a happy camper."

Dash had to grin, "Funny, how your credibility, reputation, and honor take a toll when you brush up against the truth."

Bryson Jackson was not amused. "It's not funny at all when I have a billionaire winery owner call me to tell me that an associate of mine is unprofessional and out of control."

Dash finished the cappuccino. It was so tasty that he almost asked for a refill. "I'm sorry to get you in the middle of all of this. I've never mentioned your name, nor have I cashed the latest check. If you want, I'll return it to you."

Bryson Jackson thought about it, "No—just keep it."

Dash was in no mood, "That works for me. Let's end the business relationship. Hopefully, we can continue cordial relations. I know Claudia would want us to remain friends."

The mention of Claudia's name was like a dagger to Bryson's heart, "Please, don't mention her name again. As you suspected, I was in love with her. Her presence brought me joy. We had no physical relationship, but somehow, the thought of her being gone has been the hardest thing I've ever dealt with. As we get older, we lose friends to illness, accidents, and separation. We lose our parents, pets, we have business failures, divorces, but we manage to go forward. Then we have an inexplicable loss that changes our lives. Claudia Bowers was that loss to me. I have been depressed, anxious, and have lost hope. My marriage, my family, my winery are all thriving. But I'm not."

Dash listened intently. He knew that Claudia had a profound effect on men. It wasn't her physical attributes. It was her life force, her heart, her compassion, and her wit. She took joy in everything from a sudden downpour, to a soaring hawk, to awkward gestures, to criticism. She impacted everyone, men and women, with the same sensation. They felt enriched by her friendship.

By the same token, Dash ruminated that when Claudia quit a relationship, it would be devastating.

"I'm sorry, I wish I could have brought you closure," Dash said.

Dash and Bryson shook hands, and Dash departed. The one question that he failed to ask Bryson was just what or who was Conrad's bullet-proof alibi? And who told Bryson Jackson?

Dash drove downtown to the Great Oaks police station and asked for Detective FJ Evans. It was still early in the morning. Dash was told that the detective was busy but had five minutes to spare. Dash said okay.

Detective Evans brought Dash into a room just a dozen yards from the lobby. He was all business.

"We checked out Conrad Cook. Conrad had witnesses who can account for his whereabouts during the time the murders occurred. We checked the DNA on the bandana, and all we found were your fingerprints. Frankly, I'm tired of you wasting my time. I've got a serial killer on the loose, and you've got me questioning a suspected dog poisoner. Please don't call me until this investigation is complete. We've got the Feds here, and they provided us a list of sex offenders who were in the area about the time of the murders. One word of advice—stay away from Conrad Cook, Dylan Dotson, Hernando Torres, Jasper Winery, and this building."

"If the witness was Dylan Dotson or Rex Beckett, then the alibi is bogus," Dash said to Detective Evans.

Detective Evans walked out of the room. Dash exited the room alone.

Normally, this kind of day would call for a stiff drink. It had the opposite effect on Dash. He went to the gym and swam half a mile. He did bicep curls and did the rope pull for an hour. He took a long soak in the outdoor hot tub, followed by a quick shower. Then he picked up some tacos on the way home. He was without a client and now without a contact in the police department. He was at his absolute best when he was left alone. He could think clearer, take more risks, and stay focused.

Dash took a walk with his dogs through the oaks. They rousted some rabbits. Afterward, Dash met with Rico, his ranch manager, and they discussed the projects they wanted to complete in the coming year. Dash was harboring pent up energy; he cleaned his entire house, washing the tile floors with vinegar water, getting rid of pesky spider webs, and re-organized his firewood pile. He was definitely in a manic phase—when does this phase bottom out? It came soon enough. After he cleaned the house, he ate a light lunch of a smoked salmon and cucumber sandwich, washed down with a good Chardonnay. Then fell fast asleep in his leather chair. He awoke two hours later, refreshed, but hazy. Where does he go from here with the investigation?

The notion that it's always darkest before the dawn seemed apropos. If Conrad and Dylan had bullet-proof alibis, then should Dash surrender the investigation and let the FBI arrest the perpetrators? They were the experts. Dash was an amateur, now working for free.

Who else smoked cigars? Who else drove a large grey truck? Who else was linked to Claudia and Taylor? Finally, who else had a motive for them being murdered? Was there a chance that the murders were set up to look like a serial killer to get the police off track? Dash had three female contacts who might be able to answer those questions: Ginger Rute, Amanda Jacobs, and Mona Morgan.

Dash called Ginger and asked her to come over to his house. She was reluctant, but he plied her with a pitcher of freshly-made manhattans. She arrived in her work clothes: a khaki skirt, a white blouse, and a navy blazer. She looked like a grown-up Girl Scout. She sat in a chair. Dash sat on a couch with the cocktail glasses in front of them on the broad rustic wood coffee table.

Dash wanted to catch up. "Have you been threatened again?"

Ginger smiled, "Just the opposite. I've been treated like a princess at work. Everyone's gone out of their way to be nice, so I can't complain. Even Jason, the owner, came by to thank me for the job I've done in the tasting room."

"Have they mentioned my name?" Dash asked.

Ginger laughed, "I'm sorry to break it to you, Dash. You're a non-entity. It's as if you never existed. Either they no longer consider you a threat, or they have bigger fish to fry."

"A lot of mixed metaphors to describe a fellow on the way down," Dash lamented with a twinkle in his eyes.

"I almost feel safe enough to engage in some foreplay with yiu.." Ginger moved next to Dash on the couch.

Dash laughed, "You make me sound like a quarantined inmate." He kissed her on her cheek.

Ginger took off her blazer, "But that's not why you brought me here, was it?"

"No, but I could be persuaded to change my mind. I wanted to ask you about Taylor Thorngate. What do you know about her?"

Ginger moved away from Dash on the couch, "Very little. I know she was a vendor at the winery, and she dated Conrad for barely a month. He told me he was crazy about her—that he was disheartened by their sudden break-up. I don't think he has the capacity for murder—he's too vain. He always thinks a better option is just around the corner."

Dash's head was spinning, "Everything comes back to Conrad, yet he has an alibi. I agree; being dumped is not reason enough to murder someone. Unless there is a financial reason behind it."

Ginger laughed, "You think he took out a life insurance policy on Taylor? Or someone paid him to kill her? I think you're losing it, Dash. You need a vacation." She gave him a consolation kiss on the lips.

"You're right. I do need a vacation. Remember, Conrad's ego is all based on his prowess as a winemaker for Jasper, and now Paint Horse. If he were to lose that position, he'd be devastated."

"What are you suggesting? The Perigolds are billionaires. The winery is their smallest asset. They see Great Oaks as a small hick town. They could care about Conrad, Taylor, Claudia, and me, for that matter. Their empire is global. I hate to break it to you, Dash but your conspiracy theories don't fly. I agree that Conrad Cook has the most to lose, so why would he put his career at risk? "

Dash enjoyed having someone to bounce ideas off. "I glad we agree on something. What do you know about Dylan Dotson?"

"He's your standard scum ball. Conrad is his idol. Dylan strikes out more than any guy in this town, but it doesn't stop him from trying. I heard he even signed up for dance classes hoping to get laid." Ginger laughed out loud. "When Dylan comes around the Winery, the women become invisible."

"What do you mean?"

"They hideout, take a break, pick up back stock," Ginger replied.

"That bad, I wonder if he has a bullet-proof alibi like his idol?" Dash asked Ginger.

They were into their second round of Manhattans, and Ginger was becoming more amorous. Dash responded in kind. Ginger excused herself to freshen up. Dash was left alone to ponder what they discussed. Dash heard a commotion outside. He opened the door and saw his dogs barking at a man who had just parked his truck near the house. He approached the man, who at a distance, he didn't recognize. When he got closer, he was very surprised.

"What are you doing here, Dylan?" Dash approached the younger man sporting a full beard.

"I've got a bone to pick with you, Mr. Ramblar." Dylan looked prepared to fight. He wore a down vest, and his flannel shirt was rolled up at the sleeves.

"I wished you'd called first. What is it?" Dash asked.

Dash was close enough to smell the alcohol on Dylan's breath. He sensed he'd been drinking a combo of Jack Daniels and Coca Cola (Jack & Coke).

"It got back to me that you're saying I'm a suspect in the murder of those two women." Dylan was breathing hard and visibly irritated.

"All love interests and co-workers are suspects. You knew both Claudia and Taylor?"

"Reckon I did. No matter, I didn't murder anyone. My beef is with you and your big mouth. The police brought me in, asked if I had an alibi, then asked me to do a polygraph test. I have a business to run—besides, I have a girlfriend who'd rip your throat out if she was here," Dylan said as he squared up his stance.

Dash noticed that Dylan slurred a few words. He looked over at Dylan's truck. It was a dark grey Dodge Ram with a lifted chassis.

"Your truck was positively identified as being at the dog park when Taylor was apprehended. You also went to dance classes to pick up women, and you asked Claudia repeatedly if you could drive her home. Did she let you?"

Dylan leaned forward as he headed towards Dash, showing his bulky arms, "That's our company truck—we got four more, just like it. Yep, I gave Claudia a ride home, but I didn't score."

"If you didn't touch those women, then you have nothing to worry about." Dash asserted.

Dylan was clearly unhinged, "I'm about to touch you. Does that count?" Dylan lunged at Dash, who stepped aside and let him stumble on the large flagstones. Then Ginger came out of the house and yelled at Dylan.

"Get the hell out of here. If you know what's good for you."

Dylan smirked, "You fuckin' this old man, mister blue pill? Try me— all my equipment works."

Ginger laughed, "Your equipment is attached to your body; that's the problem. Now get in your truck, go home and watch porno or whatever you do when you strike out."

Dylan was furious, lunged again at Dash, this time catching him and dragging him to the ground. Dylan was much bulkier than Dash, and his weight alone pinned Dash to the ground. Ginger went to the firewood stack right next to the door, picked up a six-inch diameter piece of oak, and struck Dylan across the neck and shoulders. He winced in pain and rolled off of Dash. Dash dusted himself off and grinned at Ginger through his teeth. Dylan was slow to get up and headed for his truck.

"If you didn't have that bitch here, you'd already be dead." Dylan drove off.

Dash and Ginger had lost that loving feeling. They went back inside; the conversation turned to Dylan.

"Thanks, Ginger, for covering my back," Dash laughed, "I had the situation under control, but you hastened the outcome."

"Dylan has you by forty pounds and twenty years. Sorry, even buzzed, that man is a load," Ginger said. They sat back on the couch a few feet apart.

"What's his story?" Dash asked. "He's feeling the heat. If he were completely innocent, he wouldn't be acting like a raving lunatic."

"He's not innocent," Ginger was adamant. "He's one of those guys with a chip on his shoulder, a sense of entitlement, and in debt—extended to the hilt. Look at this truck—cost him at least sixty thousand."

"How do you know that?" Dash asked.

"I hear things at the winery. Supposedly, he owes everyone money: Conrad, Gregg, even some of the wine pourers. He's got a good business, but somehow he's always short for payroll."

"I surprised Jasper Wines maintains his contract. They want their vendors to be model citizens—pay their employees, etc."

Ginger responded, "His crews are fast and good. He knows what he' doing. Rumor has it he's big into sports gambling. He's always talking sports to everyone."

"That can explain the indebtedness. He's vulnerable to blackmail, extortion, and being an accessory to a crime."

Ginger got up and poured them a glass of water. She walked back to the couch.

"I think I'd better be going home. This is way too much excitement for me." Ginger reached for her blazer.

Dash looked at the darkening sky, knowing he'd be spending another night alone. "How about a rain check?" he asked.

Ginger grinned, "How about a dozen?" Dash escorted Ginger to her car. Dash kissed her full on the lips. She lingered, kissing him back and hugging him. They stayed embraced for several minutes.

His two dogs, Bixby and Barney, came to his side. They all watched Ginger's car drove away. His mind wandered as he patted the dogs' heads.

Dash was convinced Dylan Dotson had a hand in the murder of Claudia and Taylor. Dylan replaced Conrad as the number one suspect. Now he'd have to build a case against him on his own. It would be no mean feat.

PART THREE: VENDANGE

Chapter Thirty-Four:

REVERSE HEIST

Dash had the fireplace roaring, a Bill Withers music track on, enjoying a nightcap with his dogs at his feet. There was a knock on his door. It was Ginger, upset.

"I got home—something didn't seem right. I don't know if someone was watching me or that someone had broken into my home. The hair was standing up on the back of my neck. I checked all the doors and windows. Nothing. There's no way I could sleep in that house—not tonight."

Ginger was standing outside on his welcome mat. She had a large leather satchel with a leather strap over her shoulder. She carried a heavy-duty canvas bag on the other arm.

Dash was in his Pendleton wool tartan robe. He opened the door and gathered her bags, "Sit down. I'll get you a drink."

Ginger smiled, "That sounds great. My nerves are shot."

Ginger settled into the same couch they were on earlier. Dash brought her a Manhattan from the glass pitcher he'd used earlier. She greedily took the glass and drank half of it. Dash had never seen her this dispirited.

"What was it—there must have been something that you saw, smelled, or heard?" Dash asked.

Ginger sobbed, "I know my house; something wasn't right." She held her drink with both hands. "I did smell something. It was your smell—when you're on the patio."

"My smell on the patio?" Dash asked

Ginger took a long drink of her cocktail. "When you're smoking cigars."

"Anything else other than my smell on the patio?" Dash asked.

She thought hard and then yawned, "The seats were up."

"The toilet seats?" Dash asked. "Off the kitchen?"

"Yes. I was the last person in the house," Ginger yawned a nervous yawn.

"An inconsiderate cigar-smoking male," Dash grinned. "I think you need some sleep."

"I could sleep through an earthquake." Ginger put down her drink.

"We've got those too." Dash gathered their drink glasses and freshened them up.

"I've camped, slept under the stars in the bed of my truck. You're not the first rancher I've bedded down," Ginger said when Dash returned.

Dash laughed, "You were glamping, no doubt. Now, you're spending the night on my poor ranch—old vineyard, propane and septic tanks, well water, no garbage service, bad internet, bad cell phone reception, gravel driveways—hoot owls, coyotes, and feral cats keeping you up all night."

Ginger snuggled up with Dash, "I thought you were supposed to keep me up at night."

"Maybe, ten years ago, now, I get up with the sun," Dash lamented.

"Please don't wake me. The rumble you hear will be an earthquake," Ginger nudged Dash with her shoulder.

They laughed, half finishing their drinks. Then they both adjourned to the bedroom.

"Which side do you want?" Dash asked, looking at the queen-sized bed.

"Side? I want the middle. You find a sliver on the bed to sleep." Ginger went to the bathroom. She returned to the bedroom, wearing just a t-shirt. The t-shirt had the Nike swash and slogan on it, Just Do It.

Already between the covers, Dash laughed, "Is that an order?"

"Yes, for another night. Tonight, it means just sleep." Ginger crawled into bed and snuggled with Dash in the middle of the bed. Dash was excited but knew he needed sleep more than play. In the morning, Dash got up to make coffee. It was an adjustment for him to have a partner, a lover, residing in the same house, the same bed, sharing the same bathroom. He knew it was short-term, but what if he got used to it? Then he'd miss her when she returned home. Ginger must have read his mind because she broached the subject when he brought coffee to her.

"You understand that this arrangement is temporary. I know I'm being watched. Until there is closure, I can't return home." Ginger sat up in the bed, having brushed her hair while Dash was getting coffee. She looked regal. She took the coffee cup from Dash, who was wearing just a robe.

"Who do you think is watching you?" Dash asked.

"If I knew, I'd tell you, or the police," Ginger was annoyed.

"I know. Let me rephrase that question. Who do you think has reason to spy on you?"

"The only reason I can think of is my involvement with you. So, you'd probably have a better notion of who that might be. My relationship with Conrad was over three years ago, and we're just casual friends now. I'm a private person. I don't hang out with other employees at Jasper. I don't have a good friend locally. My friends are from high school and college, and you're the only man I'm seeing for now."

Dash smiled, "Always a disclaimer. What time do you have to be at work?"

"Ten. I'll have to swing by my house—I forgot to bring my work shoes. I should be leaving here in fifteen minutes. I guess I'll see you tonight. Are you cooking dinner, or should I pick something up?"

Dash walked over to the bed and kissed Ginger, "One night, and we're talking like an old married couple." Dash added, "I'll cook tonight. How does grilled salmon in a lemon caper sauce, spinach with balsamic vinegar, garlic mashed potatoes, and crème brûlée for dessert sound?"

Ginger got out of bed and smiled, "I like the menu, I like the digs, I like the man. This might be the beginning of something good."

Ginger showered, dressed, and headed out the door. Dash asked her to call him when she left her house. She agreed that it would be a good idea.

At around nine-thirty, Dash got a call from Ginger.

"Everything okay?" Dash asked.

"Not really, but don't be alarmed. It looks like somebody tried to break into my house after all."

"What? How, how do you know?" Dash blurted.

"The side door that leads to my garage has been busted—there's a hole in the door where the doorknob used to be. Unfortunately, no camera on that side of the house."

Dash was alarmed, "Did they take anything?"

"Not that I could tell. I have to get to work—see you tonight. I'm looking forward to that salmon."

Dash got dressed, got into his car, taking the liberty to check out Ginger's house. He got there before eleven, saw the broken door, walked into the garage, surveyed the garage, and noticed that no attempt had been made to break into the house door from the garage. The garage door was relatively easy to go through. The doorknob and lock were standard Home Depot fare. The garage was empty except for ski equipment, bikes, gardening tools, storage boxes, with miscellaneous household stuff and wine, lots of wine. She had at least forty cases of wine, unpacked, mostly Jasper Wines and some other local wines—she probably got on industry discount. Perhaps, someone at Jasper was attempting to find cause for termination. She may have earned the wine for good performance or bought it at a discount. A case of the top Jasper Bordeaux blend would go for fifteen hundred dollars at discount, and she had ten cases. The signature Cabernet would go for a thousand a case, and she had twenty cases. She also had some other notable Cabernets from local wineries and a case of Saxum Rhone blend. Dash figured she had at least fifty thousand dollars in wine in her garage. Dash got thirsty just looking at all the premium wine.

There were stored improperly—should be stored in a temperature-controlled environment. He would have that conversation with her later.

He texted her at the winery with a wine case count. She texted right back, saying she only had about five cases of wine in the garage and only one case of Jasper. Dash texted back, "You're being set up."

Dash could not call Jasper directly, but he did call Detective Evans, telling him that there had been a break-in at Ginger Rute's house and that evidence had been deposited. Detective Evans said he didn't have time for this nonsense, but he'd send an officer over to look at break-in. The officer came over in an hour, took photos, a report, and was gone in ten minutes.

Ginger was now sleeping with the enemy.

Chapter Thirty-Five:

ESTRELLA DISTRICT

Ginger didn't lose her job. The wine was returned, along with a police report about the break-in given to Jasper Wines. Jasper Winery management didn't act overly alarmed. Ginger was confused by their reaction. Either they didn't want to take action, or they were involved in a cover-up. Ginger returned To Dash's hacienda that night after another stressful day.

Between the two of them, they drank a bottle of 2016 Etude Carneros Chardonnay and a bottle of 2016 Denner Viognier, that Dash had purloined from Ginger's garage, with her consent, to go with the salmon. After dinner, they watched a movie on Netflix. The tension in the air made for rambunctious lovemaking, including role-playing, which Ginger was adept at. She loved being seduced, then taking control.

Dash was new to role-playing, but he couldn't resist her passion. When she took control, Dash had to take the uncomfortable submissive role. Then she'd work her magic. She would tell Dash to undress, take a deep breath, and relax. He found it hard to relax under the circumstances. Then she applied coconut oil all over him, massaging him. He had to disguise his winces when she exerted pressure on his muscles and quell his pain when she dug deep into the tissue. Dash has had many massages in the past but never one where the masseuse didn't hold back. She worked out the kinks and stress replacing them with a soothing soreness. He'd never met a woman quite like Ginger.

"Where did you learn your massage technique? I haven't felt this worked over since freshman football practice," Dash asked. "I'm envious of your instructors."

"A master never betrays her mentors," Ginger smiled.

"You're correct, a woman never talks, nor should a man. Are we talking about massage instructors or lovers? Dash asked.

"Both. You should just be grateful that I've had wonderful lovers and instructors. You're just okay," Ginger laughed, "You'll do until I find someone better."

Dash was chagrined, "I'm a willing student. This old dog relishes learning new tricks."

Ginger smiled, "Attitude is ninety percent of lovemaking. The rest is just technique."

The next day, Tuesday, was City Council day and Dash was in attendance. The big development, Santa Rosa Ranch, which had previously been approved unanimously, brought another topic to the forefront: the allocation of water, and the status of 505,000 acres of the Great Oaks aquifer, among the largest on the West Coast. The Great Oaks aquifer was never mentioned in the previous meeting. It was literally the two-thousand-pound gorilla sitting on the council's bench. The discussion was about the status of the creation of a regional Estrella Water Board, which would circumvent the County and State water boards. Dash knew from the earlier meeting who was behind it and why. In the prior City Council meeting, the council recommended that they support the new water district when it appears on the ballot.

This was about controlling the million-year-old aquifer. Dash only came to see who was present and why the Estrella Water District was on the agenda. The City Council already stood behind the formation of a new water district. When the district came up for discussion, it was Bill Lyons who spoke. His winery and vineyards would be in the proposed new water district. Bill spoke about how the formation of the new water district would be vital to the east side wineries and homeowners. He spoke about the dry wells, climate change, extended droughts, and the vitality of the wine industry for the local economy and tourism.

Dash listened as Bill Lyons droned on about the Estrella Water District as a preventive measure and insurance for the future. He thanked the City Council for their support, saying he would like to introduce a measure that would circumvent the electoral process, letting the City Council rule on the measure. He brought up that the Water District would encompass unincorporated county lands and would have to be approved by the county supervisors.

Dash was intrigued. How in hell were they, Vino Veritas Investment Group, going to get this measure to fly?

Bill Lyons was prepared. He introduced former city planner and attorney, Samuel J. Dotson, who advised the City Council that it was perfectly legal for them to create a Water District without an election. The measure would have to have to go through the process of public hearings, environmental reviews, and the State Water Board. Mr. Dotson said that time is of the essence. He said the cycle of two wet years followed by five drought years is a precarious situation. The next time we're in a drought, the state would come in and try to manage our water and the aquifer. This was the first time that the Great Oaks aquifer had been mentioned.

The board did not vote or respond to Sam Dotson's and Bill Lyon's proposed measure to circumvent the election process, nor were there any expressions on their faces. Dash knew that the lack of expression meant that the measure had already been secretly discussed and lauded. This, in itself, was illegal to discuss public matters among the Council members outside of the chambers. After the hearing Dash, was curious about one matter in particular.

He approached Rex Beckett and Bill Lyons while their attorney, Sam Dotson, hobnobbed with local press. Dash approached the group standing just outside the city council chamber and directed his question to Rex Beckett. Dash knew that print media reports were in earshot.

"Hello, my name is Dash Ramblar, and I'm a concerned citizen. I'm well aware of your machinations concerning the aquifer. Don't you think the public should have the opportunity to vote on the Estrella Water District? It is their water. One other question. Is your attorney related to Dylan Dotson?"

Rex Beckett didn't want to talk to Dash, but he was in a public setting, so he had to be halfway civil. "Proudly yes, he's his son. Dylan owns a large vineyard management company. As pertains to the Estrella Water District—as we said in the meeting—local ownership will protect the community from outside interests who do not live here and couldn't give a damn about the health and safety of the water supply."

Dash smiled, "Mr. Beckett, aren't you from Orange County? You live in Newport Beach. You could give a rat's ass about the residents of Great Oaks."

Rex Beckett pretended not to hear the last statement and strode away with his partners. The trio: Sam Dotson, Rex Beckett, and Bill Lyons huddles in muted conversation.

Claudia Bowers would be proud of Dash. He was asking the question she's asked under similar circumstances. Dash was not a natural activist—he knew Claudia was better suited and easier to look at then himself—but he had to speak out.

Dash realized again what a small town Great Oaks was, where everyone is connected. Dylan Dotson may need a good attorney soon, and having a father in the profession should help. There existed a straight line between

Dylan Dotson and the Vino Veritas Investment Group. If Vino Veritas had some dirty work to be performed, Dylan was the ideal candidate.

It was now up to Dash to connect the dots. He believed Dylan was an accessory to the murders of Claudia and Taylor. He knew both women socially and possibly through work. He did vineyard management work for Jasper Wines, and he probably did work for Bill Lyons. Dylan knew Rex Beckett and all the principals in Vino Veritas. He was Dash's number one suspect since Conrad had a bulletproof alibi, according to Detective Evans.

Dash thought Dylan Dotson had the temperament of a killer: short-tempered, narcissistic, entitled, rough-hewn personality, and vengeful. Dash couldn't think of a motive, and that was the missing link.

After the City Council meeting, Dash went home. Ginger was there. She made a three-cheese lasagna with ground lamb and ground beef combined with freshly picked chanterelle mushrooms. They opened a robust 2015 Castoro Cellars Primitivo, that paired perfectly with the lasagna and the anchovy laden Caesar salad. Ginger was in a fabulous mood. They found out that Dylan Dotson had planted the wine in her garage, and Jasper Wines terminated his labor contract with the winery. Dash was worried about retribution, but Ginger wasn't concerned. The owner's son, Gregg Perigold, told Ginger that they informed Dylan Dotson that any attempt to harass Ginger would be met with legal action. Dylan signed a non-disclosure statement that protected Dylan from losing work with other wineries.

Dash was not so certain. While Ginger made the Caesar salad, he went to his gun locker and took out his Glock pistol, put bullets in the chamber, and hid it in a planter just outside the bedroom door which led outside. They finished dinner without interruption, played some Cuban music, and fondled each other like teenagers.

Dash interrupted the flow of the evening by bringing up Dylan's father, Sam Dotson.

"Did you know that Dylan's father, Sam, is a prominent local attorney who represents Vino Veritas and the Estrella Water District?" Dash asked.

"What is the Estrella Water District?" Ginger asked.

"I'm sorry. I didn't fully update you on the City Council meeting. They're forming a new water district, ostensibly to protect local water rights. But it's a grand scheme to secure water for future developments, and to tap into the Great Oaks aquifer."

Ginger was amazingly informed, "Outside groups have been trying to tap into that aquifer for years. It's illegal, but they will keep trying. You may think the Perigolds are behind this, but I think this is below them. They have more water credits in the San Joaquin Valley than any entity. That's where the big water and big money are. The state of California has paid the Perigolds millions to buy the water back."

"Then who's behind this?" Dash asked.

"Developers from Orange County, outliers—they're new to the game. They want the water action, and they know the Central Coast is the new Orange County," Ginger said with surprising clarity.

Dash was intrigued, "What do you mean?"

"I grew up in Orange County when it was just orange groves, beach towns, Disneyland, and some shopping malls. Now it's a metropolis with millions of people, and the folks that developed those orange groves are all multi-millionaires. They see the same scenario playing out here. I don't see it happening here—people are too informed, too connected to the land, too mindful, and too patient to let a group of developers from down south run roughshod over the locals," Ginger said.

Dash exhaled, "Let's hope so, but money talks, and it was apparent that the City Council is already on the payroll of Vino Veritas. Who's going to stop them?"

"Us." Ginger smiled and placed her hand on Dash's chest. It was the end of the conversation and the end of the evening. They retired to the bedroom to let the Primitivo work its wonders.

Dash asked Ginger on the journey to the bedroom, "What roles are we playing tonight?"

"You're a big bad developer from Orange County, and I'm a shy farm girl from Great Oaks," Ginger laughed. "Just kidding, we're playing ourselves—just two adults falling in love."

Dash was relieved, "I can play that part."

Ginger left early the next day because she had to drop her car off for servicing. Dash picked up the house and enjoyed a rare sunny morning in early March. All seemed right with his world, but all was not right until justice was served.

Justice for Claudia and Taylor was slipping farther away every day. Justice is a rare commodity when we have a two-tiered society. Justice is quicker for the upper class and slow, if not non-existent, for the lower class. Well-meaning, new-age folks cite karma as the great equalizer. Yet, karma works better in Hindu countries where everyone believes it than in America, where materialism is the religion. If you have more stuff, then you have good karma. If you have less, then apparently you suffer from bad karma.

Vino Veritas was not exempt from justice or karma, but it is an entity that thrives on the notion that small-town politicians will grease the skids for you. If you combine power players with financial gain, everybody wins, except for the folks who get in the way of progress.

The Hamster will go down as collateral damage—a forgotten homeless guy caught in the crosshairs. Claudia and Taylor knew too much but were not a threat. Why were they eliminated and their murders staged to look like the work of a serial killer?

Ginger used the royal "We" when she said we are going to stop the freight train of injustice perpetrated upon The Wine Sisters. She had more confidence than Dash. Sometimes the best remedy is sunshine. Dash went outside and began pruning his vineyard. It would take days, but it was food for the soul. Two years earlier, he had severely cut back the vines because they were in bad shape. Now that they were healthier, Dash was sculpting the shoulder canes for the trellising. It was an old art form. He soon grew fatigued. Just in time for lunch and a glass of white wine, Albarino. A sweet reward for two hours of labor. This was precisely the work that Dylan Dotson's crews did. During the spring, his workers would be in high demand, and he could make a small fortune in a short time.

Dylan's crews were working, and Dylan was playing. Or was he?

Dylan seemed to have little loyalty to anyone. Perhaps his real loyalty was with to his father Sam, the attorney for Vino Veritas, who probably had a stake in future developments. Normally this is called equity compensation, and it could mean a huge payout for a small-town attorney, like Samuel J. Dotson.

He once had a small office across the street from the Ranch and Farm Real Estate office.

The cement step and stoop that The Hamster favored had been the entry to Sam's office. Dotson recently moved his office to a fancier address on the square. Sam had one employee, a legal assistant, Becky Jensen. Dash went on Yelp and other online customer feedback services and found out about a dozen comments on Dotson's practice. The comments were generally good, mentioning favorable outcomes and reasonable fees.

The comments suggested that the clients were small and not sophisticated—DUI's and divorces. Vino Veritas could be Sam Dotson's ticket to the lifestyle he dreamed of.

Dash believed there were no such things as coincidences.

Chapter Thirty-Six:

RIVERBED MURDERS

Dash got a call from Ginger at work after hours. She sounded a bit stressed.

"I'm calling because I won't be coming to your place tonight. Something has come up."

"Is everything okay?" Dash pressed.

"Not really. Dylan showed up here, and he attempted to talk to me. Security intercepted him—he's now in police custody. I'm here with your friend Detective FJ Evans. He says hi."

Dash was uncomfortable being on the outside looking in, "Tell him, hi for me. Where are you spending the night?"

"That's a stupid question. At my home. Where else would I spend it, if not with you?" Ginger asked, obviously agitated.

"Do you want me to come over to your house? Do you feel safe?" Dash asked.

Ginger got impatient, "No, no, you don't understand. It was our relationship that's created this mess—I have to rethink it. It's spilled over to my workplace, to security, and now to the police. I just want to go home, drink a bottle of wine by myself, and try to get my life back. I do feel safer now that Dylan is in police custody."

Dash was not happy, "Put Detective Evans on the phone. I have some concerns."

She said okay, and she handed her cell phone to Detective Evans, "What do you want?"

"I want to make certain that Ginger is out of harm's way. I want to make certain that you don't release Dylan tonight," Dash said.

Detective Evans was audibly sarcastic, "She's safe. Number one, because she's away from you, and number two, because Dylan will spend the night with no bail hearing until tomorrow morning. We're not done with him." He ended the call.

Dash did what he did when he was out of sorts. He went to his computer, clicked on to the NY Times crossword icon, and proceeded to do a couple of mini-crossword puzzles. After that, he turned on the television to see if there were any local news stories regarding the murders. The lead story was the wet and blustery weather, a couple of playoff sports stories, but no mention of the investigation. People watch the local news for weather and sports—not for hard news. There was no mention of an arrest in the Great Oaks murders (now referred to as the "The Riverbed Murders") because the victim's bodies were dumped in the overgrown riverbed of the Salinas River.

The police did not refer to the murders of Claudia and Taylor as serial murders because they didn't want to alarm the public. They spun a backstory indicating that the women were part of The Wine Sisters group who socialized with each other. The city police chief believed that the murders were related, indicating that it could have been a love triangle gone terribly wrong—a curious take on the murders.

Dash was amused that the police agreed with his theory that the murders were related. However, the local police wanted to connect the murders, so as not to add to the speculation that a wild-eyed woman killer was on the loose. Dash believed that originally Claudia was the only target until it was determined that Taylor was Claudia's confidant.

Dash called Ginger at her home to check up her. She was calmed down and more affectionate.

"I'm sorry I blamed you for my issues at work. After the police left, Gregg Perigold came into the tasting room, opened Jasper's premium estate Cabernet, and poured everyone still working in the tasting room a glass. Gregg thanked us for remaining calm. He said that Dylan Dotson had been terminated and that a restraining order had been issued against him. Gregg stated that all contract workers would be given a set of behavior guidelines. Gregg added that there was zero tolerance for harassment of any type on the premises or at any of his vineyards.

Dash and Ginger exchanged pleasantries. Then she said that she would be moving back home because Dylan was now in custody.

On the following morning, Dash heard from Detective Evans.

"I need you to come down to the station to corroborate some evidence. We believe that Dylan Dotson was involved with the murders—his DNA matched what we found on the rope."

Dash got dressed, putting on a tightly woven wool sweater and down vest, and headed for the station on a cold foggy morning. The cold, damp mornings belied the fact that spring was around the corner. Dash found parking near the big brick police station. Detective Evans greeted him with coffee from their new Keurig machine. Dash took one sip, never taking another. He associated Keurig machines with medical offices and quick lube waiting rooms.

"Okay, what do you want me to corroborate?" Dash asked Detective Evans, who looked old and tired: dark bags under his eyes, his belly hanging over his belt, his shoulders rounded, and his back bent. Dash remembered him when he had decent posture. Dash flinched when he got close to him. He smelled old. His breath was hideous, smelling of tobacco, coffee, and stale donuts.

"You look like shit," Dash laughed. "The Feds must be putting you through hell."

"Forget what I look like. I haven't slept well in weeks, my gout is killing me, and my wife had to sleep in the other room because of my snoring and farting—sounds romantic?" Evans asked.

Evans got to business, "I need you to corroborate your positive identification of Dylan's truck at the dog park where Taylor was apprehended and that he fits the description Pedro gave you in San Miguel. Also, I need you to verify that you found the wine in Ginger's garage and that he has been harassing you since you began looking into the murders."

"How do you know about his truck matching the one at the dog park? I never mentioned it to you," Dash asked. "I got the description from an elderly woman who frequented the dog park when Taylor did. I believe she'll testify to that truck description. Dylan's description fits the one that was given to me by The Hamster. Pedro keeps changing the identities of the murderers—I think he's terrified of the consequence. I can testify to the wine in the garage—I have documented the instances of harassment." Dash did not want his testimony to carry the case.

"Dylan said they had four trucks that look like the one you described. What an idiot! We never brought up the dog park or the truck—he brought it up. We checked. They have a camera in the dog park parking lot. It showed his truck there several times. Unfortunately, the day Taylor was apprehended, his truck and her car were out of camera sight. It was dusk anyway."

"You have positively identified his DNA. You have his truck spotted in the parking lot at the dog park. You know that he knew Claudia and Taylor—so what's his motive?" Dash asked.

"That's why I brought you here today." Detective Evans continued, "We don't have enough evidence to arrest him or hold him. We need something else to hang our hat on."

Dash stood up from the conference table they were sitting at and took the terrible coffee to the sink and poured it out. He took a small bottle of water, twisted off the top, and drank. He returned to the table.

"Okay, when I was at the City Council meeting the other night, Dylan's father, Sam Dotson, was presenting for Vino Veritas out of Orange County. The City Council was in lockstep with these developers' motion to create a new water district—Estrella Water District. If you want motive, look no farther than the city fathers. They're not going to backpedal on the water district plan, and they're not going to play ball with you regarding Sam's son. In fact, I think they'll dig in, circle the wagons and fight you to the bitter end on Sam Dotson's son conviction. You can bet on it. There, I've butchered the English language with half a dozen tired metaphors. When do you release Dylan?"

"Bail for harassment is low—he'll be out by noon, today," Detective Evans said.

"What about Ginger?" Dash asked.

"She'll be okay. He has been given strict orders not to go around either her or Jasper Winery. He has too many jobs pending to blow it now. He'll need the money down the road."

"What's your plan, detective?" Dash asked sarcastically.

"Our plan is to build a case against Dylan Dotson. Murder in the first degree, two counts."

Dash threw the plastic water container in the trash and shook Detective Evans's hand.

"Good luck. I believe you've got the right man. When you've got a half dozen billionaires and millionaires on the other side of the table, your odds are pretty slim for conviction."

Detective Evans looked even worse when he left. Dash called Ginger and told her that Dylan was going to be released at noon. He told her that she was more than welcome to bunk at his place.

"I'll bring some champagne," Ginger said.

"What are we celebrating?" Dash asked.

"I've been made manager of the tasting room. Jasper Wine Estates opened a new tasting room downtown, and they want me to manage it. It's a great opportunity, and I won't have to drive forty minutes to work every day on winding roads."

Dash was pleased, "Mazel Tov!"

The day was long for Dash. He was concerned that Dylan, on the ropes, would do something reckless. He imaged the worst scenario; Dylan getting out of jail on bail, going to Jasper Winery, waiting for Ginger to come out to the parking lot after work. Dash knew that he had twice-before abducted women in, or near, their vehicles. Dash took no chance and drove out to Jasper Winery—arriving at four-thirty. He parked his car at the rear of the parking lot along the entrance road so he could have a good view of the vehicles coming and going. He opened his driver's side window, smelling the hedgerow of blooming purple rosemary. The air was fresh and sweet.

His suspicion was correct. At four-fifty-five, a dark grey Dodge Ram truck with a lifted body parked just outside the parking lot. As soon as Dash saw Dylan's truck, he called Detective Evans and left a message, "Dylan Dotson is at Jasper Winery, now." Dylan's truck was too recognizable to enter the lot. A few minutes after five, the employees departed work, got into their vehicles, and headed home. Ginger's was among the last vehicles to leave the parking lot. She drove out the exit lane and fortunately did not see Dash's vintage Range Rover. Dash started his car driving three hundred yards up Jasper's private road when he saw Ginger's Volkswagen Jetta parked along the road with Dylan's truck in front of her. He either had motioned for her to pull off the road, or he had forced her off the road. Either way, she was in immediate danger.

Dash pulled out his Glock pistol, clicked off the safety, and ran towards Dylan's truck. He arrived just as Dylan was threatening Ginger, coercing her to get into his truck. She had better sense than to obey and was retreating to her car, as Dylan waved his gun at her. Dash ran to her side, pointing his Glock at Dylan, who was just fifteen yards away. Dash motioned for Ginger to stand behind him as he spoke to Dylan.

"You're making a big mistake coming here. Don't move any closer," Dash used a law enforcement voice.

Dylan laughed, "What are you going to do, old man, shoot me? You don't have the balls." Dylan pointed his gun at Dash. Dash could tell Dylan had either been drinking or smoking weednew he was jittery.

Dylan shot wildly at Dash, missing everything. Sparks flew from the road where is bullets landed on the gravel. "That was a warning."

Dylan panicked. He walked back to his truck, got in, started the engine, and roared down the private road to the main road. He didn't get far. Police cars were waiting for him at the private road entrance. The big steel gate was closed to the main highway. Dylan surrendered.

Dylan was taken into custody and was booked on several charges, not the least of which was threatening bodily harm to Ginger with a firearm and attempted kidnapping—all felony charges. He was held without bail because he had broken his earlier bail agreement.

It was nearly eight when Dash and Ginger arrived at Dash's house. They were exhausted but managed to drink the Champagne. It was Jasper's best dry Champagne, a California Burgundian sparkling wine.

Dash lifted his empty glass, "It's not Dom Perignon, but it'll do."

"You're not James Bond, but you'll do," Ginger quipped.

Chapter Thirty-Seven:

PEDRO MENDOZA

Dylan's arrest begged the question: Who was his accomplice? The Hamster and his traveling buddy Pedro both claimed there was a second person. The Hamster described someone who looked like Conrad Cook: overweight, spiked bleached blond hair, and wearing a Hawaiian print shirt. Pedro described someone more fit. It was obvious to Dash that it would take two individuals, if not more, to pull off these murders. That's not to say that Dylan Dotson wasn't capable of single-handedly murdering Claudia Bowers and Taylor Thorngate. Still, there was no clear motive in the killings. These were the ruminations of Dash Ramblar.

Dash had never seen Ginger happier. After a career as a flight attendant for Alaska Airlines, the tasting room at Jasper was to be a respite now that she was elevated to management, she had a boyfriend of sorts.

Dash could make her laugh. He was not a good bet for the long term, but in the short term, he was just fine. Her reputation had been salvaged, she was out of danger, and she was a reliable source. Dash delivered coffee to Ginger in bed on a Friday morning. It was her last day driving out to the winery. She would open the new tasting room downtown on Monday.

Ginger took the coffee happily, pulling the covers up, "Coffee in bed, you are trainable."

Dash did his best waiter imitation, standing erect and clicking his heels, "My pleasure, madam. Is there anything else I can bring you?"

"For starters, you can get yourself a cup of coffee and join me," Ginger patted the bed and pulled the covers back, revealing her naked torso.

"I've already had two cups. I'll need a shot of brandy to calm my racing heart." Dash scurried back to the pantry for a bottle of brandy and one large balloon cognac glass.

The mornings were getting warmer as the month of March marched on. All things purple and yellow were blooming: the yellow daffodils, the Shasta daisies, the poppies, the purple irises, the lavender rosemary, and the cobalt blue California lilacs, ceanothus.

After a leisurely romp, they retired to the kitchen table. Dash was in a surprisingly talkative mood.

"Would you consider joining The Wine Sisters?" Dash asked, "You know some of the members, and since you're going to be working downtown, it would be an excellent networking opportunity to launch the new tasting room."

"It's a good idea, but you always have an ulterior motive. I've thought of joining Rotary. All the movers and shakers downtown belong."

"Busted again, I'd love to hear The Wine Sister's perspective on the murders," Dash said. "As far as the Rotary goes, maybe, but the burgermeisters are a little too staid for my taste."

"First off, I'm not going to be your mole, and I wouldn't repeat anything another woman said to me in confidence. Secondly, I like staid men. They're usually wild once their ties and starched shirts come off."

After Ginger headed to work, Dash called Mona Morgan. He told her about Ginger's Rute's new position at Jasper, and that she was interested in socializing with The Wine Sisters.

Mona said, "We meet next Wednesday for lunch. I would love to bring Ginger as my guest. She would be a good fit. Have Ginger call me."

"Will do," answered Dash.

Dash had a free day, and he chose to make the trek to San Miguel to find Pedro. He wanted a clearer description of the second suspect. He drove up on a cool sunny day. The hillsides were psychedelic green, the fruit trees had clusters of pink blossoms, with nary a cloud in the sky. Dash turned on his Bluetooth system and listened to a mix of country music, opera, and Euro-disco synthesizer. He was in a disjointed mood: euphoric, blue, and chill.

He went back to the same Dollar Store meeting with the same clerk, Cyle, but not getting the response he desired.

Cyle responded to Dash's inquiry, "Haven't seen Pedro since the last time you were here. He's disappeared."

"Do you know anyone who might know where he is?" Dash asked.

"His girlfriend, Cecelia, drops by for a six-pack on occasion. I'd check Rudy's Bar down the street. I think she's a day time drinker."

Dash laughed, "I didn't know there was a difference."

The bar was full. It was too early for St. Patrick's Day, and there wasn't a person of Irish descent in the bar. Rudy's reflected the town demographics: ninety percent Hispanic and ten percent ex-cons. There were half a dozen women playing pool, drinking at the bar, and socializing. It was not a pick-up scene. The women were treated with deference. In the Hispanic culture, mature women were treated with great respect.

Dash went to the bartender, who had a shaved head and some prison quality tattoos. San Miguel was only a hundred miles south of Soledad State Prison. San Miguel was the cheapest place to live south of Soledad on the coast. Dash handed the bartender a ten-dollar bill and asked if he'd seen Cecelia.

"That was easy money," the bartender laughed, "That's her playing pool." He motioned his head towards the only pool table in the joint.

Dash went over to the pool table, putting a five-dollar bill on the table, "I'm up next."

Cecelia laughed, "Put your money away Gringo—we're playing just to pass the time. You can play me—he's gotta' go back to work." She looked at the other player who looked like a shorter version of Pedro."

The player took the hint, gathered his coat, and settled up with the barkeep then left. Dash introduced himself, "I'm Dash. What's your name?"

"Don't give me that bullshit, you know who I am. I heard you ask for me—you want to know where Pedro is, don't you? You're the gringo that buys him cigarettes. I saw you when I was waiting for him in my car. You're responsible for him going to jail for that outstanding warrant—what a fucking tool. I should have you thrown out, but I want to take a little of your money first."

She racked the billiard balls and handed Dash her pool cue. "This is the only decent one—the others are all banged up."

Cecelia was in her early forties, still attractive, but on the downhill slope. She wore too much mascara, her lipstick was too red, and her hair was dyed too black. She had a decent figure, a broad mischievous smile— the kind of sex appeal that sneaks up on you.

"So, where is he?" Dash asked after he broke the table. None of the balls dropped in a pocket. He handed Cecelia back the cue.

"I think he went back to Mexico. He's got a condominium down in San José del Cabo, that his buddy The Hamster left to him."

"Living large. Why didn't he take you with him?" Dash asked.

"He doesn't ever take me with him—he says it's like taking sand to the beach." Anyway, I've got kids here to take care of. He'll come back looking for me; I'm his American wife." Cecelia proceeded to drop five billiard balls in a row and left the cue ball just an inch from the corner.

"We didn't decide how much we're playing for," Dash smiled. "So if I went down to Cabo, could I find him?" Cecelia put another two balls in the pockets and handed Dash back the cue. "One hundred dollars. I don't know the exact address, but it's at a fancy place called La Profundo Mar Azul." He says it sits right on the Sea of Cortez. Good luck finding him—I think he's worried that he'll end up like The Hamster," she said, looking up at Dash from the pool table.

"Why is that?" Dash asked.

"You wouldn't be looking for him if you didn't know the answer. Everyone is looking for him. Do you think you're the only gringo looking for him?"

"Who else?" Dash asked.

"Guys in nice suits—younger than you—better looking," Cecelia laughed. "You're all right looking—too skinny for me. I like a man with a little meat around the middle—a life raft so I won't fall out of bed."

"I'll take that as a compliment," Dash smiled. "So, give me a better description of the guys in suits." Dash handed Cecelia five twenty-dollar bills, "That should cover the bet."

She took the money, "You like throwing money around. Not a good idea here. You might not make it out of the parking lot. Those guys were not really in suits, just nicely dressed, pressed shirts and pants—lots of starch. Two guys, both on the tall side—both with dark hair. One guy had a messed-up hand."

"What did you mean—'messed up'?" Dash asked.

"Bandaged up like he cut it bad. Not broke. No cast." Cecelia lifted one hand to illustrate. "He had a bad attitude. The other guy was laughing and kidding him. "

"Did you get a name?"

"No, but the way they talked, they weren't from here."

"How did they talk?" Dash asked.

"You know, like Southern California rich guys," Cecelia answered, looking around the bar furtively. "Do you want to play another game, same bet? My kids are coming home from school soon."

Dash thanked her, and he left before she did. She had already racked up the balls and found another guy to play with. She wasn't going home anytime soon.

Dash drove home listening to Bach on Pandora, trying to calm his thoughts, getting a picture of the two new suspects in his head. Southern California rich guys is not a clear description of anyone, other than gender, race, and spoken vernacular. Hearing a generalized description of a white man is a fair turnabout for a Latina who gets typecast constantly.

Rex Beckett had a bandaged hand. Dash couldn't see him going to dive bars in San Miguel to locate Pedro unless he thought he could get him to yield. If indeed Rex Beckett was searching for Pedro, then Pedro was now in the crosshairs.

Descriptions based on gender and race tend to be vague and generalized. Someone that laughs is perceived to be happy. Someone who doesn't smile has a "bad attitude."

The prime suspect, Dylan Dotson, was in jail. Other suspects were working the back channels to make certain that no new information emerges. Pedro was smart to go to Mexico.

Before he had arrived home, Dash had made a reservation to fly out the next day to San José del Cabo and find Pedro. He bought a one-way ticket. There were some cool courtyard hotels in downtown San José. Too small to book online, he'd find a room when he got there.

Dash turned on the radio, heard the song "Ventura Highway," and cranked up the volume.

Chapter Thirty-Eight:

BAJA CALIFORNIA

When Dash got off the plane in Baja, smelling the redolent air, breathing in the warmth, gazing upon the sun-drenched mountains, and hearing the gaiety of the Spanish language, his heart brightened. Dash then had to get through the gauntlet of timeshare hawkers at the San José airport to locate a cab into town.

San José del Cabo is less glitzy then Cabo San Lucas to the south, and definitely more authentic. A large church and plaza make up the center of town, surrounded by restaurants, bars, and curio shops. An art district has formed just blocks from the main plaza where many American ex-pats reside operating galleries in the area. Dash found a small courtyard hotel just eight blocks from the plaza. It was rundown, clean, tired, warm and its charm was its humility. Dash just wanted to lie down on the bed, open the wood shutters on to the street, and watch the overhead fan rotate. It wasn't going to happen today. He had to locate Pedro.

He took a taxi to the La Profundo Mar Azul Resort. The taxi cab driver called it "Mar Azul San José." Dash figured every beach town in Mexico had a Mar Azul Resort. Dash thought about the absurdity of looking for a man knowing only his first name and living in a condo owned by a man known only as The Hamster. There was something about that absurdity that enlivened Dash. A wild goose chase was better than a caged chicken hunt. The resort was as expected. The entry was notable. You arrived at valet parking, walked up half a dozen stairs to a large arched entry. The main lobby looked directly out to the Sea of Cortez—a completely unobstructed and awe-inspiring view. Dash found a bar just past the reception area and settled into his first mojito. Rum is only drinkable in Mexico, Key West, or Cuba. Bartenders also might know Pedro by his nickname, Pepe.

After his mojito was delivered, he gave the bartender a ten-dollar tip asking him if he knew a Filipino man named Pedro, or Pepe, who arrived two weeks ago.

The bartender took the money, "Everybody in San José is named Pedro or Pepe. Filipinos look like Mexicans?" The bartender's sarcasm was barely inauspicious to the weary traveler.

Dash put down an additional twenty-dollar bill, "Pedro speaks Spanish, but not Mexican Spanish—he has almond-shaped eyes. You might mistake him for Asian." Dash returned with scant sarcasm.

"I work here twelve years. I see everybody from everywhere—only your President can't tell the difference," the bartender grinned.

Dash smiled, "So, do you know him? Pedro, the Filipino?"

"Everybody does—he smokes all day, Lucky Strikes—flirts with everyone. He smells like an ashtray—bad tipper."

Dash was delighted, "So where can I find smoky Pedro?"

The bartender was beginning to warm up to Dash, "Not until tomorrow morning. He drinks a beer for breakfast then takes a walk on the beach. No one sees him until the next morning. I think he's hiding. Are you with the Federales?"

Dash laughed, "No, I'm a tourist. We have a mutual friend—I'm trying to track him down."

The bartender made him another mojito on the house, "Be here at seven in the morning. By seven-thirty, he's gone."

Dash had not eaten or showered since he'd arrived in Cabo. He bought a bathing suit and towel at the resort gift shop, then headed for the pool changing rooms. Within minutes, he was swimming in the Sea of Cortez and later, lounging by the pool. He ordered ceviche, made with fresh marlin, accompanied by a bottle of Modelo Especial, with the anticipated effect of a restorative nap. When he awoke, he had no idea where he was. It took him a couple of minutes to realize he was in paradise—he didn't even have to die. He changed back into his clothes, took a taxi back to San José del Cabo, and had dinner at Mi Casa, devouring chicken enchiladas in their renowned mole sauce. The mole sauce is cocoa-based and has the sweet chalky taste of chocolate made piquant with the addition of spices. The mole sauce in America never tastes quite like it does in Mexico. He walked back to his small hotel, set his phone alarm to six, and slept like a reptile under a hot rock.

He made it back to the resort by seven the next morning with a couple of minutes to spare. Dash walked to the outdoor café overlooking the pool and the sea. A light breeze coming off the sea delivered the subtle smell of its inhabitants. The waiters all wore white with colorful sashes. It was a morning of sunshine, warmth, relaxation, and gratitude. Dash immediately recognized Pedro, clean-shaven, wearing a golf hat, looking like a prosperous man of leisure. He ordered "huevos rancheros" with the self-assurance of somebody with a roll of cash in their pocket. Dash was the only person to know that Pedro was basically homeless and destitute prior to meeting The Hamster.

When Dash approached the table, Pedro panicked.

Dash motioned for him to relax, "I'm not here to harm you. Cecilia told me where to find you. No one else knows."

Pedro was not amused, "I told that bitch not to talk to anyone."

Dash spoke in a calm voice, "She only told me because she's concerned for your safety."

A waiter brought Pedro a big breakfast of huevos rancheros with fresh avocado and orange juice with a slice of lime. Dash told the waiter to order him the same breakfast. The waiter asked if he wanted the Tequila Sunrise too. Dash nodded.

Pedro looked at Dash in disbelief. "You show up here—sit at my table—order my breakfast. What next?"

Dash tried to put Pedro at ease. He poured himself a cup of coffee.

"I know you're in danger. Cecilia told me that two men came looking for you. She didn't tell them where you went. I've come here to get a positive identity on the men you saw in the riverbed the day before Claudia Bowers was murdered. They have one man in custody, thirty-five years old. His name is Dylan Dotson. Do you know him?"

Pedro was not convinced, "I'm not telling you anything, mister. After The Hamster got killed, you showed up in San Miquel. Then they showed up. I said too much already. My vacation is done—I'm gonna' have to leave here now. Your friends will find me and cut my throat."

"They're not my friends—describe them to me. No one has followed me here. You're not in any danger—you're in the clear," Dash said.

Dash's breakfast came. He devoured it. Something about Mexico, maybe the humidity, gave him a big appetite. Pedro picked at his food, looking over his shoulder like he expected to be taken out at any second.

"Your friends, the gringos—not cops—had on expensive shoes. I always look at the shoes." He looked down at Dash's canvas boat shoes, "You got on vacation shoes. Those fellas— they were all business. They wanted to know what The Hamster knew. I told them. I know nothing, and The Hamster told me nothing. They didn't believe me. They told me they'd be back. I was on a plane to Cabo that night. Now you're here—I'm fucked."

Pedro took a long swallow of his tequila sunrise. He looked around the café. There were only the wait staff and a few older tourists.

"Were they fat, thin, tall, short, old, young—anything you can tell me?" Dash asked.

"You really don't know who they are?" Pedro grinned. "I could tell you anything—you'd believe me. Wouldn't you?"

"That's why I'm down here. I was hired to find Claudia's killers. You and The Hamster are the only witnesses. Otherwise, they get a pass. Tell me this—do the fellas that showed up in San Miguel trying to get information look anything like the killers you saw on the riverbed?"

"You're not paying attention." Pedro ordered another tequila sunrise and lit up a cigarette even though signs that said No Fumar were posted everywhere. Pedro was more relaxed. "The killers were the odd couple: the young guy with the beard and the older guy with the baseball cap."

Dash raised his hands. "Hold on. First, I hear there's a big guy with blonde spikey hair wearing a Hawaiian shirt; then, you tell me there was a fit guy. Now you tell me about a baseball cap? We have the guy with the beard in custody. I just need to know who his accomplice was."

Pedro inhaled the cigarette smoke like it was his last, putting the cigarette butt on the tile floor, smashing it with his foot. "You mean the guy that canvassed the place with him or the guy that brought the body by himself?

"Are you saying there are now three suspects?" Dash was frustrated. "Let's start with the two suspects who left the rope casing the location. Can you describe them?"

"I told you two big guys, one with a beard in hoodies, jeans. They came when it was almost dark. I didn't get a good look at them."

"Did you see anyone else?" Dash asked.

"Yes and no. I saw them leave the body. They were dressed differently. It was dark."

"How were they dressed?" Dash asked.

"The older guy with the baseball cap was wearing a black leather jacket—the guy with the bandaged hand. The other guy, with the beard, had a watch cap pulled over his ears, dark sweater, dark pants."

"The Hamster talked about a guy in a Hawaiian shirt with spiked blonde hair. Did you see him?"

"He was talking about a different guy," Pedro answered

"What different guy?" Dash was exasperated.

"Guys that would take lunch break down at the riverbed park. He saw the same guys all summer. It was like their little getaway. They were workers. I never saw 'em. I never went near that park. The cops would patrol it. They left The Hamster alone."

"Why?"

"Because he gave them information—that's what he got him killed," Pedro answered.

Dash was curious. "Do you think the workers who had lunch at the park were the same guys who dumped the women's bodies?"

Pedro looked at him like he was stupid. "You're not paying attention—they were the same guys. They knew the riverbed; they hiked all over it. The Hamster told me all about them. We should have stayed in Mexico. We come back, and he gets his throat cut. I ain't going back."

"You won't testify if they're arrested?" Dash asked.

Pedro finished his Tequila Sunrise, laid down a five-hundred-peso bill, and headed out of the restaurant. "Them ain't common workers—they're connected to some powerful people. You're dead if you testify against 'em. I'm surprised they didn't get you yet." Pedro left at exactly seven-thirty before his next tequila sunrise arrived. Dash was left alone with remnants of cold tortillas, eggs, coffee, and a drink that was more tequila than sunrise. Dash would never get Pedro back to the Central Coast.

Dash relaxed the rest of the day, swimming, eating, drinking cervezas, dreaming of Ginger, and contemplating his next move. He called Ginger—she was okay. He flew home the next day.

Leaving Mexico was always hard for Dash. Work in America paid for the relaxation of Mexico, but you couldn't take it back with you. You left behind the beauty, the poverty, the music, the food, the crummy roads, the greywater smells, the native stoicism, the wisdom, the poetry, and the corruption when you boarded the flight home. Home was familiar—familiarity is contemptible, boring, and predictable.

Dash couldn't predict what awaited him.

Chapter Thirty-Nine:

SAM DOTSON

Dash was greeted by incessant March rains ensuring a "super bloom" on the Carrizo Plain in April. The fruit trees were laden with pink blossoms, the grass was a neon green, and the Salinas River was plump with runoff.

Ginger had returned home basking in the opening of the new Jasper Tasting Room in downtown Great Oaks. Her picture had appeared in the local weekly, and she'd been interviewed on a local radio show. She was busy, but not too busy to entertain Dash.

Dash called Detective FJ Evans the day after he arrived, telling him that he had narrowed the suspects to three individuals, one of whom was in custody, Dylan Dotson. Detective Evans told Dash that Dylan had been released on bail, and his restraining order was still in place. Detective Evans further said that they didn't have enough evidence to charge him with the murders.

Dash was incensed. "What about his damn DNA on the rope? His truck identified at the dog park? His weapon? His threats to Ginger? You said he was arrested on multiple felony charges. Who got to you?"

Detective Evans wasn't taking the abuse from Dash, "I told you. We've dropped the charges—not enough evidence. Ginger said she wouldn't press charges—same with Jasper Winery."

Dash got in his last lick, "Very tidy work detective. You've got the killer in custody. You get a couple of calls and bingo. It won't make your retirement any sweeter knowing you let the bastard go free."

Dash did manual labor when he was done with people and the games they play. He cut back vines, planted grass seed, power washed the outside patios, and replaced the outdoor cushions—general maintenance for spring. The busy work didn't allay his frustration. Dash decided to take matters into his own hands. He would set himself up as bait, hoping to catch a big fish. He knew that Dylan Dotson was the perpetrator, and Conrad Cook was complicit if not an accessory. So who was the puppet master? Dash had narrowed it down to two individuals. He was going to draw him out.

Dash followed his nose, eliminating suspects, following leads, honing in on the motives. Why had Claudia Bowers, The Hamster, and Taylor Thorngate been murdered? All three had their throats cut with a sharp blade in one swift motion. Claudia and Taylor were part of the casual drinking and dining group called The Wine Sisters. The Hamster was collateral damage.

Dash believed that only Claudia's murder was intentional. Taylor's murder was to create a pattern to throw off the police and create a new narrative. Then why was Claudia murdered?

Dash had to set a trap. He knew that Dylan's father Sam was on Vino Veritas's payroll. He called Sam's office to set up an appointment claiming to be a developer who wanted to develop a huge swath of Great Oaks near the train station. The area was about eight blocks from downtown and not that desirable until recently when the downtown core had been built out. Sam Dotson thought that developers were his new ticket to wealth and power. Prior to Vino Veritas, Sam Dotson had been a small business attorney who dabbled in DUI arrests for his clients. When a client would call with a DUI arrest, he would blithely admonish them with, "You've joined a big club."

Dash arrived at his appointment in the New Century building. Sam had recently moved from his dreary office on Fiftieth Street to his new digs in the heart of downtown on the park block. He had a shiny oak door with his name embossed on the glass. Dash entered the handsome brick building that had been rebuilt after the 2003 earthquake. His office on the second floor overlooked the park. The lively restaurant and bar scene was just a few paces away. Sam Dotson was living his dream.

Dash stopped by the county building and picked up a parcel map showing the old lumber yard, which he was supposedly going to develop. The lumber yard was in property tax default and was up for sale.

Dash was dressed for success. He wore a Brioni navy blue suit, a Talbott green and blue club tie, Ferragamo lace-up dress shoes, and carried a Coach leather briefcase. These were clothes he kept for precisely these occasions when he knew the parties were impressed by labels.

Sam was shorter than his son, maybe five feet nine inches tall, stocky build with a receding hairline. He kept his remaining hair buzz cut. He wore a new suit that hung badly off his frame like a napkin on a brick. His office looked like it had been recently refurbished, giving the air of recent prosperity. Dash introduced himself as Derek Rumsfield.

"Mr. Rumsfield, a pleasure to meet you. Are you new to the area? You look familiar."

"Yes, and no. I live in Laguna Beach. I'm in the process of purchasing a large tract downtown. I've been spending a lot of time with city planning. I think I saw you at a recent City Council meeting." Dash had rehearsed his lines.

"Sit down," Sam moved to the sitting area next to his desk, "Tell me about your plans."

Dash laid out the parcel map on the large coffee table, "Mixed-use, commercial and residential. First, we're building a high-end boutique hotel, restaurant, and third-floor pool with a rooftop bar. Then we're adding apartments and condominiums. The whole project is projected to be around thirty-five million dollars." Dash laughed, "We expect overruns, etc."

"Certainly," Sam smiled broadly, "I work with several developers in the area, and I could probably help you get through the permit process, the environmental regulations, and the water issues."

"Tell me about the water issues," Dash asked.

"As you may know, the main issue for development is getting water permits. The city is under scrutiny since this last drought. They are very cautious in approving any large-scale development. Your project would require a water variance permit and some shepherding through the process. I imagine that's why you're here."

Dash smiled, "Your very prescient, Mr. Dotson. I understood that you're working with another Orange County Development Group, and you've managed to get them permitted."

Sam Dotson was visibly proud, "Yes, Vino Veritas is right on track to be one of the biggest landowners, builders, and developers in Great Oaks in all areas—commercial, residential, and agricultural. We're forming a water district to accommodate the development."

"Perfect," Dash added. "Is there any chance we could piggyback that effort?"

"Certainly," Sam leaned forward, "Membership is expensive but let's not use the expression piggyback. All projects must stand on their own merits." Sam winked at Dash pathetically. "There are no guarantees; however, we have our sights on the aquifer."

"The aquifer?" Dash played dumb.

"Yes, half a million-acre feet just below us. When we get access to that aquifer, then we can greenlight your project, as well as others."

Dash didn't flinch, "What are the obstacles to the water district?"

"They've mostly been removed. We've worked closely with the city council, the opinion makers, and our membership is rock solid."

"What obstacles have been removed?" Dash asked."

"Mostly political, some do-gooders have been silenced, and the court of public opinion has turned in our favor," Sam boasted.

"How so?" Dash leaned in.

"We have portrayed our water district as a local grassroots organization intent on preserving water for generations to come, and good stewards of the resource. We are trying to suspend the election process—go directly through the city council and county supervisors. We have incredible influence on both bodies." Sam Dotson boasted.

"What do-gooders did you have silenced?" Dash asked.

Sam had a twinkle in his eye, "Just a figure of speech. This is a small town. Money talks—the outliers usually come around."

Dash responded, "I'm all in. I'd like to employ you—put your firm on retainer. What are we talking about, money and time-wise?"

Dash thought he saw Sam lick his lips, "The upfront fee is fifty thousand, the retainer is ten thousand a month until you're permitted. We'll need to meet bi-weekly for about two hours. All court fees, expenses, etc., are additional. You said you are negotiating the purchase of the property. Do you have a timeline?"

"I'd like to break ground a year from now, next March. I need you to do something for me straight away. If I write you a check for five thousand today, can we proceed?" Dash asked.

Dash wrote the check in front of Sam on a check with only a phone number on it. He handed it to Sam, who was grinning ear to ear. "What is it I can do for you, Mr. Rumsfield? He looked at the signature, which was scribbled.

Dash lowered his voice, "I need for you to scare off one of the other bidders for the project."

Sam Dotson was intrigued, "Who would that be?"

"Bill Lyons, owner of Lyons Wine Estates," Dash said without emotion.

Sam Dotson laughed out loud, "You're kidding me. Do you know who he is? He owns the biggest winery locally by far. He's involved in Vino Veritas, which I also represent. I can't touch him, nor would I. I'm afraid you're just going to out-bid him."

Dash knew the minute he left the office that Sam Dotson would be on the phone with Bill Lyons. Then the ruse would be up. Dash attempted another tactic.

"If you can't touch him, can you tell me what you know about Amanda Jacobs? I met her at the Polo Lounge, and she wants to work for me," Dash grinned mischievously. "If you get my drift. She says she's well connected."

"I know of her, but be forewarned. She's involved with another Orange County guy. He might not like it if you mess with his gal. I would stay clear. She's a Wine Sister. They're trouble."

Dash was now digging deeper. "What do you mean by trouble?"

Sam took another long look at Dash, "You came in here for help with your development. I can't help you with your employee situation. I have one word of advice for you—stay away from The Wine Sisters. They created problems for other clients, which we had to rectify."

"What do you mean?" Dash asked.

Sam became suspicious, "I won't answer that. You don't sound like a developer. Take your check back. I don't think we can do business." Sam slid the check back to Dash.

Dash had heard the expression for attorneys who handle clients' personal issues. They call them fixers. Dash was convinced that Sam Dotson was a "Fixer." Now he had to determine to what length Sam would go to "fix" a problem.

"I'm sorry to hear that," Dash responded. "What client had you eliminate Claudia Bowers?"

Sam's cheeks turned beet red, "What, what did you say?"

"I know your son was involved in the murder of Taylor Thorngate. I'm not clear what your role was," Dash said with all malice.

Sam Dotson got up and went to his desk, opening a drawer bringing out a handgun. He was shaking badly.

"I don't know who you are, but you're way out of line. I have my rights. If someone threatens me in my office, I have the right to shoot them." He lowered his small-caliber handgun waist high with a direct line to Dash's abdomen. "Now leave."

"I'll leave. You're wrong—you just can't shoot an unarmed man in your office. You have no proof that there was a threat. I won't leave until you answer my question."

Sam was flabbergasted by Dash's audacity. "That wasn't a question. It was an outrageous accusation. My son, Dylan, hasn't been charged with any murders. He's working as we speak. I think you are mentally unstable. Please leave."

"You've answered my questions by your demeanor. You and your son are guilty. It is my charge to get you both convicted."

Dash left the office. Sam Dotson returned the gun to his desk drawer, noting that the safety was on, and there were no bullets in the chamber. The first call he made was to Rex Beckett.

"We have a problem."

Chapter Forty:

LAS VEGAS

Dash drove the half dozen blocks to Fiftieth Street to the Farm and Ranch Realty office and parked his car where he'd have a good view of the vehicle departures from their parking lot. Dash waited for Beckett's SUV to leave the office. Beckett came out the back door wearing casual attire (linen tan slacks, a blue and white checkered button-down shirt, loafers) carrying a small suitcase. Dash followed Rex Beckett's black Cadillac Escalade. The Escalade took the Twelfth Street ramp on to Highway 101 south. He followed it to San Luis Obispo down Broad Street to the airport. He was heading out of town, not on his private jet back to Orange County. For whatever reason, Rex Beckett was flying commercial. Dash watched him park in short term parking, take a parking ticket from a machine and walk into the terminal.

Dash did the same. He got into the terminal, looking for Beckett at the Alaska Airlines desk. Alaska Airlines had one daily direct flight to Las Vegas. Dash waited while Beckett chatted with the Airline employee who sold him the ticket. Dash looked at the schedule. The flight to Las Vegas was not for another forty minutes. As Dash suspected, another passenger would show up and join Rex Beckett.

Amanda Jacobs looked stunning in her buff-colored short-waisted denim jacket, black jeans, and Tony Llama boots. It was just days past the vernal equinox, and she was donning small frame sunglasses on a very overcast day. Dash watched as she embraced him. They both looked happy to be with one another. Beckett held out his right hand for Amanda. Dash noticed that Beckett's hand was no longer bandaged. Amanda's presence didn't surprise Dash, but the next couple that showed up did.

Dash's former client, Bryson Jackson and his wife Jackie Jackson, arrived and greeted Rex Beckett and Amanda. They were taking all taking a junket to Las Vegas.

Dash had been terminated by Bryson Jackson before he finished his investigation into Claudia's murder. He was supposedly fired because Taylor Thorngate's murder furthered the reasoning that both women had been killed by the same man. The prime suspect, Dylan Dotson, had been detained, but eventually, his charges were dropped due to lack of evidence. Dylan was now free to murder again.

The suspected ring leader, Rex Beckett, who may have orchestrated both Wine Sister murders, appeared to be the new besties with his former clients, the Jacksons. Dash had never told Bryson and Jackie that Rex Beckett was a prime suspect, nor had he mentioned to him his liaison with Claudia and perhaps Taylor. The fact that they were all Moonies—lovers that were bestowed moonstone jewelry—was prima facie evidence of the links.

Dash watched as they left the main terminal for their gate and their flight to Las Vegas. Dash was fatigued and hungry. He decided to go downtown to Giuseppe's, which was his favorite haunt for good Italian food and a great Negroni (gin, Campari liqueur, vermouth) cocktail. The restaurant was in an old landmark building: high ceilings with a narrow corridor past the bustling bar to the courtyard. The sun had come out, so Dash had lunch outside in the courtyard. The sun, combined with a few cocktails, induced that delectable zone halfway between sleep and nirvana. One of the few pleasures of growing older is appreciating that zone. Dash let his laziness overtake his consciousness. Justice for Claudia, Taylor, and The Hamster seemed to be drifting farther and farther away.

Dash combined appetizers to make a meal: steamed clams in a white wine broth, fried Calamari, roasted portabella mushrooms, and an arugula and cucumber salad washed down with a glass of Sangiovese. Dash took a walk after lunch in the mission district in downtown San Luis Obispo along the creek. It was not Paris, but as a true flâneur, he tried to get lost walking down an unfamiliar dark street out of the commercial area to an old residential area. The air was damp and seductive. The early ripe smell of spring erupting from the decay of winter gave succor to his thoughts. He stopped and admired the architecture, which ranged from old California craftsman to New England clapboard.

He left SLO town and headed north home, totally relaxed. He called Ginger and made a date for the following night while he devised a strategy to close the curtain on Beckett and friends.

What was Beckett's motive for eliminating Claudia? She was an erstwhile girlfriend, a notorious gossip, especially about past lovers, and a perceived obstacle to the machinations fomented by Vino Veritas and the Estrella Water District. Claudia had a brief encounter with Beckett but quickly retreated, ending the relationship despite his protestations and gifts of jewelry. He put the full-court press on Claudia and came up a basket short. Claudia was also an obstacle between Amanda and Beckett. Claudia dismissed Beckett because he was married, albeit a political piranha. How did Dash know all this other than supposition? Taylor Thorngate was clear, "Claudia was sleeping with the enemy." Taylor was in love with Bill Lyons, never getting involved with Beckett. Now Beckett had his sights on the Jacksons—Beckett's intentions were always less than honorable.

Dash had no evidence to take to Detective Evans. Claudia was apprehended in front of the law offices of Sam Dotson on Fiftieth Street across the street from the Farm and Ranch Real Estate Offices, where Rex Beckett had an office on the third floor. The Hamster was killed on the stoop in front of Sam's office. Sam's son, Dylan, was the primary suspect in the murders. His friend and cohort, Conrad Cook, was also a suspect. Dash was not told what Conrad's unreproachable alibi was nor why he was no longer a suspect by the local police.

Dash had two eyewitnesses, one dead, the other in Mexico, who described Conrad, Dylan, and Rex Beckett accurately. Dash believed that Taylor was trying to point Dash in the direction of Rex Beckett before she was killed. Now his former clients were with Beckett in Las Vegas. A smart man would give the investigation a rest, let the police do their work, and enjoy his new girlfriend, Ginger, his two dogs, and the tranquility of residing on a working vineyard. Dash should bank his checks, forget about his sorry clients, and go back to Mexico for another month. Bryson Jackson was a shrewd man. He wouldn't be misled by Rex Beckett, or would he? Unless the Jacksons were trying to sell their winery, retire and travel. Red Fox Winery had a four-hundred-acre estate vineyard, a new production facility, a grand tasting room, brand recognition, all worth in the tens of millions of dollars. If Beckett's group, Vino Veritas, was offering to buy— who wouldn't consider their offer.

It didn't fit Vino Veritas' business model. They usually bought properties on the east side in foreclosure, under-capitalized, with a dry well or underproducing wells. They would buy these properties on the cheap, secure their water credits, put in deeper wells, and sell them when they appreciated. A simple formula, not illegal, just shrewd and profitable.

Dash thought of the teal bandana, the moonstone jewelry, the method of murder, the suspects, and the motivation. None of it connected or made sense. That was the key. Claudia's murder was personal, and Taylor's was a cover-up. That is the only explanation Dash could conjure up until he spoke to Sam Dotson.

Chapter Forty-One:

GREAT OAKS

Dash decided to follow the most feckless suspect in the murders of Claudia and Taylor, Sam Dotson. A small-town attorney who befriends out of town players, believing that he was now playing in the big leagues. An oversized ego, an undersized intellect, a criminal for a son, and a belief that he was now untouchable. Whether Sam was part of the "Riverbed Murders" conspiracy or simply a useful idiot was reason enough to focus on his activities.

It was Thursday, lunchtime. Sam Dotson would be at the local Rotary noontime meeting. It was a big Rotary club held in a big ballroom, and Dash patiently waited for him outside. Sam could walk to the hotel ballroom to the meeting from his office, crossing the town square. Dash sat in the bar lobby, waiting for the meeting to finish. He heard the applause for the speaker then the silence for the final words—culminating in the din from a hundred and fifty voices at once after the applause. The Rotarians, men and women, walked out en masse, mostly dressed in business attire. Sam was easy to spot. His short, stocky stature was not made for suits. He wore a big red tie mimicking the President. He was jovial and self-aware of his new status as a prominent attorney. He was engaged in conversation with the mayor, Pete Ligotti, and a couple of other Rotarians. Rotarians looked the same nationwide, be it Grand Rapids, Missoula, or Great Oaks. They were well-meaning, prosperous, middle-aged, and over-fed. The real power players like Bill Lyons, Jason Perigold, or Rex Beckett wouldn't be caught dead at a Rotary meeting unless they were invited as a speaker.

Dash followed Sam as he cut across the square to his office. He walked briskly, on a mission, deep in thought. He did not see Dash. Dash stopped and waited when he approached the door and the stairs up to his second-floor office.

Sam was met at the top of the stairs by his son, Dylan, who was quite agitated. Dylan had been waiting for him. Dash could hear Dylan yelling at his father. He could not see Sam take him by the nape of his shirt forcibly shoving him inside the doorway, out of the view. Dash went up the stairs just outside the office door. He could hear them screaming obscenities at one another. After a few minutes, Dash opened the heavy oak door to the law office of Samuel J. Dotson. Dash walked through the doors to find Dylan on top of his father on the lobby carpet pummeling him with fists and accusations. No one else was around. Neither Sam nor Dylan were aware that Dash had entered the office.

All Dash heard over and over again from an incensed Dylan was, "You've destroyed my life. I'm ruined."

Sam lay nearly unconscious on the floor when Dylan finally got up off his father and saw Dash. He glared at him with visceral anger, then charged at Dash. He pulled out his long serrated pocket knife taking two swipes at Dash's face, missed both times. Dash was cornered up against the entry door. He dove to the floor towards the reception desk as Dylan wildly lunged after him. Sam was now up off the floor and had retreated quickly to his office just beyond the reception area.

Dash crawled around the desk on his hands and knees to escape Dylan's blade like a deadly child's game of hide and seek. Dylan reached Dash and jumped on him, attempting to slash his neck but missing, slicing his shoulder instead. Dash was unarmed, not thinking he'd need a gun at a Rotary meeting.

Sam Dotson emerged wild-eyed from his office, grasping his revolver. Sam took two quick shots at Dash. The first bullet missed completely penetrating the wall. The second bullet hit his son just three feet away from Dash. Sam ran over to his fallen son. Dash tripped him en route. Dash easily poached Sam's handgun. Sam got up and stumbled to his son's side, who lay on the floor. Sam moaned like a just castrated steer. Dash looked on unemotionally, pulled out his cell phone, and dialed 911.

Dylan Dotson's wound entered his back and found a home in his aorta at the top of the left ventricle. He was dead before the EMTs arrived.

Detective FJ Evans arrived with the other two detectives in the Great Oaks Police Department. Sam Dotson was despondent at first, then accusatory, blaming Dash for his son's death.

Pointing at Dash, Sam blurted out, "This intruder broke into our office. My son tried to stop him with his knife. I accidentally shot my son trying to shoot him."

Detective Evans determined that the shooting was an accident. He arrested Dash for unlawful entry and trespassing into Sam's law office. Dash was released the same day when it was determined that the office wasn't locked, and the law office lobby was a public space, whereas anyone could walk in off the street and go up the stairs to the office. Too occupied with grief, Sam Dotson did not press charges against Dash.

Dylan's knife was taken in for evidence. Dash contended that the knife was the murder weapon in the Riverbed Murders, confirmed by State of California forensics. Dylan Dotson was named posthumously as the murderer of Claudia Bowers and Taylor Thorngate. The case was closed, and the small community of Great Oaks on the Salinas River was relieved. Sam Dotson closed his office for remodeling and moved to a new office near the private airport after he took six months off.

Dash Ramblar met with Detective Evans at their favorite bakery café. They sat discussing the detective's ensuing retirement, the cheapest online site to buy cigars, and put the investigation to bed. Detective Evans was in an ebullient mood. "Less than a year before retirement and the most publicized homicide case in our history was resolved, thanks in part to you, Dash."

Dash was less enthusiastic. "I guess that means you're buying the donuts today," Dash added. "You still have some unfinished business. You have one suspect who conveniently is dead, no motive for the murders, and two accomplices who have been given a pass. Let's not forget the murder of The Hamster, who originally described Dylan Dotson."

Detective Evans was defensive, "Let's be clear. There was no case and no motive prior to Dylan's death. Fortunately, he brandished his knife. We secured it for evidence, and it turned out to be positively identified. If he hadn't been shot by his father, he'd still be free. I know it's not a complete victory, but he definitely was responsible for slitting those poor women's throats. He grew up on a ranch near Creston, working summers at the nearby slaughterhouse. He bragged to anyone that would listen that he personally had killed over a thousand animals. As far as a motive, it was pure and simple jealousy. We have witnesses that he attempted to take Claudia home from a dance lesson in Atascadero. She declined his offer, accepting a ride from his friend Conrad. She embarrassed him and eventually dating Conrad Cook. He then killed Taylor because she knew all about Dylan's back story with Claudia. He had to squash her testimony and provide cover." Detective Evans was smug in his depiction of events.

"From the beginning, I believed it was about the old dance: sex, lust, and jealousy, but I was dead wrong. I heard Dylan say to his father that 'he had ruined his life.' Why would he say that unless he had knowledge or was complicit in the women's murders? You know damn well this was less about the old dance and more about the new dance: money, greed, and power," Dash asserted.

Dash leaned back in his chair, looking around to see if anyone was within earshot, "Floyd, this is all too tidy even for a small-town police department. Have you given up looking for other accomplices?"

"Without a confession by the deceased, we have no way to proceed. I know your concerns, but we are handcuffed," Detective Evans chuckled at his use of the word "handcuffed."

"That means that Conrad Cook is free to stalk other women, work for a prestigious wine group -knowing damn well that he was an accomplice in two murders. Also, I contend that Rex Beckett orchestrated and planned the murders. Dylan was his fall guy. You won't admit it, but we both know that to be true."

Detective Evans was not convinced, "Okay, smart guy, prove it. Your only witness is hiding out in Mexico and will never testify. You have vague ideas about a wild conspiracy—water rights, developers, and politicians. I can guarantee you, even if Claudia was a thorn in Rex Beckett's side, he wouldn't have killed her for her political views. Damn it, Dash, you're losing your grasp on reality."

"It was the combination. He wanted her in the worst way. She had qualms about playing with a married man. Beckett couldn't have her, so no one would have her. She also had loose lips, and was determined to spill the beans on the whole Vino Veritas-Estrella Water District plans." Dash's words sounded empty and unconvincing.

Dash was frustrated, "Okay. The motives for Rex Beckett's involvement sound weak, I'll give you that. If his machinations play out, he'll be a very rich man, enough to push Beckett over the edge. I believe that Bill Lyons was using Claudia and Taylor to gain inside information and eventually ace Beckett out of Vino Veritas and the whole equation. I was at the city council meeting. It was Bill Lyons who spoke on behalf of the new water district. Remember, Bill Lyons was a sponsor of the Save the Oaks campaign. Taylor said that Claudia was sleeping with the enemy: the enemy being Rex Beckett. She did that in an effort to gain information and cripple

Vino Veritas." Dash was exhausted by his rambling soliloquy and drooped back into his chair.

"As I've said before, you watch too much TV. This is Great Oaks. People don't get killed over a planning issue. They might get sued, they might go bankrupt, but nobody gets murdered. We may be a Wal-Mart redneck, big butt town. Folks here aren't that stupid."

Dash laughed at Detective Evans's depiction of a lowly unsophisticated town on the verge of becoming a tourist mecca with rampant development everywhere, "Maybe it was true when millionaire ranchers controlled the city. Now we have billionaires from all over the world here trying to get a piece of the action. The stakes are much higher. Don't ever underestimate corruption, greed, and hubris."

Detective Evans asked, "Hubris?"

"You know—an operatic expression; the pride that is transparent to others but not to the prideful. The pride that gets people killed. The pride that lets two murder accomplices go free."

"Talking about transparency, you said you would tell me who you were working for when the case was closed," Detective Evans smiled broadly.

"It's interesting you should ask," Dash grinned, "Bryson Jackson, the owner of Red Fox Winery and a brand-new partner in Vino Veritas. I believe Jackson hired me to find out if Beckett could be linked to Claudia's murder. Conrad Cook, a friend and confidant to Bryson Jackson, was an accomplice. I believe that Bryson Jackson introduced Conrad Cook to Rex Beckett."

Detective Evans groaned, "Enough with your spin, Dash. Go home. Prune your vines, have a glass of wine, play fetch with your dogs, relax and enjoy the sunset. You're not going to fix Great Oaks anytime soon."

Dash couldn't hold back a grin, "You're the one retiring. I'm just getting started in this game."

"You think it's a game. These old ranchers, developers, winery own-ers play hardball. You won't be needing your softball glove," Detective Evans said.

"Enough of the baseball talk. I won't rest until Claudia and Taylor's murders are fully resolved. That goes for The Hamster's too," Dash looked upward, "Sorry, Hamster—I let you down."

"You're talking to ghosts now; maybe you need an early retirement." Detective Evans pushed himself away from the table, got up out of his chair, waiting for Dash to get up.

Dash got up from his chair, left some money on the table, walked around the table, and touched Detective Evans on the elbow.

"I know you, Floyd. You won't retire until there's closure. You know Dylan didn't act alone," Dash said, using FJ's formal name to beguile him one more time.

Detective FJ Evans winked at Dash, "Please don't call me Floyd." Detective Evans walked out of the coffee shop. Dash noticed a little bounce in his step. He wasn't going to retire.

Chapter Forty-Two:

EVER VIGILANCE

The days were warming. The vines were pruned, and the weeds were winning the terrain battle after a wet winter. To regain the terrain would require weed-whacking, high weed mowing, and the implements: gloves, mower, shovel, garden fork, and perspiration. Dash convinced himself these ordinary, repetitive tasks were very Buddhist in nature. Beer was antithetical, water was replenishing, food was a bother, and a nap was sublime.

Dash smiled while cutting weeds because the activity had a parallel connotation to the Orange County developers who were multiplying like acorn woodpeckers. It was a bad metaphor because development meant the erasure of the oak woodlands where the acorn woodpeckers thrived. That was the battle that the Save the Oaks committee was presumably fighting.

The regional news covered the story for about a week. There wasn't an impending trial, and the evildoer was now buried. The news anchors covered Easter bunny stories and the Kentucky Derby. Dash was not content to let it rest. Ginger was on a different bent; she'd joined The Wine Sisters, who had a combination remembrance lunch for Claudia and Taylor and a celebratory toast for the police following the closure of the case. No mention was made of Dylan Dotson.

Ginger talked to Amanda, who boasted of a marvelous weekend in Las Vegas with Rex Beckett. She said his marriage was a convenient inconvenience because they could just have fun and not bother with stage two fuss. She did mention traveling with the Jacksons, whom she found to be delightful and wacky. Dash asked Ginger if Amanda had an anecdote to illustrate the Jacksons' wackiness. She had none.

Dash did meet with the Jacksons under the premise that it was a wrap-up meeting. They were in a good mood as the spring wine tourist season was in super bloom, and sales were up over last year.

Dash showed up in a salmon-colored polo shirt, khaki slacks, reddish-brown loafers, and a tan acquired from outdoor chores. He was greeted like a champion, of sorts, given that he was a witness to Dylan's killing, during Dash's ongoing investigation.

"You were right all along, Dash. We knew you were the best man for the job," Bryson said, presenting Dash with his latest GSM (Rhone blend) release. Dash swirled his glass, putting it to his nose, swallowing appreciatively.

"This is excellent," Dash said, putting his glass down. "As you know, the police have concluded that Dylan was the lone perpetrator and the case is closed. I believe differently, but I do concur with their conclusion. He was the man who did the deed. He had accomplices who are now free to go about their lives."

Bryson and Jackie frowned with Dash's pronouncement, "What are you talking about, Dash? Give it a rest. I know you worked hard on this, putting yourself in danger, nearly getting shot, and barely surviving with your reputation in tack. You came close to losing it all with your wild accusations about Vino Veritas, the Jasper Wine Group, and Conrad Cook. Don't tell me you still think Conrad was involved?" Bryson asked.

Dash took another swallow of wine, letting the young wine wander from his taste buds to the back of his mouth. He thought better of pursuing it with the Jacksons.

"No, I won't go that far. I do think he had some knowledge. I'll let the conspiracy bear hibernate for the time being," Dash said.

Bryson pursued the inquiry, "That would be wise if you plan to remain in this city and continue working as a private detective—live as a gentleman farmer and vintner. What would you gain from opening up another can of worms?"

Dash was surprised by his tone, "I hope that's not a veiled threat. As you know, Claudia was very keen on the notion that Vino Veritas desired to form the Estrella Water District. She knew that the Estrella Water District was predatory, detrimental to the community at large, to the balance of nature and the water table. I do believe it was part of the reason she was murdered."

Bryson responded defensively, "No. I would never threaten you or anyone else—just cautionary advice."

"You won't deny, you had a discussion about the water district with Claudia at the Save the Oaks committee' meetings?"

"She was young, idealistic, barrel salesperson. She was not an environmentalist, nor was she completely informed on these matters. It didn't get her killed. To suggest otherwise is pure idiocy." Bryson's jawline firmed, and his eyes steeled.

Dash understood, "Okay, I will concede that she was a novice. You must admit she was a powerful advocate against rampant development. Let's change the subject."

Bryson looked relieved, "Good, we remember her as such, and we won't diminish her legacy."

They discussed the heavy winter rains, the upcoming summer wine events and stayed clear of Claudia, Taylor, Dylan, Conrad, and Rex Beckett. Dash did not disclose that he knew that they went to Las Vegas with Rex

Beckett and Amanda Jacobs. He surmised that Bryson and Jackie were investors and partners in Vino Veritas and that Bryson's activity in the Save the Oaks committee was more as a spy and disinformation plant than as a true advocate for the oaks.

Dash took Ginger to dinner in town for a celebratory dinner. Ginger disguised her femininity whenever possible, but when she let it flourish, she was a sight to behold. She wore an olive-colored off the shoulder blouse, baring her lovely décolletage, a longish dark green silk skirt that showcased her ankles and smart heels. She wore her auburn hair in a messy bun and a simple jade pendant around her neck. Dash dressed modestly, trying not to upstage his dinner companion. They went to a renowned Italian restaurant in Great Oaks famous for their truffle risottos, wild venison, and veal.

They celebrated with champagne along with an array of artisan olives, cheeses, and slivers of Italian meats before dinner. The discussion was warm but direct.

"I spoke to the Jacksons, and they essentially told me to back off the investigation, to let sleeping dogs lie, and build on my new reputation as a tough guy," Dash added the tough guy for effect.

Dash was surprised by Ginger's response. "That disappoints me. I thought the Jacksons had more integrity. I hope you don't heed their advice."

Dash smiled sweetly, obviously smitten with Ginger, "That was the response I was looking for."

"If I thought you would retreat from this, then I would retreat. The man I hope you are will not back down from a fight or battle an injustice. I know Conrad. I know what he is capable of, and I think he should watch his back. Vino Veritas will come after him eventually," Ginger said.

Dash enjoyed Ginger's company, her resolve, the champagne. He relaxed, knowing she was on board with his quixotic investigations. "I will keep a low profile in the meantime."

Ginger warned, "Please don't let your guard down. They still may come after you."

They lifted their glasses as one. Dash toasted, "Here's to us and ever vigilance."

"To us." Ginger smiled.

Chapter Forty-Three:

UNFINISHED BUSINESS

Dash had not been entirely truthful with Ginger; he had no intention of curtailing the investigation. He was determined to find justice for The Hamster. Dylan Dotson was posthumously tried, convicted, and sentenced for the murders of Claudia Bowers and Taylor Thorngate. Dash was certain that Dylan did not kill The Hamster.

Dash booked a flight to San José del Cabo. He told Ginger he was flying to Los Angeles to see his daughter Amber, which he did. But then he flew out of LAX to Cabo. There was a risk involved, and he didn't want Ginger upset. He arrived on a quiet Sunday afternoon at the normally busy international airport. Dash booked a suite at the Hotel Playa Azul. Dash was flush with money after cashing Bryson Jackson's check.

The Hotel Playa Azul was as close to a four-star hotel as you can get in Mexico. The maids wore pink and white uniforms, the bartenders wore short coats and white shirts, and the tile floors were constantly being polished. The Hotel Playa Azul was adjacent to La Profundo Mar Azul, the condominium hotel where Pedro Mendoza stayed.

Dash checked into his hotel, took a short nap, and then went downstairs to the open-air dining room, which had an uninterrupted view of the Sea of Cortez. Dash ordered the ceviche, which came with fresh marlin, ripe avocado, olive oil, lime juice, and a hint of vinegar. He also ordered the grilled swordfish served on a plank. He drank only one Dos Equis lager with dinner. After dinner, he took a short walk on the beach to Pedro's condominium. He went up to the condominium bar and ordered a Mexican brandy. It was Sunday night, and the bar was dead. The bartender was finishing his shift and wasn't talkative. Dash engaged him and asked about Pedro Mendoza, the Filipino tourist. The bartender said he hadn't seen him recently. He heard that Pedro had traveled back to California, but he didn't know if he'd returned. Dash gave him a good tip and headed back down the beach to his hotel. He asked the front desk to give him a six am wake up call and settled in.

Dash got up at six, went down to the beach, swam to the buoys, drank a pot of coffee, and got dressed. He had no appetite. His gut was full of anticipation.

Dash strode down the beach to the condominium complex and headed to the dining room. He ordered avocado toast. Pedro appeared at seven dressed in white linen pants, a green and white embroidered shirt, and a woven Panama hat. He gave the appearance of being a wealthy chilango, a derogatory nickname for tourists from Mexico City. Dash watched as Pedro ordered a Corona with breakfast. Pedro signed la cuenta and then headed out of the dining room. Dash followed him.

Pedro did not take his morning beach walk but went directly to the street out front where a new Toyota 4Runner was waiting for him. Dash waived at the line of taxis squatting in the shade across from the condominium entrance. A faded blue Honda pulled up. Dash got in, telling the driver to follow the Toyota 4Runner.

The 4Runner followed the main highway south to Cabo San Lucas, then exited into the Twin Dolphins Resort, where wealthy Americans stay. It has a private beach on a private cove, but most hotel guests spend their time surrounding the infinity pool overlooking the sea.

Dash told the valet that he was checking into the hotel. Pedro had already entered the hotel. Dash walked through the lobby unnoticed. It was a Monday morning, and the resort was buzzing with activity. The crowd was the Hollywood set: attractive people wearing expensive clothing sporting tans, cosmetic enhancements, and accessory dogs. Dash blended in wearing canvas shoes and a Tommy Bahama shirt off the rack. His Jack Spade large frame sunglasses lent him a modicum of credibility. He could've been an out of work actor or writer vacationing on royalties.

Dash walked out to the pool area looking for Pedro, but he'd disappeared. The pool was littered with the beautiful people. Behind a wavy stucco wall was a private club pool that featured cabana bar service, a fresh taco bar, where clothing was optional. Dash could see Pedro's Panama hat at the private bar holding court, but two attendants blocked Dash from proceeding. He retreated to the large resort bar near the largest of the pools, not a bad venue for surveillance. He waited for an hour sipping a Cuba Libre. He grew impatient and asked the bartender how much it would cost him to enter the private club. The bartender said it was by invitation only, but he could manage a day pass for Dash for a hundred US dollars. Dash handed him the money, and the bartender gave him a plastic key card. He learned it was for the employee entrance to the club.

Dash walked into the private club through the employee entrance. Like all private clubs, it wasn't that special. The service wasn't any better, the drinks weren't any stronger, the food wasn't any more delectable, but it was exclusive. Pedro didn't recognize Dash as he approached him. Dash took a seat at the bar. One man and a woman stood between Dash and Pedro. When they turned to acknowledge his presence, they both recognized Dash immediately.

The couple was Amanda Jacobs and Rex Beckett. They wore bathing suits and pool robes.

Dash greeted them formerly, "Hello Pedro, so pleased to see you in the company of Rex and Amanda. I thought you were staying up in The Hamster's condo up the road in San José del Cabo. What brings you to Cabo San Lucas, amigo?"

Pedro let Rex do the speaking, "We're vacationing. What brings you here?"

"The same reason that brought Pedro here—to spend down some money for services rendered."

Pedro was not having any of it, "What are you implying, amigo?" I can't remember you're fucking name—you have no business here."

"Dash Ramblar, private investigator, from Great Oaks. My business here pertains to The Hamster and his untimely murder," he leveled his gaze at Pedro. "I believe you're responsible. When I was last here, you said that you were staying at The Hamster's condominium. You also said that you were in Oregon when he was murdered. I checked with Cyle at the Dollar Store in San Miguel. He said that you were in town on Halloween. He remembered that you bought some Halloween candy for Cecelia's kids. The Hamster never intended for you to have his condominium, especially after you told the detectives that he was an eyewitness to Claudia's murder."

Pedro rose from his chair, taking off his Panama hat. He walked around Amanda and Rex so he was face to face with Dash. "No one accuses me of nothing and gets away with it.

"Are you going to cut my throat with the knife in your pocket like you did to The Hamster?" Dash asked.

Rex Beckett rose from his chair, getting between Dash and Pedro.

"Stop it, Pedro. Leave now. I'll handle Mr. Ramblar."

Dash spoke, "You know Pedro identified you as being at the site prior to Claudia's murder. He said that a more fit man with a bandaged hand was Dylan's accomplice."

Pedro was angry and shaken, "Bullshit, I never said that." He left the club, forgetting his hat.

Rex Beckett was less emotional. "Amanda and I were enjoying our little getaway before you interrupted us." Beckett motioned to the attendant, "I believe that Mr. Ramblar is not a member of this club."

Dash got up, "I'm leaving. Don't bother. I know that you paid Pedro to murder The Hamster. It would be in your best interest to deal with him before he testifies in court. I will deal with you later."

Amanda was upset, "Why, why are you saying this? Are you crazy? Why would Rex have a homeless man murdered? It makes no sense. You're ruining everything."

Dash looked at Amanda with her Moonstone pendant. "Have a wonderful stay here in Cabo. I'm sure Rex can explain everything to you and to his wife."

Dash left the Twin Dolphins Resort and took a taxi back to his hotel. When he returned, he went down to the broad public beach, took another swim, ate some raw oysters from a beach vendor, and took a nap in the shade of a rented palapa.

Chapter Forty-Four:

THE AQUIFER

Dash figured that he'd be on the hot seat when he got back to Great Oaks.
He was right. Rex Beckett would surely have notified Conrad Cook with
instructions to make life uncomfortable for Dash.

Dash found everything in order at his hacienda when he returned.
Bixby and Barney were overjoyed to see him unpack his suitcase. Ginger
couldn't take his call at work, so Dash went to her house and waited for her
to get home.

She was immediately suspicious, "Where did you get that tan, certainly not in overcast Los Angeles?"

"I had a little business to attend to in Cabo," Dash uttered.

"Thanks for telling me. If something happened there, would have
been no way to contact you." Ginger stammered.

"I left all the Cabo information with Amber." Dash finally got around
to kissing Ginger. She was still unhappy.

"You're okay. I guess that's all that really matters. Or are you?" Ginger
glared at him while keeping a firm grip on his hand.

"I ran into Rex and Amanda vacationing with Pedro—not the usual suspects. My hunch was right. The Hamster was killed or set up by Pedro, who was working for Rex and Vino Veritas. I put them on notice that I knew about their whole scheme, and I could prove it."

"That wasn't a smart move," Ginger said. "Now, you have those bastards wanting to kill you, and I have to deal with Amanda at the next fucking Wine Sisters dinner."

Dash was taken aback, "When do you learn to swear like a sailor?"

"When I fell in love with you. It seems like the only weather you like is a shitstorm."

Dash laughed hard, holding Ginger tightly. He kissed her. "You're my umbrella."

Ginger pulled away from Dash's embrace. "No, you've got that wrong. I'm nobody's umbrella. Before I spend the night with you again, I want this mess cleaned up. That should be incentive enough."

Dash returned home. He knew he'd have to deal with Conrad sooner than later. The sooner was the following morning. Dash texted Conrad and copied Detective Evans with the message, "I met with Rex and Pedro in Cabo. They said that you were the accomplice in the murders."

Detective Evans immediately called Dash. "I told you to back off. We have zero evidence linking Conrad to the murders, no DNA, no weapon, and he has an alibi."

"It was his teal bandana at the murder site. When Ginger's house got broken into, she smelled cigar smoke. Conrad smokes two to three cigars a day. I would bet my ranch on it," Dash asserted.

Detective Evans laughed. "Your ranch and five bucks would get you a cappuccino at Starbucks. I smoke four cigars a day—does that make me a suspect?"

Dash knew he was right. He had only one move left. He called Mona and told her that he had a story for her. She agreed to meet with him. In the interim, Dash got a text back from Conrad. It was a smiley face emoji next to a rat emoji with the message, "You got nothing."

He met Mona at the Berlin coffee house, the only place that had strong enough coffee for Mona. She was glad to see Dash.

"You must be pleased. I understand you're a bit of a hero," Mona extended her hand.

"Not really. Right place, wrong time. I was lucky I didn't get shot." Dash shook her hand. "I'm not pleased. Vino Veritas is forging ahead with its plan to form the Estrella Water District. One accomplice in the murders is on vacation, and the other is getting new labor contracts."

Mona looked at Dash. He appeared tan but not rested. "I thought you'd be happy. Dylan Dotson is dead, and he was positively identified as the killer. Tell me what you know about the accomplices."

"Two names, Rexford Beckett and Conrad Cook. I'm sure you know them both. I don't want you to write about the murders—I want you to expose Vino Veritas. That would give Claudia peace."

Mona smiled, "I'm way ahead of you. I've already written it. I've been doing the legwork and research for months. My publisher says that the article will be on the front page, above the fold."

"Splendid," Dash beamed. "Is there anything I can help you with?"

"As a matter of fact, you can. You said that you've been harassed, your dogs have been poisoned—all since you starting investigating Vino Veritas. Will you let me tell your story? I need anecdotal material for the article."

Dash thought about the consequences of being quoted in an expose of this magnitude. He would be blackballed by the local Vino Veritas investors, and most importantly, he would betray the first tenet of private investigation: keep all information in your confidence, only to be shared with your client.

Dash thought of Claudia, The Hamster, and Taylor. He knew he was doing right by them.

"Yes. You can quote me and tell my story," Dash said.

Mona looked concerned. "I can make you anonymous if you'd prefer. I like you. I wouldn't want you to have to move out of town."

Dash laughed, "Whatever works. They'll know who the source was straight away."

Dash told Mona the complete story, including his thoughts on the accomplices which weren't going to be published. He wanted a record in the event that he got knocked off. Mona filled her notebook while Dash spoke.

"I think I have enough for now. I call you if I need more material," Mona said. They left the coffee shop into the bright spring sunlight. It was going to be another sizzling hot day in Great Oaks.

Dash smiled to himself. He knew that this article would stop the Estrella Water District cold. He also knew that there'd be others. The aquifer was never going to be safe from exploitation. But for once, Claudia prevailed.

Dash was correct. Vino Veritas closed down its operation in Great Oaks after the release of the article. Mona didn't pull any punches naming all the principles and connecting the murders of Claudia Bowers and Taylor Thorngate to the attempted cover-up, relating to the attempted heist of the local water supply. Rex Beckett left the Central Coast for good and returned to his home in Newport Beach, where Vino Veritas was shuttered.

Conrad Cook was mentioned as having a contract with Vino Veritas for dubious activity not related to vineyard management. His association with Vino Veritas made him a pariah within the industry. When his contracts were canceled, he resorted to selling pain killers laced with Fentanyl. Cook was arrested for first-degree murder when a twenty-year-old overdosed thinking he'd bought Percocet for a toothache. Cook pleaded no contest and was convicted on a manslaughter charge.

Dash's antidotal quotes in the article also gave him some breathing room, scaring off potential clients. He gained a temporary reputation as an unreliable confidant and had to resort to insurance fraud cases to pay the bills. He and Ginger kept a low profile in Great Oaks and savored a modicum of domestic tranquility.

Chloe, Taylor's dog, was adopted by an active senior, who frequented the dog park where Chloe could see her chums.

THE END

EPILOGUE

The setting for the Dash Ramblar Mystery Series is on the Central Coast of California. This unique part of America is blessed with a Mediterranean climate, oak-studded hillsides, a dramatic coastline dotted with charming towns and villages. It evokes the mythical sun strewn California dreaming, an eternally youthful place in our psyches.

This tourist mecca can be described as primarily rural and kicked back, not to be confused with unsophisticated or sleepy. The region bears an abundance of characters, some natives, but mostly transplants, seeking to reinvent themselves or escape their cruel pasts. The Central Coast, unlike the rest of the country, cares little about your resume, your religion, or your bank account; judgments are made on the person in front of them and their deeds.

Many movements and individuals gravitated to the tranquil Central Coast for its unsurpassed natural beauty and mild climate, discovering a magical magnetism about the place. Alternative communities have erupted here for years from the "California Colony of the American Woman's Republic" originating in Atascadero in 1913, Esalen Institute in Big Sur in 1962, Tassajara Zen Mountain Center founded in 1965 near Carmel Valley, Halcyon in Arroyo Grande founded by Theosophists in

1903, and the Sunburst Sanctuary near Lompoc followed the teachings of Paramahansa Yogananda.

The real pioneers of the Central Coast, however, were ranchers and cowboys. Their ranches are among the biggest in California, with Hearst Ranch being the largest. The cowboy heritage is now an expensive hobby; the Rancheros Vistadores in Santa Ynez is one of the most exclusive and expensive horse-riding clubs in the world. The Vaqueros, Mexican cowboys, were the mainstay of the ranches.

Big Sur, Montana de Oro, and The Pinnacles are places that stretch the imagination. The mythology of the Central Coast exists because of dreamers and artists like Robert Lewis Stevenson, Ansel Adams, Ignacy Paderewski, and Henry Miller, who came for enlightenment and succor. Homegrown artists like John Steinbeck captured the tension between the landscape and its inhabitants. The over-arching scenic beauty can squash the creativity of timid and cowardly, empowering the fearless.

For thousands of years, Native Americans enjoyed this paradise living in harmony with the earth. The Chumash Indians from the Channel Islands settled throughout the coastal areas, surviving on the bounty of the Pacific. The Salinan Indians lived on meal made from the oak nuts and the game that thrived in the fertile Salinas Valley.

Father Junipero Serra arrived in California from Majorca in 1769, charged with establishing a network of missions spanning California, and converting the Indians to Catholicism. There are eight missions on the Central Coast from Santa Barbara to Carmel, where Father Junipero Serra is buried. Red tile roofs, white stucco walls, and wood beam ceilings are synonymous with the preponderance of Spanish Colonial and Mission Revival architecture seen throughout the Central Coast.

The gold rush never came to the Central Coast, as it was the last region of the state to see an influx of Europeans and Americans from the East. Mexican laborers built this region with their skills in stonework, tile, carpentry, and stucco. The "braceros" were crucial to establishing and maintaining the Central Coast's agricultural economic base.

Agriculture has always been vital to the Central Coast long before tourism. Cattle and sheep have grazed the large tracts of land for centuries. Dairy cows brought a wave of Swiss Italian farmers who settled along the coast, eventually closing their dairies when land and water became too expensive. Growers planted walnut, almond, and olive trees on the hillsides. In the rich Salinas River Valley, "America's Salad Bowl" that runs South to North emptying into Monterey Bay. The robust produce industry never had the cachet of wine grapes.

It was the wine grapes that put this region on the map. From the Santa Ynez Valley and Santa Rita Hills in Santa Barbara County to the Santa Lucia Mountains in Monterey County, the wine grapes flourished within dozens of microclimates and terroir surpassing the elegance of the Old World.

Great Oaks, Dash Ramblar's fictional hometown, is depicted as a town transformed from being a "cow town" to a destination for weekenders and wine aficionados. The remarkable transformation was literally overnight, or so it seemed to the locals who could no longer recognize their environs.

A wine region brings a surfeit of material for the mystery writer. The potent blend of money, prestige, and romance brings a myriad of carpetbaggers, misfits, developers, artists, addicts, ex-felons, gold diggers, and con men attempting to make good.

The San Simeon earthquake of 2003 killed two in downtown Paso Robles, destroying several landmark buildings. The earthquake kickstarted the ensuing renaissance around the plaza, bringing a new vitality to the Central Coast.

The Character Log
THE WINE MENAGERIE

Great Oaks:

Dash Ramblar	Protagonist P.I.
Amber Ramblar	Dash's daughter
Bixby, Barnaby (Barney)	Dash's dogs
Rexford Beckett (Rex)	President, Vino Veritas Inc.
Conrad Cook	Paint Horse Winemaker
Detective FJ Evans	Detective, Great Oaks P.D.
Sam Dotson, father	Attorney, Great Oaks
Dylan Dotson, son	Dotson Vineyard Management Great Oaks
The Hamster	Homeless: Salinas Riverbed
Pedro Mendoza	Homeless: Salinas Riverbed
Cecelia	Pedro's girlfriend in San Miguel
Pete Ligotti	Great Oaks mayor
Hernando Torres	Dotson Vineyard Management
Sara Hutchins	Broker: Ranch and Farm Real Estate
Ginger Rute	Jasper Winery Tasting Room

Wine Industry:

Bryson Jackson, husband	Red Fox Winery
Jackie Jackson, wife	Red Fox Winery
Bill Lyons	Wine Estates
Gregg Perigold, son	Jasper Winery, heir
Jason Perigold, father	Jasper Winery, owner

Wine Sisters:

Claudia Bowers	Wine Sister (barrel sales)
Taylor Thorngate	Graphic artist
Brenda Brown	Owner of Oliver Twist Restaurant
Mona Morgan	Wine writer
Amanda Jacobs	Rex Beckett's girlfriend